Praise for Connie Brockway

"Romance with strength, wit, and intelligence. Connie Brockway delivers!"

—*New York Times* bestselling author Tami Hoag

"This frothy literary confection sparkles with insouciant charm. Characters, setting, and plot are all handled with perfect aplomb by Brockway, who displays a true gift for humor. Witty and wonderful!"

—*Booklist* (starred review) on *The Bridal Season*

"An undercurrent of danger ripples through this exquisite romance, and Brockway's lush, lyrical writing style is a perfect match for her vivid characters, beautifully atmospheric settings, and sensuous love scenes."

—*Library Journal* on *McClairen's Isle: The Passionate One*

"Those looking for a little more substance in their plots will relish this one; there's intrigue, adventure and betrayal, all woven into a story with characters you won't soon forget."

—*The Oakland Press* on *McClairen's Isle: The Reckless One*

"Intricately plotted, with highly inventive lead characters, Brockway's latest is an intense and complicated romance . . . Everything works in this cat-and-mouse tale—there is excitement, chemistry, obsession."

—*Publishers Weekly* (starred review) on *All Through the Night*

CHRISTINA DODD
AND
CONNIE BROCKWAY

Once Upon
a Pillow

POCKET BOOKS

New York London Toronto Sydney Singapore

An *Original* Publication of POCKET BOOKS

 POCKET BOOKS, a division of Simon & Schuster, Inc.
1230 Avenue of the Americas, New York, NY 10020

Copyright © 2002 by Connie Brockway and Christina Dodd

ISBN: 0-7434-3680-6

First Pocket Books trade paperback printing July 2002

10 9 8 7 6 5 4 3 2 1

POCKET and colophon are registered trademarks of Simon & Schuster, Inc.

For information regarding special discounts for bulk purchases, please contact Simon & Schuster Special Sales at 1-800-456-6798 or business@simonandschuster.com

Printed in the U.S.A.

To Scott. Forever.
—Christina

For Judith Johnson,
luge wannabe and best of friends.
With lots of love,
Connette

Dear Reader,

Even though our husbands have never met and live two thousand miles apart, we were amazed to discover that they are constantly asking us the same question: "What can you two possibly have to say to each other so often and for so long?" Coincidentally enough, they usually ask us this while holding a phone bill.

We always answer, "We're talking about writing. Yeah, uh, writing."

Because neither of us is a liar, merely a tale-spinner, and there is a difference, here, at last, is incontrovertible proof that we really do talk about writing—*Once Upon a Pillow*. In a fit of creativity, we conceived the idea of writing a series of romances centered on a bed constructed in medieval times and treasured by generation after generation of the Masterson family until it is finally retired (ha) into a modern-day museum.

So, it is our pleasure to present you four luscious tales in one wonderful story. We had a fabulous time writing *Once Upon a Pillow* and we hope you have just as much fun reading it.

Love,
Christina Dodd and Connie Brockway

M arking the border of Cornwall and Devon, a small, inconsequential river runs out of the moors. Like a royal courier on a vital mission, the river Cabot gains impetus as it goes, ultimately flying past the tiny village of Trecombe before plummeting over the steep cliffs into the sea. Of late, the banks of the inconsequential river have yielded an unforeseen boon in the form of a particularly fine clay which has, in turn, given rise to a new cottage industry in Trecombe.

Most people would concede it is a long overdue reward for the faithful Trecombians who have long lived in this grand, often austere, but always beautiful land. Indeed, there are families who claim they are descendants of the town's founding father, a knight who, on his mandatory quest to find the Holy Grail, fell asleep beside the river and was awakened by a tall, green-eyed maiden who bade him stay . . . along with a number of interesting things which in no way affect this story.

Needless to say, stay he did and whether the tale is based in actuality or not, the fact remains that even today Trecombe boasts a greater number of green-eyed residents per capita than any other place in England. It was one of the few things

German bombing and severe economic depression failed to destroy. In fact, few of the neat, picturesque cottages here are over a hundred years old and the town, pretty though it is, would seem to have little to recommend itself to an archeologist or social historian.

However, a small way out of Trecombe, as if distancing themselves from the town's pedestrian concerns, stand two ancient buildings. Roosting atop the cliffs is St. Albion's chapel, complacent at having escaped the dissolution that claimed its adjacent abbey. The other building, a short distance inland, is Masterson Manor, once the home of the town's first—and as far as anyone knows, only crusader, Sir Nicholas.

From behind the manor's stalwart walls, Sir Nicholas had directed the fortification of Trecombe against brigands. In its high-ceilinged rooms he had sired eight sons, all of whom had lived to adulthood. From its graceful mullioned windows he had watched his castle being built above the cliff walls. And while the castle, the emblem of his might and power, has been reduced to a few ruins, the manor still stands, noble and handsome in its antiquity.

In its current incarnation, Masterson Manor is a private museum. Regrettably, the house isn't the stuff from which successful private museums are made. It is small as house museums go, having only twenty rooms, and set in a wildly beautiful, untamed landscape, not the manicured Disney gardens day-trippers with kiddies prefer. And while the assortment of Masterson heirlooms the current curator has so lovingly and painstakingly collected is impressive, there is only one item unique to Masterson Manor, one item which has drawn the museologist along the twisted lanes and remote byways that lead to Trecombe: The Masterson Bed.

But even this gem has not been able to generate enough money to keep the doors open, the taxes paid, and the current owners in treacle pudding. And so, The Masterson Museum is closing. Indeed, it has already been sold. And this is the last tour of the last day.

Laurel Whitney, the museum's curator, house sitter, and social historian, closed her eyes briefly as the group she was leading murmured appreciatively over the contents of the dining room. She would have few opportunities left in which to soak up the atmosphere of the place, an atmosphere she was in great part responsible for creating. For Laurel had found the Chippendale dining table that exactly fit an earlier Masterson lady's description of the one her family had owned. Just as Laurel had painstakingly hunted down the complete silver service placed on that table, located and had hung the exact pattern William Morris paper she'd seen gracing these walls in nineteenth-century daguerreotypes and through sheer perseverance, had bullied a local family into relinquishing the original Tabriz carpet that lay on the floor.

She adored Masterson Manor.

It was the stuff of dreams for a doctoral candidate in Social History because manor houses of this vintage were much harder to come by than castles. In fact, she couldn't remember being happier than since she'd come here . . . Well, in point of fact, she could. But that hadn't been *real* happiness; it had been sex. *This* was happiness with staying power: The happiness that comes only with the Acquisition of Knowledge.

In the library she'd found a sixteenth-century diary and a pair of black candlesticks that a good cleaning had revealed to be fourteenth-century silver candelabra. In the bedroom she'd discovered a secret drawer containing a fan written over in a tiny delicate scrawl with the names of Regency gentlemen. And in a rosewood chest she'd found artifacts from the long gone abbey, including a ninth-century cross and a gold *paten*.

She'd identified at least eighteen clothing eras from examples pulled from the attic's mothball-cushioned trunks and had begun to sift through a cache of ledgers she'd found in the basement when the current owners had announced that they had sold the manor to a private party who intended to make it his summer home and that all the contents were being auctioned off.

Laurel had been aghast. *Was* aghast. She'd spent the month since the announcement frantically trying to complete a rough transcription of the ledgers she'd found before the new owner arrived. If only there had been more time. But there wasn't. There wouldn't be.

She glanced briefly out the window to the west where the sun made a spectacular orchid and magenta display behind the tumbled castle walls. An hour at most before the tour ended and then what did the future hold for her? Would she go back to America? Move to London? Or Glastonbury?

The thought caused her stomach to twist in knots. She *belonged* here. Knowing she drank from the same gilt and rose-patterned Wedgewood teacups as Lady Meredith Masterson gave her a sense of continuity. When she took the footpath to the castle ruins and stared out across the sea as the wind rushed up from the breakers and whipped her dark hair, she felt an exhilaration no place on earth had ever engendered in her. And sometimes late at night, when the house was closed and the owners gone, and she'd wrapped herself in a cashmere shawl and was toasting her toes at the hearth, she could almost hear the sounds of those earlier Mastersons moving about on upper floors, quiet of foot, deliberate in movement. She would miss those discreet ghosts.

Unconsciously she straightened. She couldn't think of the future. She *wouldn't*. It was too hard. Just as the past had been too hard to contemplate when she'd first arrived here under the excuse of researching her doctoral thesis: "*The Medieval*

Bed, A Study of Matrimonial and Social Obligation." It was too hard, just like the presence of that . . . that *handyman* was too hard to think about.

If it had been her decision, Max Ashton wouldn't have spent ten minutes in this house. But it wasn't her decision. The new owners had hired him to "make the place half-way habitable" before their arrival. *Habitable.* They'd probably tear up the ancient flagstones in the kitchen and install no-wax linoleum. She quelled the urge to shudder and fixed a smile on her face as she turned back to the tour group.

"If no one has any other questions for me regarding the dining room, we'll proceed upstairs," she said.

The little group, a trio of American women, the blonde one's teenage son, and a honeymooning couple shook their heads in the negative as Laurel ushered them into the hall. She stopped at the foot of the staircase and gestured around.

"As I pointed out earlier, Masterson Manor is built in the traditional hall style, with family area distinctly separate from public rooms. But over the centuries, the house has been renovated and altered. The barrel vaulting overhead, however, contains the original three load-bearing beams, each cut from a single piece of wood and weighing over half a ton."

The young husband, John, looked suitably impressed while the bride, Meghan appeared anxious. Tenderly, he pulled her against his side. "It's stood nine hundred years, pet. I don't think she's about to come down now."

His bride laughed at herself and shook her head and Laurel felt a pang of envy for them. Once she'd felt like Meghan . . . She refused to entertain the thought. "If you'll follow me?" she said briskly, moving up the staircase.

She pointed out the Chinese vases in the niches at the top of the stairs, pristine and gleaming red and cobalt. She was not the only one who took pride in her work here. The housekeeper, Grace, could easily have let these small things go untended, unlike the butler, Kenneth, who should have retired years ago but couldn't because of an unfortunate predilection for the racetrack. As Laurel started down the gallery, she heard the sound of pounding behind the door at the very end. Blast. *He* was still working.

"When are we going to see this bed you've all been talking about?" the teenage boy, Brian, suddenly asked.

"Shh," his mother Mrs. Plante said.

Laurel turned, smiling. "It's all right. Everyone wants to see the Masterson bed. I was hoping the handyman would finish before we got to it, but time is flying and I should hate for you to be rushed through. It is the highlight of the tour."

And you wouldn't mind seeing him again, either, would you, Laurel? she asked herself derisively.

The group assured her they did indeed want to see the bed, settling the matter. She led them to the master bedchamber and stopped in front of the door. "Very well. Here she is, live for your entertainment and edification, the one, the only . . ." She paused dramatically, her eyes twinkling. She always loved the look on the faces of the tourists when they got their first glimpse of The Bed. "The Masterson Bed."

She pushed open the door and stood back. Inside, Max Ashton stood up, wiping dusty hands on his jeans. Without a glance at him, Laurel hustled her group into the room. The one-time solar was a large chamber, the walls covered with Masterson family portraits, furnished in authentic Regency era artifacts, a painted screen and cherry tallboy, a carved bombe chest and black japaned inlaid desk, twin settees covered in cream and green print, drapes of heavy green damask. Still, all the sumptuous furnishings paled before the overpowering presence of the room's centerpiece: the Masterson bed.

Eight feet tall by eight feet wide by eight feet in length, the ancient walnut beauty presided over the room with the contented, slightly disreputable air of one who has weathered any number of pretenders to its crown as the oldest surviving bed in England. The deeply carved posts rising from the corners were as thick as her waist—indeed, one legend had it that they were actually dryads, transformed and hewn while in their wooden state—while the rails and canopy frame glowed darkly, polished by thousands of hands over eight hundred years. Sumptuous, detailed, and faintly exotic, the carvings covering it had provoked centuries of debate over the bed's origins.

Whatever its beginnings, the sheer weight of the thing must have been instrumental in its continued existence. Simply put, no one could get it out of the bedroom. Centuries had pretty much petrified the wood into something closer resembling stone than fiber. It certainly weighed as much as stone. Laurel could attest. She and Kenneth and Grace had once tried to shove it to the back wall in an attempt to get to the floorboards beneath. They had not been successful.

She eyed the epic proportions fondly. The years had taken their toll, and generations of former owners had left their scars on it, but these was only to be expected. What male Masterson had ever been able to resist marking anything that came into his possession? Still, it was a handsome, grand old thing and just looking at it filled her with a sort of reverence. One the *handyman* obviously didn't share, since he was regarding the group with the indulgence an adult generally saves for tots at a cartoon matinee.

She didn't spare him more than a glance but that didn't keep her from realizing that he was now sparing her plenty.

And why not? At five and a half feet, packing a well-toned hundred and thirty pounds into a pair of well-cut navy slacks and snug cream-colored cashmere sweater, with hair as black and shiny as a raven's eye, and a face some men called piquant, the one thing she wasn't insecure about was her looks.

"Come have a good look-see," Laurel invited her group.

The middle-aged American ladies made a beeline for the bed. The smallest one, Mrs. Stradling, red-haired and comfortable-looking, began a minute inspection of the headboard. Brian—more interested in power tools than antiques—wandered over to where Max had exposed the wall's internal wiring.

"She's a grand old thing, isn't she?" Miss Ferguson, buxom and pert, asked.

"How do you know it's a 'she'?" the honeymooning groom asked curiously.

Miss Ferguson regarded the younger man with the conde-scension of the *cognoscenti*. "Honey, it gets made, it gets rum-pled up, and it gets walked away from in the morning. Of course, it's a 'she'."

Meghan blushed. The other ladies chuckled and even Max Ashton grinned. Only Brian didn't seem to get the joke and that was because he was backing into Max.

"Oops! Geez, I'm sorry, Mister," the boy exclaimed guiltily. He'd been trying to peer through the hole in the wall.

"Think nothing of it, lad," Max replied.

At once, the three female American faces swung toward him.

"You sound just like Laurence Olivier," Mrs. Plante breathed.

"Only you're taller, and fairer, of course," Mrs. Stradling pronounced, eyeing Max speculatively.

"And while the voice is refined, the look is definitely rugged," Miss Ferguson nodded sagely.

"A duke," Miss Ferguson clipped out, "with an agenda."

"Or a vendetta," Mrs. Plante mused quietly.

"Or a past," proposed Mrs. Stradling.

Even the starry-eyed Meghan was eyeing Max in friendly, if objective, appreciation. The tour was definitely getting side-tracked and Laurel did not want to spend any unnecessary time weaving fantasies about Max Ashton. She'd woven one too many in that area already.

"Please," Laurel said in barely suppressed exasperation. The women turned around from their contemplation of Max and looked at her.

"He's not Heath Ledger, you know," she said, trying for jocularity and ending up sounding tense. "Mr. Ashton, would you mind finding something else to do while we're in here? We won't be but a short while."

Max shrugged, his smile lazy and knowing. "Not a bit. But since you won't be long, and I was going to call it a day after I was done in here, why don't I just hang about while you lecture? Might even learn something interesting."

"I am sure nothing I have to say could interest you."

"Are you?" His smile had become gentler. His dark eyes darker. She felt a little breathless, a little cornered by the look in his eyes . . . *Nonsense!*

"Yes. Besides, I wouldn't want to bore you."

His smile faded and his gaze became even more focused on her. "Never."

She felt herself flush and to cover her sudden confusion, she turned her back on him. "As you will. Now, what say we turn our attention to the star of this show?"

"Yeah," agreed Brian.

"Good." Laurel smiled at the boy. "First off, anyone have any questions?"

This wasn't how this part of the tour was supposed to go. Usually, she did a five-minute chronology of the bed and *"hasta la vista,* tourists." But today she wasn't in any hurry to have them leave and the museum close for the last time. She wanted to extend this rare sense of ownership, and more, deep within her was welling a strange feeling of urgency that there were a million stories in her that needed to be told, or else they would be silenced forever.

"Come on," she urged them. "Anything. This bed is a legend. How often do you get to sit on a legend and ask a Legend-Meister questions?"

Miss Ferguson raised a hand.

"Shoot," Laurel said.

"Okay. When was the bed made and who made it?"

"Good question." Laurel nodded sagely. "The fact is, we don't know for certain who made the Masterson bed. It's first mentioned in historical annals in the late thirteenth century, when a visiting nobleman wrote about his sojourn in Trecombe and how his host gave up 'a wondrously carved, magnificently foreign bed for my comfort.'

"'Magnificently foreign' is a direct translation and our best clue as to its origins."

Laurel knew she was good at this, not because she was smart or conscientious, but because she loved it. As she spoke, she could feel the decades and centuries slip away, a world form in her imagination that she only needed to close her eyes to see, feel, smell, and hear.

"From this reference and judging from the motifs in the carving, we can gather that the bed was made somewhere near Jerusalem at the beginning of the same century," she went on. "Undoubtedly it was brought back to England by a crusading knight."

She smiled happily. "That's right. The first recorded Masterson was a *bona fide* knight."

A knight in shining armor, a man who understood and lived by a code of chivalry, a 'flower of manhood,' she thought wistfully. And while logically she knew she would have found a thirteenth-century knight chauvinistic, egocentric, and violent, she wished there were men about today—she glanced at Max—who treated a lady as well as they did, with respect and consideration.

"Just think of what it must have been like to be a knight in those days," she went on dreamily. "It was like being a rock star today, only the jousting field was his concert hall and noblemen and noblewomen were his groupies.

"And a tournament! The ultimate concert! It would have been fabulous. Imagine one in which the Masterson knight rode." She sighed deeply, her eyes fixed on an interior vision she alone could see.

"He enters the field on his prancing destrier, his armor shimmering in the sun. The pennants ringing the field snap beneath a cerise-colored sky as the crowds dressed in silks and satins cheer. The children throw him flowers while the ladies toss him their silk scarves."

She closed her eyes. "I wish I could have seen it. . . ."

The Bed Is Made . . .

Trecombe, Cornwall circa 1200

CHAPTER 1

Get those pigs off the tilting field!" Simon Gundry, sheriff of Trecombe, hollered at the children.

The two boys, eager not to postpone the promised entertainment, complied without complaint, hieing after their father's escaped sows, sliding and whooping across the icy uneven ground.

Simon watched until they'd cordoned the pigs off by the tanner's stall and turned back to the task at hand.

"It is agreed then," he bellowed with as much authority as he could muster, "whoever is unhorsed by his opponent first, will withdraw his claim for the lands abutting the river."

Simon watched as the knights mounted their destriers at opposite ends of the long jousting field which was separated lengthwise by a low rail. He blew into his hands and shivered in the raw March wind. It was early in the day yet and the field was still frozen. Later, the sun would turn the ground into an ice-clotted mire. Not that the cold had kept spectators from turning out.

The young gentlemen from Teague Manor milled about the far end of the list, while their ladies, wrapped snug in rabbit-lined pelisses, their hoods drawn tight about rosy faces, roosted on rough benches hauled out by their servants. Along the rest of the field's length stood the free folk of Trecombe. Even the holy brothers from tiny St. Albion's Abbey stood in the crowd.

And why not? Simon thought. Trecombe was too small and remote to attract tournaments the way the cathedral cities and market towns did. Trecombe's only annual tournament was the one held on Saint Neot's name day. Therefore, for the common people of Trecombe, this was a rare holiday, while for manor-born sons and daughters, it was an escape from a long winter of boredom.

Simon, however, being neither manor-born nor bored, but instead in charge of all the civil justice in the shire, was unhappy. He did not like this. Not at all.

A dispute between knights regarding property should properly await the king's assize. Unhappily, as knights, the two combatants had every right to demand judgment by combat rather than await the king's justice, and consequentially endure the loss of a valuable planting season.

Aye, Simon understood the reasoning behind the challenge. But he liked it no more for the understanding. He stomped his feet and offered a quick prayer that his role here did not come back to haunt him. Then he cupped his hands and hollered, "Are you ready, Sir Moore?"

Pretty as a maid with his golden hair and ruddy cheeks, Sir Guy Moore looked born to the brilliant raiment he wore, presents his proud parent had bestowed upon him at his knighting nine months past. Since then, he'd already won three tournaments. Now, he dug his golden spurs into his destrier's milk-white sides. The brute arched its neck, rolling its eyes and drumming its hooves anxiously upon the hoar-touched ground.

A cheer rose from the crowd in response. Simon, who'd seen his share of knightly posturing and had known Guy Moore when he was a spoiled bit of snot hanging from his father's nose, wasn't so easily impressed.

"I am ready!" Guy shouted, his voice ripe with confidence.

Simon turned toward where the other knight, a stranger here, fought his borrowed war-horse to a standstill. It was woefully apparent that he was not ready. The crowd eyed him without warmth. A few snickered.

The stranger looked like Hotfoot compared to Guy Moore's Gabriel. Where Moore was fair, smooth, and light, this one was dark, bearded, and huge. Where Moore looked like greenwood, supple and tensile, this man looked to be carved from a bole, hard and obdurate.

He was a crusader, knighted, rumor had it, upon a bloody battlefield by Richard himself before following that same Richard to the Holy Lands. It was a good story, Simon admitted, but Trecombe had seen crusaders before and knew all too well that knightly armor as oft shielded vice as virtue. After all, Sir Gerent Corbet had been a knight, and only think on the years of terror his tenure had wrought in Trecombe.

No, what stimulated curiosity about this man wasn't *what* he was, but *who* he was: Sir Nicholas, whose origins were so humble and obscure they did not even boast a proper sur-name, the newly found heir to Corbet Manor. Once it had been Sir Gerent's demesne and now it was the richest in the land.

Making this Sir Nicholas No-Name, as the town's brats had dubbed him, even more fascinating was the fact that he'd never actually *seen* the lands to which he held title—not until he'd ridden into Trecombe two days ago. Because before he'd come into his inheritance, he'd been lost on the crusade and presumed dead. Indeed, even now perpetually lit candles graced the altar at St. Albion's, assuring his soul's ascension to heaven.

He'd come on the Sabbath, entering church as bold as brass, and announced himself. Amid a cacophony of amazement, Father Timothy and Father Eidart had vouchsafed that this Sir Nicholas was who he said he was, having known him from Glastonbury and having been instrumental in the events that had led to Sir Nicholas's inheriting Corbet lands.

But before Sir Nicholas could even retire to spend a night at his newly claimed manor, Guy Moore had arrived and challenged the stranger to ownership of the orchard by the river. When Sir Nicholas had disclosed that he owned no steed, the holy brothers had come to his aid yet again, finding within their snug stables the destrier of a knight they'd lost to God's grace this past winter. Unridden since then, the horse had grown unruly and Sir Nicholas now had all he could do to keep the creature under control.

No wonder the people of Trecombe, great and small, were willing to forsake their work to see this particular joust. 'Twas not often a man returned from the grave—particularly a Syrian grave. If only he'd looked the part of God's returned champion. He did not.

For while Guy Moore looked every inch his position, not even the most accomplished troubadour could have found much in Sir Nicholas's person worth romanticizing. Nicholas's dull mail—again the deceased knight's—was as ill-fitting as his horse was ill-tempered. Even his lance was borrowed; its history, like his own, a mystery; its strength and straightness as suspect as the man who wielded it.

Simon shook his head despairingly. It would be, he feared, a short tournament.

"Sir? Are you agreed?" Simon shouted to the newfound lord of Corbet Manor.

In answer, Sir Nicholas raised his arm. Impossible to read his expression. His already dark visage was further obscured by a thick, untrimmed beard and the black locks that fell unkempt upon his shoulders.

But his green eyes were clear and his gaze seemed steady enough. If he felt at a disadvantage on his vexatious mount with his borrowed lance, he did not reveal it. He wore composure like a mantle.

"By the thighs of the poxy bitch that whelped you, Simon, get on with it!" Moore shouted.

"Ride!"

Both men's lances rose in brief salute and then Moore's steed reared, silhouetted against the blinding blue of the newly flushed day. Then he was flying down the field, his mail shimmering, the red silk ribbons braided in his horse's mane rippling, his young body canted forward.

As for Sir Nicholas. . . . Well, no one would be writing odes to Sir Nicholas's prowess this day, that was a certainty. His mount plunged forward, unbalancing his rider and sending the point of Nicholas's lance pitching earthward. For an instant, Simon thought it would impale the ground, unseating Nicholas before Moore drew near enough to take credit for it.

Pity, Simon thought morosely. Then, slowly, amazingly, the battered knight pulled the tip of the thirteen foot lance from its perilous drop. Alas, not in time to guide its path.

Still, The Virgin must have favored her resurrected knight, for in heaving back to keep his lance from falling, Nicholas's shield shifted, slanting sideways so that when Moore's lance struck it, it skittered along the shield's surface, its force deflected.

Moore cursed roundly and the riders thundered past one another to their respective ends of the list. Moore wheeled his mount sharply and adroitly while Sir Nicholas fought his mount into a looping turn.

"Ready!" Moore shouted and, without awaiting his opponent's consent, spurred his destrier forth, once more charging down the tilting rail. And once more, Sir Nicholas's mount gathered its haunches and bolted.

This time, however, Sir Nicholas was ready. He crouched low over the beast's withers, his lance steady.

The crowd held its collective breath. Only the thunder of hoofbeats and the squeal of the incarcerated pigs broke the quiet. The air frosted over with the spectators' mingled breath. Flecks of mud sprayed from beneath flying hooves. Somewhere a baby squalled.

Twenty feet from his adversary, Nicholas abruptly stood up in his stirrups. It was a bold ploy. Raised thus, if Guy struck true, Nicholas would easily be toppled. *But,* the stance also allowed Nicholas a few precious inches of height which he used to his advantage, leaning out and over the tilt rail, risking all on the gamble that by doing so his lance would reach Guy a split second before Guy's reached him.

Close . . . closer . . .

The lances seemed to strike the knights' shields at the same instant. Nicholas fell back into his seat, pitching sideways, his lance swinging up as he tried to right himself. Guy, quick to seize advantage, yanked savagely at his reins, trying to wheel his mount on his rear legs in order to finish off his flailing opponent from behind.

He had almost turned his horse, dropping his shield to do so, when suddenly Nicholas spun around, his leg swinging over the pommel so that he circled round in the saddle without bothering to turn his mount to match his direction. His seemingly uncontrolled lance suddenly sliced through the air in a deadly up-swinging arc, colliding into Guy's unprotected side.

And with that, it was over.

Like a bothersome fly, Guy Moore was brushed from his destier's back and landed in a clatter of metal on the muddy ground.

Either the hammers pounding against his temples or the taste of rotted wool in his mouth woke Nicholas. Neither was pleasant and the knowledge that he'd willfully pursued both did not make them any more appealing. He'd never been a man to lose his caution in drink, and less the sort to deliberately spend his joy after having dulled his senses. Pleasures—in his limited experience with them—were too rare to enjoy with less than a full complement of faculties.

But his triumph at having won the joust, and the release that came of having yet again cheated death, had for once overwhelmed him. He'd started drinking as soon as he'd found a tavern. Now he was paying the price, learning anew that self-indulgence was a luxury he could scant afford.

He squinted into the shadowed interior of the only proper bed he'd found in Cabot Manor, noting the plain dark curtains hanging about it and the rough texture of the pinewood surface, hand-planed and unadorned. 'Twas far cruder furnishings than one would expect in so well-made and well-tended a manor house—at least, he recalled thinking it well-tended after he'd finally found his way here early this morning. Still, he thought with a sweet sense of ownership, it was *his* bed.

He had never owned anything in his life besides his honor, the skills to do bodily injury to another man, and his fearlessness in doing so. Or rather, there'd been a time he'd been fearless. No more.

Once more he felt fear gnaw in his gut, fear that he no longer remembered the art of jousting, that it, along with so much else, had been lost in the Saracen dungeons or baked to dust under the Holy Land's sun-blistered sky; fear that he'd escaped that blasted land to slave and beg and labor three thousand miles only to have it end on a rural tilting field, killed by a pretty boy in silver mail.

But he hadn't lost.

Nicholas let his head roll back and smiled into the shrouded darkness. Finally, he was someone. No matter how short a time he held Cabot Manor, history must forever bear witness that he had existed, he had *been*. For he was lord of this manor, master of three thousand acres upon which lived thirty serfs, a mill, a granary, a buttery, a stable . . . and a bed.

The tightness in his gut relaxed and the thundering in his head abated. He sighed and, stretching his arm out, brushed against something soft and yielding. A female breast. He looked over, startled.

Ah, yes. He remembered now. As a newly christened debauchee, he had apparently decided to make up for the years he'd lain fallow in a Syrian dungeon. He studied the ripe figure sprawled beneath the blankets at his side. She was snoring and the scent of ale and peat smoke rose from her pink and grimy skin along with a mélange of other odors which, he suspected, had taken up residence on her person long ago.

Sowenna? Aye, Sowenna. Warm, full-bosomed, avaricious, blonde Sowenna. After six years gone from England, he had been stirred by the sight of blonde hair. He had promised her a trinket for her company and while he knew that in the eyes of the church offering "a trinket for company" was no different than offering a coin for prostitution, well, he'd had what he wanted and she'd gotten what she needed.

Need and want. He'd always considered them separate, but of late he'd come to wonder how far apart they really stood.

Still, the reminder that he was paying for her favors dimmed his initial pleasure. He scratched his chest, hoping she hadn't given him fleas, and remembered an exotic room filled with steaming pools and ladles of clear water. Not every memory he'd brought back from the crusades was cursed with bleakness or fraught with peril.

He closed his eyes and Sowenna rolled atop him.

"You're awake!" she crowed and fumbled between their bodies. "Good. Now let's see what I 'ave here. Nuthin' I like better than to start the day with a nice—"

Whatever Sowenna liked to start the day with was to be forever lost, for at that second the bed hangings snapped open and sunlight poured in, blinding him with brilliance. A slender figure stood by the side of the bed, her features eclipsed by the sunlight behind her, a nimbus of fiery darkness about her head, her hands on narrow hips. Her chin jerked up, as though she'd been slapped, bringing her features into view. She was lovely, lovely and careworn and proud. Like some displaced faerie lass, slight but strong, with a wisdom that belied her youthful visage.

Sowenna blinked crossly, her playful demeanor wilting like harebells before a frost. "What do you think you're doing?" she squawked, scooting upright without bothering to cover herself. "Who do you think you are, anyway, you scrawny get of a scrawny whore!"

Nicholas closed his eyes, Sowenna's shrill battle cry renewing the drumbeat in his head.

"Who am I?" The slender beauty asked, pointing her finger at him. "I'm *his* wife."

CHAPTER 2

As Jocelyn Cabot stood in the master's chamber fuming, she felt as if she'd walked straight into her life seven years ago. The clothing lying in heaps about the room, the yeasty stench of ale underpinned by the thick pervasive aroma of sex, it was all the same. From the spilt tankard on the floor to the look of sluttish triumph on the face of the woman peering over the man's muscular chest, it was familiar.

It could have been her uncle Gerent lying there with his latest woman, too drunk to meet with the guild masters, too stupid to rely on diplomacy to listen to them. Instead, he'd sent her out to feed them his threats. Not again. Never again.

"Get out!"

With alacrity, the woman scuttled from the bed, grabbed up her clothes and bolted out the door.

The man, her *husband,* Sir Nicholas *No-Name,* swung his muscular hairy legs over the side of the bed and glowered at her. That, too, sharply brought back a memory. She flinched reflexively, expecting at any second to be struck and sent careening across the room.

But he did not raise his hand to her. Instead, heedless of the fact that he was unclad, he rose and stood over her, naked and huge. Not huge like Gerent who'd been a grizzled, filth-encrusted bear of a man. Nay, this knight was a stallion in his prime, so flat of belly one could see the muscles clearly delineated beneath the dark fur that started at his chest and covered him all the way down to the sex hanging heavy and turgid between his legs.

Jocelyn flushed, averting her eyes. With a scowl, Nicholas looked around and snatched the sheet from the bed, securing it low around his hips.

Resentment and despair vied within Jocelyn. Resentment, because she'd kept her part of the bargain. She'd honored her husband's memory, kept candles lit for his salvation, paid for masses to be said for his soul. Despair, because after six years of rectifying all the wrongs Gerent had heaped on this tiny village, once more a whoring, drunken, knight was lord of this fief.

"You are supposed to be dead!" The words burst unbidden from her lips. Again, she cringed, certain now that she'd won not merely a smack across the face, but a graver punishment. One would think that after her years as Gerent's ward, she would have learned to keep a still tongue in her head. Not so. And the people of Trecombe had on more than one occasion thanked the good Lord for her inability to let any miscarriage of justice pass unremarked.

She closed her eyes and waited, fighting back tears of anger, trying desperately to ignore the fact that they were also tears of fear.

"Pardon me for returning alive," Nicholas finally answered.

She opened her eyes and looked up. He looked grim and dangerous, but his arms remained at his side. He was *so* big. Father Timothy had never mentioned that the man he'd wed her to by proxy was so physically intimidating.

No wonder this man had been knighted on the battlefield. He'd only need to stand over his enemy—as he was standing over her now—to have him quaking like a leaf in the wind— as she was shaking now. The reality of her situation came back to her with breath-stealing force. *This was her husband.* He could do with her anything he wanted. She was his chattel.

What *would* he do to her? Impossible to say what lay behind those bright green eyes. Impossible to discern the expression on that dark, bearded visage surrounded by those long, matted locks of hair. She swallowed, deciding the best course would be to retreat while she could.

"I will leave you to dress, sir," she said with as much dignity as she could manage. She began to back away.

At once, he followed. Her eyes widened and she backed up more quickly. He matched her pace for pace, deliberately herding her backward across the room until her shoulders banged into the wall.

He raised his hand and she turned her head sharply. His eyes narrowed a fraction but he only lifted the braid that hung over her shoulder and looked down at it a second before turning his cool, uncompromising gaze to hers.

"Why do you want me dead?"

"Why?" *Because you are a blight on this land, a curse on these people and they have been cursed enough.* The words trembled in her throat, waiting to be spoken, but she managed to keep them back.

"We were informed of your death. We have grown accustomed to it," she said breathlessly, albeit accusingly, for his fingers still played idly with her braid, like a merchant testing the quality of a suspect bolt of silk. "King Richard himself sent word of your capture. And later we learned that knights whose families could not pay their ransom were killed. We were *certain* you were dead."

"I assume a ransom was demanded for me," he said carefully. "Why wasn't it paid?"

"There was no money," she answered. "Gerent left nothing but the land and that enfeoffed save the demesne which had been overworked and yielded few crops."

"You could have sold some land."

How dare he lecture her on husbandry and economics? She had done more for Trecombe in six years than her uncle had in the thirty. "To whom, pray thee tell?"

"Perchance, that flower of manhood, Sir Guy Moore?"

Her mouth flattened. "Guy Moore has never paid for anything in his life. What he wants, he takes."

"How is it then that he hasn't taken the lands by the river?"

"Everyone knows King Richard honors the memory of his fallen knights. He would look sorely on any who tried to wrest land from the family of a crusader who'd died in the Lord's—and Richard's—service," she replied. "That is why I have been able to achieve some small prosperity for this demesne, for these people. Your *death* has protected us from jackals."

"I can hold the demesne," he said. Once again, he reminded her strongly of Gerent and yet, there was a difference. True, Gerent would have made such a statement, but where Gerent would have swaggered and sneered, there was not even a tincture of the braggart in Nicholas's voice. He was simply stating a fact.

And she did not doubt him. He looked every inch the ready warrior. Before he'd covered himself she'd seen a long white jagged scar on his left flank. More scars puckered on his shoulder and left arm. They only accentuated the impression he gave of strength and power.

"You mistake my meaning, sir," she said roughly, too aware of how close she was to his naked chest. "Because there has not been a need to hold this demesne, we turned our eyes to greater purpose than keeping and taking. We built and cultivated."

She'd been convent-raised, torn from the holy sisters' care at the age of twelve when she'd been hauled off by her sterile, vile, drunken uncle Gerent who had installed her in Cabot Manor as his heir. Fresh from religious instruction, she'd taken one look at the decrepit manor and the miserable, cowed faces of Gerent's serfs and villeins and immediately understood her role in life.

She was to be these people's liberator. Nine years later, she knew herself to have been a good liberator, a good mistress, a wise and prudent steward. But now, for some unknown reason, God had seen fit to test these poor folk—and herself— with a new ordeal. She glared at the ordeal.

"*That* is why the buildings are in good repair, the fields fertile, the cattle plump, and the people content. In short, because you were dead and there wasn't anyone an ambitious knight could challenge for what we have."

"But now there is," he said.

"Aye. Only look what your return has already brought! Not two days here and blood already shed, and more than like, every jackal within a day's ride sniffing that spilt blood and ready to come a-running."

A renewed sense of injury filled her, not for herself, but for the people who would be trampled in any clash of knightly conceit. And there was always knightly conceit.

"And you would rather I had died than return to share with you that which your uncle bequeathed me along with your hand."

"Might I speak plainly, sir?"

At this, the huge warrior gave a short bark of laughter. "Blind me, Madame, but if your last words were an example of honeyed words, I fear I shall be smote asunder by your 'plain-speaking.'"

She gazed at him, subtly comforted by that brief sardonic speech. He had wit then. Gerent wouldn't have known irony if it had given him a written introduction. She straightened her shoulders. When she left this room, they would both know exactly where they stood.

He sighed. "Speak, girl, before you bite through your tongue."

"We covet peace, sir, not riches. We are not political, we are not significant, nor do we stand in the path of ambitious princes." The words rushed from her, severe and accusatory. "We are a tiny fief of God-serving people who raise good wool and make a decent cheese and who, because the king treated us with benign neglect, were treated likewise by all men.

"But now you are here and I will have you know that the ghost of your arm was better protection and far better guarantee of peace than your living arm can ever hope to be. And if your sword arm benefits us not, but instead brings only woe, what good are you to us then? To me?"

He regarded her impassively. "You think a knight's value does not extend beyond a hard arm and a long sword? You are quick to judge."

She eyed him with barely masked disdain. "Excuse me, sir. I have only had the example of a hundred or so knights from which to learn my prejudices. But I will endeavor not to fly to judgment."

He laughed again, this time with more humor and less rancor. "I am not sure that the edge of your tongue isn't sharp enough to daunt any knight's resolve. You are . . ." He trailed off abruptly as she smiled at what she'd perceived to be the honest appreciation in his tone.

He looked amazed, and if he was, it would not be more than she. The last thing she expected was to be smiling at this unlooked-for and unwanted husband.

He blinked, becoming mindful that he was staring at her. "Come, wife, I am sure you will find some use for me."

She darted a quick glance over his body and in that brief survey realized anew how large he was, how well-proportioned and clean-limbed, how dense his furry chest and broad and hard his shoulders. How masculine he was.

And how close. She could feel his heat.

She wet her lips, feeling suddenly a little breathless. "I only have yokes enough for two oxen, sir."

At this, he burst into laughter, throwing his great, bearded head back, the long, black hair swinging down his back. Suddenly he looked young and . . . and liberated.

It was an odd thing to think, but she could not refute the impression. He looked down into her face, still smiling, his teeth flashing white in his dark bearded face and she met his gaze and was bewitched.

She was caught in time, held in his eyes' summer bower green, transfixed, exposed and shielded, all at once. She had never experienced anything like it; she could barely remember why she stood here, or who she was.

"Your name is Jocelyn, is it not?" he asked.

She blinked. His question broke the spell, roughly recalling her to the present.

Had she meant so little to him that he hadn't fixed his wife's name in his mind? And why should that surprise her? He'd married her by proxy because he'd been promised a fiefdom should he survive the crusade. He'd forgotten her.

All her grievances, the essential unfairness of his being alive, rushed back to her. Father Timothy had gone on ad nauseum about how fierce and ungovernable this man's blood lust was and, because of that, how likely he was not only to die in battle, but be first to die.

The man standing before her didn't look intemperate and hotheaded. He looked like a man who had every ounce of his will under the strictest self-mastery. Indeed, she doubted his beard grew without first begging his indulgence.

"Aye," she said sullenly, winning a scowl from him. "Jocelyn. Was it only my name you mislaid or was it the fact that you had a wife at all?"

He flushed bronze but replied with affronted pride, "If I had remembered I had a wife, I would not have bedded Sowenna."

Sowenna? Fury made her tremble. He had no trouble recalling *her* name. "Is your defective memory supposed to make your whoring more palatable to me? For if that is your intent, you have failed."

"It wasn't my intent to make anything more palatable, simply to state a fact. I am no adulterer."

Her eyes narrowed. "Tell that to Sowenna."

His skin darkened to a shade behind the bush of his beard. "I am telling it to you."

For a long minute their gazes locked. His cold, hers hot. "Tell me, wife," he finally said, in tones which made it clear that they had done with that subject. Or so he thought. "Are you responsible for the manor's repair, the fief and the crops, the rents and the aids?"

Her pride made her forget her ire. "I would not pay a reeve for what I could do myself. And I trowe I have done better for this holding than any man has yet to do."

"Aye," he murmured. "You've been a very good steward. Were you as assiduous and devout a widow?"

"Of course," she replied indignantly. No one had ever accused Jocelyn Cabot of shirking an obligation.

"From the day we had word of your capture, I have had candles lit in supplication for your soul." She eyed him severely. "The cost of such a tribute has been seven shillings a year. That is eight crowns gone from the demesne ledgers for the salvation of your perdition-bound soul. A soul," she added darkly, "that your body still harbors!"

"And this was done because you mourned my loss, not, perhaps, out of," he paused, "gratitude?"

She flushed, unhappily aware that his words struck close.

"Don't vex yourself over the price of those candles, Joceyln," he finally said. "Perhaps the Good Lord will think you meant it as an indulgence, though I've a full complement of indulgences already." There was bitterness in his voice. "There is nothing like a crusade to earn indulgences.

"Still, I'd hate to see all those candles go to waste. Perhaps I should pursue fresh vices to ensure that your coin was well spent?" The laughter, suspect and subtle, flickered in his gaze. "Perhaps, my lady, you'd care to join me?"

His gaze warmed, inviting her. For a second she wondered what sort of sins a man like him indulged in? Then she remembered that Sowenna already knew.

"I shall say a novena for your blasphemy," she said coldly.

"My, you *are* a dutiful wife. How ever did I come to deserve such?"

There was that word "wife" again, spoken in that disconcertingly intimate voice, a voice that stroked the senses and sauced the mind. And had he moved closer? Because his body closed her off from the room as effectively as a wall, and the movement of that living wall with each deep inhalation fascinated her nearly as much as the word "wife."

"Yes, wife," he murmured.

Had she spoken? She couldn't recall. She wondered if that dark fur was silky or coarse to the touch.

"Jocelyn, my wife." His voice was quiet and low, a holy voice, a mystic's and a saint's voice . . . the devil's voice? "Aye, my wife who was never my bride."

She averted her eyes. He shouldn't say these things to her. 'Twas unseemly, scandalous.

"What's this? A blush? But then, you'd be a maid, wouldn't you?" he murmured. A scowl tipped his dark brows inward. "And would like to stay that way, I troth."

She could think of no answer. She wasn't sure she had one. When she'd heard Nicholas's fate, she'd put behind her all thoughts of what a man and a maid did. She'd thought she'd done so with relief, but now she wondered if there hadn't also been some small, unexplored ort of regret.

He watched the emotions play across her face and answered what he thought he read, his gaze becoming shuttered and flat.

"Don't annoy heaven with pleas that you might escape the inevitable, Jocelyn," he said. "You can't."

And he kissed her.

Jocelyn broke away from him and fled, leaving Nicholas staring after her, bemused and cautious and thoughtful.

For one intense instant she had melted into his arms, sweet and supple as a green willow. Her mouth had yielded, her hand had lain quiescent against his breast. But all too quickly she'd realized the brief breech in her formidable defenses. 'Twas a shame.

The scent of wood smoke and horse sweat rose from the drab surcoat she wore over a threadbare, dusty chemise. She was not blonde. She was not ripely made. She was tall and angular and her hair was like burnished midnight and her lips as sweet as figs. And when she'd stood over him as he lay abed, so angry the tears shimmered in her dark eyes, her voice low and passionate and alone, like the call of some night bird, he'd been overwhelmed.

He'd known who she was before she spoke, before he realized that the laws of God and men had already bequeathed her to him. Though in truth, she'd had it correct. He had forgotten he'd had a wife.

Which wasn't surpassingly strange, since he'd never seen her. He had only wed her by proxy in order to save her from some vague threat Brother Timothy, now Prior Timothy, had told him about—*and* to gain himself a fief. Yes. He had wanted something for himself, something tangible and real, something lasting. He did not want to die Sir No-Name.

So he'd made that marriage half-sotted on the eve of leaving on crusade. And, he admitted, unworthy though it was, he'd been more interested in the proposed wife's prospects than the wife herself.

But now he'd found something he wanted even more than her dowry, more than Cabot Manor, more than the land itself. He wanted Jocelyn, including her well-guarded heart.

He'd spent a lifetime in a dungeon learning to guard his tongue, avert his eyes, play the necessary game of weights and measures. She hadn't. Her valiance still shone as bright as a lodestar, even though he would have wagered much that she paid in her own blood for the privilege of championing the weak and defenseless. A woman like that, a woman of passion and courage, was worth any ten holdings.

But how to woo her? He could lay claim to her body, he'd every right and she, dutiful wife that she was, would doubtless suffer him. But he did not want her to *suffer* him. He'd never owned anything but what he carried within himself, and of that a good deal was made up of pride.

It would be a difficult campaign. She had made very clear what value she put on his knightly skills. Why she found the matter of his being alive troublesome, a vexation at best, a plague at worst. Added to which, he had been in bed with another woman.

That might take some time to repair.

CHAPTER 3

Since Nicholas wanted to talk to the matchmaking clerics, he returned the foul-tempered destrier to St. Albion's himself. Like the rest of what he had seen of the small abbey, he found the stables as snugly wrought as the wealthiest lord's manor. In truth, the saddles and bridles that a tonsured lad was oiling were far more ornately fashioned than any he'd seen in his own stables.

Aye, little St. Albion's did well for itself, Nicholas thought. As he approached the small abbey's exterior, a young, husky female voice raised in panic issued forth from an open window. It was Jocelyn. Nicholas slowed.

"What am I to do, Father?" Jocelyn asked.

"I do not see there is anything to do, child," Prior Timothy said, his tone troubled. "He is your husband, returned from a certain grave to take his place at your side as the master of this fief. God's will be done." Never had a priest sounded less convinced of God's will.

Jocelyn made an impatient sound. "I refuse to believe that this is His will. Why would He allow me to make right all the wrongs Gerent Cabot heaped upon Trecombe, only to set in Gerent's place a creature of similar temper and like habits?"

"Now, daughter." This time the voice belonged to the round and childlike Father Eidart. "Not all men are beasts."

"This one is." She spat the statement with such conviction Nicholas was taken aback.

"He is not in residence twenty-four hours and already he cavorts in bed, my *only* bed, with women whom he pays—"

"Enough!" Father Timothy cut in.

"How do you know that?" Father Eidart asked curiously. Nicholas was curious himself.

"Last night, he borrowed money from my miller at the tavern for his . . . entertainment," she ground out. "The miller came to me this morning to settle the account."

Ah, yes, Nicholas remembered. He had borrowed a few coins to buy the woman some wretched bauble. Little had he realized his villeins would go to Jocelyn for repayment. It appeared he would have to explain the concept of discretion to his newly adopted people.

"Then, indeed, he has proved himself an untamed, uncouth creature," Prior Timothy was saying. "But we knew this when we arranged the marriage."

"It is *why* we arranged the marriage," Father Eidart added penitently.

"I know, Father!" Jocelyn burst out. "I know. 'A man so bold and savage and fierce must invite death.'"

"A martyr's death," Father Eidart said solemnly. "It is what we anticipated."

"A dead sainted husband for me, reprieve from a tyrant's rule for Trecombe, and yearly donations to the Church for arranging it," she clipped out.

Nicholas was stunned for a moment. She had *paid* the priests to find her a husband likely to die on the battlefield?

No wonder St. Albion's was so well provisioned. Its riches had been bought with his death. Nicholas settled his shoulders against the warm stone wall. My, what an interesting wife he'd found himself.

"We only *trusted* that Nicholas's death would be God's will. We never gave any guarantees," Father Timothy said mildly. There was a moment's silence and Nicholas could picture Jocelyn standing there in her threadbare finery scowling crossly because God's will and her own hadn't been in accord.

"It's a test, isn't it?" she asked suddenly.

"A test?"

"Yes. The Lord is trying to determine if I am worthy to preside over the holding."

"How do you discern this?" Father Timothy asked.

"Well," she said slowly. "Nicholas is the final obstacle to my establishing a lasting peace and prosperity in Trecombe."

"He might not be an obstacle," Father Eidart suggested. "He might want peace and prosperity himself."

Nicholas could only imagine the flat look of contempt that statement brokered.

"He returns home and within a day is involved in a brawl over the disposition of land I have held peacefully for six years," Jocelyn said. "A few hours later he is debauching at the inn with the most disreputable hounds Trecombe breeds and, speaking of breeding, I return from my pilgrimage to find him with a woman drunk in *my only bed!* I swear by Neot's toe, that whatever happens, I will never sleep in that bed again—"

Father Timothy, like Nicholas, seized on that last bit. "'Whatever happens'? What do you mean by that? What do you imagine is going to happen?"

"Well," she said angrily. "We cannot allow all my, er, God's hard work to be destroyed. He would not want that. Would He?"

Neither holy brother had an immediate answer.

"It is clear. A wolf has been set amongst your flock and someone must get rid of him."

Nicholas's mouth dropped open, partly in amazement, but with a good deal of admiration, too. The woman would have made a fine warrior. She identified her enemy and had already decided the most expedient way to deal with him: Kill him. *If* she could bring herself to do it. Or she might talk the holy brothers into dealing with him.

For though she sounded resolute enough, her voice shook. A general she might have been, but a murderess? He doubted it.

This time the moment of silence stretched longer.

"You are not suggesting that we take a human life?" Father Timothy finally whispered. "We are monks, daughter. Not warriors. It is evil to even contemplate asking us. Convent-bred as you are, you know this."

Nicholas could hear her shuffling unhappily in place. "Forgive me, Father. You do right to chastise me, for if I am to be worthy of the honor and duty with which I have been invested, than I must be willing to do whatever deed needs be done in order to preserve this place, these people, and your holy selves."

"You must not sacrifice your immortal soul!" gasped Father Eidart.

"You remember my uncle's tyranny, the poverty and depriva-tion in which he kept St. Albion's? The disdain and humiliation he heaped upon your heads? The many ways he undermined and mocked the Church's authority?"

Father Eidart muttered a horrified, "God help us!"

Nicholas crossed his arms over his chest and scowled. More and more he wished his dead uncle-in-law were alive so that he could make his acquaintance and, not coincidentally, have the pleasure of making him not alive.

"In theory," Father Timothy murmured, "if a person was to commit a sin in order that graver sins were not committed, perhaps that person might be granted an indulgence . . ."

"An indulgence?" Jocelyn echoed in an odd tone.

At this, Nicholas's head shot up and his eyes narrowed. Until now, he'd thought himself listening to the ravings of someone grievously wronged, knowing that ravings seldom translated into action.

Now, with the monk's whispered hint, all that had changed.

Jocelyn was quiet. Indeed, for many minutes he could hear nothing but the sound of her breathing, quick with anxiety.

"I must go," she finally said, in harried tones.

"No. Wait." It was Father Timothy again. "I mean, I didn't mean . . . These are extenuating circumstances. I only meant to point out that God blesses his warriors in whatever battle they fight. As long as their cause is just. As a crusader, Nicholas is already assured a heavenly seat. How many of us can make that claim?"

"Yes," she said in a hollow voice. Apparently, the holy brothers had stunned her. "We should honor him for his service to God."

"Indeed, and he has been. For many years. It would be nice if he never had the opportunity to eradicate the good he has done. For his soul's sake, you understand," Father Timothy said desperately.

At this, Nicholas nearly choked. *Nice?* It would be *nice* if he died before he had the opportunity to sin again?

"I understand."

"That is not to say that he shouldn't be treated with respect, deference, and honor until . . . well, for the rest of his life. His wishes should be indulged and his hours easy, filled with convivial company and pleasant conversation."

Nicholas listened in amazement. He felt like a prize boar

being readied for market. He was surprised the holy brother hadn't added something about his diet.

"And make certain he eats to satiation those things sweet to the palate and agreeable to the stomach."

"I . . ." Jocelyn began in a distressed voice. Nicholas waited, willing his wife to repudiate the hinted plan. It would also be *nice* if someone chose to stand between him and those who would do him evil. It would be *nice* to have a champion.

She said nothing, however, and while he was disappointed, he was not surprised. From the little he had gleaned from this conversation, living under her uncle's auspices had been a misery of shame from which she'd only been free after her proxy marriage. Now the husband who was to have died had returned, a man demonstrably cut from the same base cloth as Gerent. How *could* she be pleased that he lived?

The rationale didn't cheer him greatly. Less so, when he heard her quickly excuse herself and flee her spiritual advisers. Still, he tarried.

"You do not think she'll actually . . . ?" Father Eidart gulped.

"I don't know."

"It is a sin."

"Is it? Jocelyn said that the wolf must be kept from the flock. Perhaps she is right. Come now, brother. Remember her desperation as her uncle lay dying? How she begged us to find a way that she might escape the wifely yoke her uncle's three brides knew? How grateful she has been since?

"With her patronage we have built this small and humble church up into a place worthy of Our Lord. With her continued patronage, we will build a reliquary fit for St. Neot and then, God willing, we will be able to persuade the bishops to release his sainted toe to us."

Nicholas started in amazement. This was all about a shriveled relic? His life was being traded for a *toe?* The absurdity of it nearly made him laugh.

"Think of the pilgrims such a relic will bring here!" Father Timothy went on. "Think of all the good we might do administering to these pilgrims."

Think of all the wealth such pilgrims would bring to Trecombe and St. Albion's, Nicholas silently added.

"Should Sir Nicholas live, do you think he will provide the reliquary such a hallowed relic requires? The reliquary Jocelyn has promised to have made?" Father Timothy snorted. "No."

Eidart sighed. "I do not doubt you are right."

"And Sir Nicholas would certainly not leave the holding to the Church upon his death as Jocelyn has publicly announced is her intention should she go to her grave without issue."

"No," Eidart agreed. "It is the way of such men to hoard in death that which they owned in life. Still, I am unhappy in this role."

"I am not very comfortable with it, either. Sometimes it is quite difficult to discern the Divine Plan. We must trust Providence will dictate Jocelyn's actions."

And with an unhappy demur from the guilt-stricken Eidart, the two moved off, leaving Nicholas to muse over what exactly one does with a potentially murderous wife and a pair of holy brothers who have an unholy interest in his demise.

Such thoughts occupied him as he headed back, passing the abbey garden patch being weeded by a young man. Clearly, Nicholas would do well to try to understand better what manner of woman he'd wed, of what she was capable, and what she was likely to do.

He stopped at the fence surrounding the little garden and leaned over it, hailing the fresh-faced lad. "Here, boy, what is your name?"

The lad looked up, smiling at the excuse of a short respite, and came willingly enough to the fence where he leaned on his hoe. "I be Keveran, sir."

"And are you an acolyte, Keveran?"

"Not yet, sir. I work for the holy fathers every Thursday so they will keep my ma in their prayers."

"I see. And do you know who I am?" Nicholas asked.

The boy grinned. "Aye, sir, I do. You're Sir Nicholas, returned from a heathen's cell in the Holy Land." There was a touch of hero worship in the lad's gaze. Obviously, a bright boy.

"Then you know my wife."

"Aye, sir. My father is weaver here in Trecombe as was his father before him. I've known Lady Jocelyn all my life."

"And what sort of lady is she?" Nicholas asked, carefully watching the boy's face. He had grown adept in reading the expressions of others. His survival had oft depended on it.

"She's a fine lady," Keveran avowed at once. "Devout and pure and just."

"I've married a saint!" Nicholas said and smiled.

Keveran laughed and then blushed. "Forgive me, sir. I didn't mean to laugh. Your lady is as quick to a kindness as a bird is to song, and as fair a mistress as ever a body could want . . ."

"But . . . ?"

"But when she's crossed, she's fierce as a hornet what's nest is been toppled, though as quick to regret her temper as she is to come into it."

"A pliant lass, though," Nicholas suggested. "Easily led."

The boy snorted. "Like yon boulder."

Nicholas could well imagine that. He looked at Cabot Manor standing over the riverbank, the fields being turned by men and a team of oxen. She would have to be resolute to direct the holding.

"She's a fair steward, my wife." He left just enough question in the statement to invite comment.

"No man could do better," the boy avowed.

"Aye. But she hasn't much dignity, I think."

The boy looked surprised. "Lady Jocelyn? As dignified as a bishop in his miter. Why would you think different?"

Nicholas waved his hand toward the holding. "The land look fertile, the cattle fat, the orchards well-tended, but the house is as bare as a hermit's cave and she's dressed with no greater consequence than yourself. I trow she knows not how to outfit herself as befits her consequence."

"Oh, she could turn a fair hand to it, if she'd the will," Keveran said with a sly, knowing smile. "But she has always spent any spare coin on you, sir."

"Me?" Nicholas asked in surprise.

"Aye. Have you not been in the church? Is it not a work of art glorifying the Lord? Your wife is responsible for it. She has endowed the church most generously in order for masses to be said for you, candles burned for you, prayers offered for you. She was overcome with grief at your loss. It was a wondrously poignant thing to see."

She had been overcome with *guilt* at his death, Nicholas thought and found some comfort there. For if she felt guilty simply because she'd bought a husband she wanted dead, well then, didn't it stand to reason that her conscience would never allow her to actually kill that same husband?

If she did, her self-imposed penance would be enormous. He could not help grinning. A few years after his murder and St. Albion's would rival Shrewsbury Cathedral.

"I own myself amazed such a paragon has gone unclaimed in her widowhood," Nicholas said casually.

"Oh, there's many a man thought to court her, Guy Moore being the most persistent, what with his lands abutting hers, er, yours, sir. But she has been most faithful to your memory."

So, it was not only priests and his wife whom he should have a care not to turn his back to. A surge of jealousy ripped through Nicholas.

"She must be overjoyed that you have returned," Keveran said sincerely.

"Oh, she is," Nicholas said. "She is."

CHAPTER 4

"Y ou look like a servant," Nicholas said.

Jocelyn, distracted by the list the weavers had left for Nicholas's inspection, nodded distractedly, neither offended nor interested in his assessment of her clothing. She had other things to contemplate. In the week since his arrival, Nicholas had asked her advice in his dealings with the people of Trecombe often. She took the responsibility seriously.

Besides, he could scarce fault her for one of his own most outstanding deficiencies. He didn't dress any better than a servant either, though, she admitted grudgingly, he was a good deal cleaner. She shot a quick glance at her big, dark husband. And hairier.

"Therefore," he went on, seeing that she wasn't going to respond further, "I have sent for the seamstress in order to have some new gowns made for you."

Now, he had her attention. She put down the accounts. "Why would you do that? We can put the coin to better use than to augment my vanity."

"*Whose* vanity?" he inquired mildly, the corner of his mouth lifting in that impossibly boyish manner. His emerald gaze flowed along the lines of her shabby gown making her feel shabbier still, and a number of other things that she'd as lief ignore.

"My vanity, Madame. Your image reflects on me as much as yourself. I would have it imbue the proper respect."

She vacillated miserably, knowing she should simply tell him she would *not* have a new gown. But the ignominious truth was that she wanted a new gown. Frankly, she *lusted* after a new gown.

It had been years since she'd owned something pretty and frivolous and fine. Which is precisely why she lowered her eyes and crossed her hands piously. Because one ought to make every effort to resist prideful self-ornamentation. Oughtn't one? "Men and women should command respect by their deeds, not by their apparel."

He smiled at her, and once again she had the odd notion that he knew and was amused by this, her latest in a series of increasingly frequent bouts of moral wrestling. She was being fanciful, she knew. How could he know her thoughts? It simply seemed so because his face was half obscured by his thick beard, thus making his green eyes seem brighter and more knowing.

"Have her make three new gowns for you," he said.

She made one last feeble attempt at humility. "Why?"

"Because I am the master and I say so," he replied equitably.

"Your will be done," she demurred. After all, Father Timothy had specifically charged her to be accommodating and pleasant to her husband and well, though she had found it a ridiculously easy undertaking, there was no reason to arbitrarily make it harder.

"Now, my lady, if you wouldst pour me more wine, I will fetch us a last bit of meat from the sideboard. Then I'll be gone to the village."

"Gone?" she echoed, surprised by the ripple of disappointment his statement provoked. True, he left her every day. Sometimes he went into town where she knew that as the lord of the holding and Master of Cabot Manor there were many things he needed to know about Trecombe.

Oft times he and his new protégé, Keveran, spent the mornings on the second floor in a little used section of the manor where, from the poundings and occasional crash, she assumed Nicholas was tutoring the lad in swordplay. But usually, none of this occurred until after sext. Mornings were hers.

"I want to see if this tanner is fouling the water as the villagers contend or if, as he claims, the water runs as pure downstream from his shop as above."

He handed her his goblet and winked. *Winked!*

Blood poured into her cheeks. She'd never been treated playfully before. She'd never been close enough to someone in either age or circumstance not to have both elements interfere with the relationship.

But Nicholas was her equal, if not in birth, definitely in status. He could say things to her no other person dared. Such intimacy was intoxicating, freeing, and . . . And something she would have to do without, she forced herself to recall, fingering the vial of poison she'd secreted beneath her tunic. Nonchalantly, he rose to go to the carving table.

Blast the man for providing her with so many opportunities to do him harm! It was almost as if he was daring someone to try to take his life. Had he no care for his person? Did he not realize that enemies lurked all about? That with the flick of her wrist she could empty this hideous elixir in his goblet and send him well and truly to his just reward?

Only she didn't want to send him anywhere. Not before lunch.

She forced herself to recall all the reasons why Trecombe,

St. Albion's, and she were all better off without her husband. But the only honest one she could come up with was that if something was not done soon, Sir Nicholas was going to impoverish them with his profligate ways. His years in that dungeon seemed to have bled from him all appreciation for the value of a coin.

He ate apples fresh which should have been stored for winter. He'd sent a man to Glastonbury who'd returned with exotic spices such as ginger and cinnamon with which to flavor their food. The same man brought back the tapestries that now hung on the chamber walls, soaking up the cold and pleasing the eye.

Jocelyn rotated her shoulders, working the twinge in her neck. The cold was helped greatly by the new hangings but a soft feather bed . . . Aye! That would be a luxury, indeed.

She'd gifted the only one in the manor, despoiled as it was by the memory of the slatternly blonde wench, to her husband. And while she had no regrets of that, she did regret there had been none to replace it. The pallet she lay on now was close to the cold floor, hard and mean. But beds, especially lofty, high feather beds, were prohibitively expensive. Even Nicholas would never waste money there.

But he had ordered her dresses.

Miserably, she studied her husband's broad back. Wretched creature that she was, part of her *wanted* new gowns and fur-lined pelisses like the ladies from Teague Manor wore; wanted stockings to keep her legs warm; and candles, bright beautiful lights, to fill the halls.

He'd brought those things.

No. She reminded herself. He didn't bring them. He simply took money *she'd* saved, money earmarked for the reliquary for St. Neot's toe, and spent it on . . . on her.

For, honesty compelled her to admit, he hadn't spent it on

himself. No fat destrier gobbled oats in her stable. No vain-glorious banners hung in the hall. No shiny new mail or freshly fashioned swords had appeared since his arrival.

Everything he owned or bought or traded for he seemed content to share. *Seemed.* She must remind herself that it was young days yet, that Gerent had had occasional bouts of pleas-antness. She frowned, disliking the comparison of Nicholas to Gerent. It felt too like betrayal. And there was no reason for her to feel that way. She'd betrayed no one. Yet.

She looked up as Nicholas returned with a succulent slice of beef, the aroma of cloves hanging above it like incense, the opportunity to poison him lost. Happily, she regarded the plate he carried.

Her eyelids narrowed in bliss and she inhaled. Spices. He loved spices and had introduced them to her and now she loved them, too. Cinnamon, cloves, and nutmeg were an indulgent revelation, a feast for the senses and a bounty for the palate. She'd never dreamed things could taste as pretty as their aroma, but they did.

With one brow cocked inquiringly, Nicholas sawed off a piece of beef and speared it with the end of his knife. Enticingly, he dangled it before her mouth. She'd already eaten. To eat more would be gluttony.

"My lady looks piqued," he said, waving the meat nearer. "It would be a sin to waste this."

"It needn't go to waste," she answered faintly, trying not to lick her lips. "We could break fast on the remains tomorrow."

He shrugged and popped the morsel into his own mouth, chewing thoroughly, savoring it. He did everything with such *appreciation:* eating, drinking, even the manner in which he lis-tened was intent, paying full heed to what was said to him, giving the speaker a sense of importance.

Aye, and the way he walked, too, with his shoulders held

back, his dark face lifted to the sun, or the breeze, or even the shadows, seemed as if he was the recipient of favors received. He was a rare pleasure to watch move.

He was also a conundrum and Jocelyn had learned to be wary of puzzles. In the past, the answers were invariably not to her liking. Most likely, Nicholas was simply being pleasant preparatory to demanding his connubial rights.

In truth, it relieved her that he troubled himself over that which he could simply take. Gerent certainly never bothered to court his women. *If* that was what all this pleasantness was about.

She'd begun to have her doubts. Because for eight nights running now, she'd laid awake on her pallet, stiff with an anticipation that had never been answered. Each night she'd prayed he would simply come in, do the deed, and be done with it, done with the act, done with the sweetening, done with the questions that he created simply by all his cosseting and spoiling of her.

Od's bodkin! Why couldn't he just reveal himself as the man she'd found drunk and malodorous in her bed with another wench, not this solicitous giant with his cool composure and his overwhelming patience and the infrequent smile that caused her heartbeat to race and her skin to flush?

Besides, the fact that he hadn't come to her pallet was beginning to vex her with decidedly worldly speculation. What would it be like to be bedded by a creature so overtly masculine, so big and muscled?

Maybe, she should *offer* what he didn't demand? Surely, she owed him that. Hadn't Father Timothy all but suggested it?

It was this conjecture that stayed with her after Nicholas bid her a respectful adieu and went off to town. Jocelyn left the table and wandered, uncharacteristically vague in her destination and uncertain of her plans, finding as the hours passed and the day wore on that a terrible fascination had taken root in her imagination, but one impossible to ignore.

Finally, her thoughts chased her from her room and down into the kitchen where the servants had already begun preparing the evening meal. A pair of girls washed and peeled vegetables while a lad was already turning the haunch spitted over the fire in the hearth. The head of the kitchen, Gwen, stopped kneading the dark mass of bread on the big table and looked up.

"Aye?" the older woman asked.

She had no real reason to be here. The staff was well-trained and loyal and the weekly tallying of food stores already done. "I . . . I came to make certain there was enough to eat this evening. Last night, Sir Nicholas looked like he could have eaten more."

"Oh, aye," Gwen said complacently, returning to her kneading. A smile turned her lips, even though her gaze was fixed deliberately on the bread dough. "Tha' one is a man with an appetite to be sure. And with a hungry look about 'im. But I'm not certain it's food he pines after. Mayhap, you can satisfy him where my cooking can't, Milady."

The girls tittered and Jocelyn, unwilling to let them see how their words brought the blood boiling to her cheeks, cleared her throat, nodded sharply, and spun around, fleeing the warm kitchen.

A few moments later, she found herself walking toward the sea path. Often when Gerent had been alive, she'd sought refuge here above the sea cliffs, where seabirds wheeled through the mist and plumes of water erupted on the breakers far below.

She had nearly reached the path when she spotted a lone figure standing atop a prominent boulder, one foot resting higher, his hand on his hip. At once, she recognized her husband. The wind plastered his shirt against his broad chest and set his cape swirling about him. He looked so very masculine, so strong and dauntless. Something inside of her yearned to go nearer and because she mistrusted that impulse she'd been about to disobey it and turn when he spied her.

"Jocelyn," he called. "Come. Join me."

As she hesitantly approached the base of the boulder, he walked to the edge and leaned down, holding out his hand. His smile was brilliant against his dark beard. "Here. Hold on to my wrists with both your hands."

She did so, and with no noticeable effort at all, he lifted her to his side and released her. At once she stumbled on the sloping surface and he caught her to his side. He was solid and big, his arm a steel band about her waist.

"Careful," he whispered against her temple, his breath warm and sweet. "I wouldn't want to become a widower before I was a husband."

Her breathing stumbled as had her footing. His words too closely echoed her recent thoughts. What would it be like to be made love to by Sir Nicholas?

She pulled away in confusion and he let her go.

"What are you doing here?" she asked.

He sighed, as if she'd disappointed him and then, smiled, biting back that disappointment. "I'm going to build a castle here," he said.

She stopped and stared at him. "A castle?" she asked disbelievingly. "Why? We've never been troubled by the barons. Indeed, few even know we exist."

He turned a troubled face toward her. "If there is one thing I have learned in my journeys, it is that what someone holds, no matter how small or seemingly inconsequential, others will want to take.

"There are powers greater than barons, Jocelyn. Men who

would steadily accrue loyalties and allegiances from all class and type of man, nobleman, merchant, and freeman. A time will come when we will be forced to choose between one great lord and another. We may not wish to make a choice, but we will be forced to it. And then . . ." He stopped and sighed again and this time his sigh was rife with weariness.

"And then?" she prompted quietly.

"Then I must be able to hold against those men that we will someday call enemies. We must be prepared."

He looked resolute but so saddened and troubled that before she realized what she had done, she touched her fingertips lightly to his cheek. "Then build your castle, Nicholas," she said softly.

She had never called him by his Christian name without his title attached. He gazed steadily into her eyes, communicating with her in ways she had never realized were possible. He turned his head slowly and pressed his lips to the tips of her fingers. His eyelids shut, the thick fringe of lash sweeping against his dark cheek.

Her skin tingled and her pulse quickened. She felt her mouth grow moist and her lips part on a whisper of surprise. He stepped closer. His eyes opened, questioning. She did not have an answer. Not yet . . . Her hand dropped.

"I . . . best leave. I have . . . I have duties to attend to."

"I would never have taken you for a coward, Jocelyn," he said.

But she was a coward and they were standing in full sight of the manor and she was not yet ready to admit what she contemplated. She did not answer and before he could react, she scrambled down off the boulder and started off at a brisk pace. He would probably follow her. Back to the manor. Up the stairs. To her room and from there . . . ? Her skin began to prickle all over again.

Only when she'd gone a few dozen paces did she realize she didn't hear his pursuit. Furtively, she glanced back over her shoulder. He was still standing where she'd left him, watching her with an ironic smile on his darkly handsome face.

Damnation!

Back at the manor, the encounter with Nicholas provoked fleeting, unruly, and decidedly unholy imaginings. She tried earnestly to keep her thoughts pure, but the memory of his breadth and stature, his smile and his green eyes kept intruding until she finally gave up.

To wonder about what sort of lover one's husband was was not unnatural, she told herself. She'd been a wife six years without having a wife's knowledge. She had seen countless giggling and blushing girls turn into countless women, some whose eyes shone whenever their man was about, others wont to duck at the sight of anything that sprouted hair upon its chin. Jocelyn wanted to know why.

She had no illusions about how she was viewed. Trecombe thought her a saint but she'd never desired sainthood. Sainthood had been foisted upon her by her convent training, her uncle's depravity, and the wretchedness of the people she'd inherited.

If she *had* wanted sainthood, her nature was more likely to have chosen a martial path to it, one with swords and confrontation and battles. She'd never have opted for sainthood via chastity.

Yet, here she was, twenty-one years of age and still a maid. And decidedly not a saint, whatever Trecombe thought. Saints didn't dwell on things like the size of their husbands' hands or the oiled ease with which their hips moved when they walked, or the memory of their male organ.

She did.

And as the day turned into evening and her imaginings

grew more fevered, frustration begat desperation. And desperation is the mother of sophistry.

So that when Jocelyn considered it carefully, it became clear to her that Father Timothy had meant to address her unnatural state when he'd urged her to comfort Nicholas in *every* possible manner. No abbey wants an unnatural lady-lord as their patron, nor does a town wish to think its lady-lord an aberration and what was a wife who was a virgin, if not that?

She *owed* losing her virginity not only to Nicholas, who was slated to die, but to the church, to Trecombe itself.

With such happily unassailable logic guiding her, Jocelyn made early for her chamber that night, leaving Nicholas still at the table, talking with the sheriff who'd returned with him. Jocelyn hadn't heeded much of their conversation. Her thoughts were unraveling along lines that left her flushed and light-headed, so much so that at one point Nicholas remarked upon her state and asked if she was feeling well. Soon after, she excused herself.

But thinking and planning a thing, she soon discovered, were not the same as doing it. She made for her room and removed her threadbare gown, wishing that she had something handsome to wear, settling instead for a loose chemise that tied at the throat and fell straight to her feet.

She hesitated a moment before having the girl unbraid her hair and comb it out, so that it lay like a sheet of darkness about her shoulders. She bit her lips and stared at her reflection in the polished metal before dismissing the servant.

Then, taking a deep breath, she lit the rush torch from the hearth fire and, like a soldier entering the battlefield, stalked down to the chambers Nicholas had commandeered as his own. Marshaling her courage, she entered his room quickly and stopped inside the door. She looked about in surprise.

The small chamber was as Spartan as a novitiate's cell. The

bed, a chest, a table, and a chair composed the lot of his furnishings. No tapestries covered his walls. No vessel filled with wine stood awaiting his pleasure. No fire burned in the hearth, only a few sullenly glowing coals. Alongside the chest stood a dented but well-oiled sword, standing in its worn scabbard.

The reminders that the man she'd come to give herself to was a warrior nearly sent her scurrying back to her room. But she was no coward and feared the loss of what she'd not yet known worse than blows. She stayed.

She glanced at his bed, but could not bring herself to lie where another woman had been with her husband. Instead, she quickly piled blankets and a thick sheepskin in her arms. She could make a bed in front of the fire, but she was not comfortable with the thought of being so blatantly exposed by its light. Instead, she chose a place beside the great chest, within the fire's warm circle, but shadowed.

She lay down flat on her back, folding her hands at her waist and closing her eyes. Intently, she listened to the sound of her own breathing and forced it to a slower pace. She waited.

He didn't tarry long with the sheriff. Within a short while she heard heavy footsteps in the outer hall. Then the door swung open and a light appeared. He stood huge and masculine in the doorway, his back to her as he addressed someone in the hall. Her heartbeat tripped over itself. Would he be gentle? Would he be swift? Would he take any care at all with her?

"Nay, I've never had a squire, young Keveran, nor do I intend to start. To bed with you, boy." The tone of Nicholas's voice was good-natured but unutterably weary. "Tomorrow you'll wish you'd stayed at the wainwright's for I am unused to waiting for what I want, and unwilling to wait more than a second longer than necessary for what I'll have. We'll put in a full day and then some."

She frowned, pondering what this meant but then she heard the door close. She squeezed her eyelids tightly shut, feigning sleep, and heard the sounds, somehow lonely, of a man moving about a nearly empty room.

She knew the moment he saw her.

For a long moment there was silence. Then she heard the whisper of leather sole boots moving near. Then the heat from his body washed over her and his breath fanned her cheek. Why didn't he do something? Why didn't he—

Fingertips brushed her cheek, a gossamer touch of such delicacy she would have sworn butterfly wings drifted across her skin. She held her breath. The touch returned and lingered this time, trailing sensation across her lower lip.

No one had ever caressed her before. There had been awkward kindliness in some of the nuns' rare embraces, and Gerent's occasional rib-bruising, drunken jocularity, but never tenderness, never this breath-stealing care. Her neck arched, her lips parted, and she sighed.

His fingertips played along her jaw, his thumb tipped her face up . . . For a kiss? *Please.* She wanted so much to be kissed.

Instead, his touch drifted down her throat to the pulse beating wildly at its base. With a simple, deft movement, he twitched the knot, loosening the collar. His hand slipped beneath the cool cloth, trespassing lower still, gently pulling the neckline down lower . . . lower . . .

Her breath caught in her throat. His fingertips brushed gently across the full upper swell of her breast, teasingly close to exposing its crest and the nipple that strained tight and swollen, eager for his touch.

She kept her eyes shut, closed against the reality of him, the dense, masculine actuality of him, steeping herself in the fantastical sensations. It was easier this way, imagining a phantom lover bestowing these gentle caresses, a phantom lover with slender, graceful hands and a peace-loving nature. Not this dark giant with blood in his past . . . and his future.

His hand moved back up to her shoulder, slipping under her neck and cradling the back of her head. Then, light and ephemeral as April snow, his lips touched hers.

It was surpassingly wondrous his kiss, as enticing as his spices, honeyed and delectable and addictive. She sighed as his lips burnished hers, opening to sip his mint-sweetened breath. He held his lips softly against her parting lips, trembling slightly. And then . . . ? Then he eased her gently back to her pallet. And released her.

She waited for something more. She wanted more. She wanted whatever a husband and wife might do in the privacy of their chamber. Her heart pounded in her chest, her skin prickled, hot and tight, her thoughts seemed mired in a pool of anticipation and anxiety.

But nothing happened.

She opened her eyes, looking about accusingly for the man to whom she'd offered herself. He stood by the hearth, turned away from her, his hand braced on the lintel, his head bowed. She twisted in frustration and her eye was caught by the glint of metal on the chair beside his pallet. His dagger. Unsheathed.

She nearly groaned as yet another opportunity to dispatch this huge, masculine problem presented itself. Once more, the reckless brute had his back to her.

Silently, she slid from the pallet, moving on cat's feet behind him. He didn't move. He simply stood with an inexplicable air of resigned vigilance in the tension of his broad shoulders, the cant of his big body. He looked as alone as she so often had felt.

Amazed at herself, she placed her hand gingerly upon his

back. The muscles beneath her fingers jumped. She wet her lips.

"Sirrah, you are tired. You should sleep."

For a moment he did not answer.

"Sir?"

"Sleep does not come easily to me of late," he finally answered. "Do you have some wifely draught that might aid me in my search of peace?"

By the saint! He might as well just *ask* her to murder him. She spoke shortly, angered more with him for his lack of caution or with herself for her cowardice she could not say. "No! No, I have no herb craft."

"A pity," he said, and turning she saw that he smiled and that there was a new warmth in his smile and that the odd assessing quality she'd sometimes seen in his gaze had fled before it. "But then, the night holds wonders a sleeping man cannot enjoy."

Her breath caught in her throat. The look he bent on her was suddenly searching and faintly predatory. And it was this slight, irrefutable resemblance to Gerent, the stalking quality in the way he turned toward her, that sent her back apace. His eyes narrowed.

She marshaled her courage. She lifted her chin. "I have come to fulfill my wifely obligation," she said staunchly.

He did not seem surprised. He only regarded her between narrowed forest green eyes that glinted in the firelight. "Have you? How dutiful of you.. But you are dutiful, are you not, Jocelyn? Dutiful and virtuous."

He laughed slightly, but it was a humorless sound. "Keep your virtue, Jocelyn. I'm not Gerent. I learned self-mastery from the harshest of teachers."

She stared at him wide-eyed. "I don't understand."

He leaned back against the wall next to the hearth, the

shadows immediately covering him, leaving his voice discon-
nected from his corporal form. He had a beautiful voice.

"I've been many places in the world and I have seen countless sacrifices. Too many. But this, dear wife, isn't an altar and
I'm not a priest."

"But . . . I don't understand," she repeated. She was bewil-
dered, somewhat provoked, a good deal more humiliated, but
she'd never been one to let pride guide her actions. Trecombe
would have never survived Gerent if she had.

He cocked his head and even in the darkness she could see
the gravity of his expression. "I will not say that I do not want
you, Jocelyn. My body trembles with want. My loins are afire
to feel the sweet release promised by your body's embrace.

"But in a Saracen dungeon, Jocelyn, I saw men who'd had
everything taken from them, pride, hope, and dreams. I've
had a lifetime of taking what I wanted and having what I
needed taken from me. No one will ever take what I treasure
away from me again. Be that honor, hope, this holding. Or
you."

She shivered at the sudden ferocity in his gaze. He saw it
and banked the fires he kept so well hidden, his face once
more composed and calm. "But I'll not *take* either. I'll only
accept what you give.

"So go back to your pallet, Jocelyn, or take off your gown
and touch me like a wife touches her husband."

She couldn't do it. He asked too much. She'd been a maid
too long.

She turned and fled his room, racing down the corridor to
her own chambers. Only once there did she pause, her
thoughts a maelstrom. He roused her admiration with his dignity and her fear with the desire she'd seen burning in his eyes.

Thenceforth, whatever else happened, she would never
again confuse Nicholas with Gerent Cabot.

CHAPTER 5

D
o you think it too ostentatious?" Jocelyn asked, the honest worry in her voice vying with the pleasure lighting her eyes as she whirled about in her new gown.

The sunlight pouring through the solar windows glinted off the raven dark braids that swung out as she spun. The soft blue color of the gown brought out the apricot hue in her cheeks, the ripe, succulent tint of her lips. She fairly glowed with pleasure.

Nicholas struggled for a smile but had to settle for a nod before forcibly returning his attention to the heavy ornate staff the guild masters had presented him with that morning. As a tribute of appreciation, they'd said. As a token of their approval, Jocelyn had remarked under her breath.

"It's fetching," he said shortly, hoping she'd not take offense at his shortness, but unable to say more when she looked like that and stood so near and toyed so heedlessly with his heart. "Perfect."

"Come, sir?" she said, her teasing tone irresistible. "Perfect? Perfection is not found this side of heaven."

He looked up, catching her eye and holding her gaze. "Isn't it? I could have sworn different." She turned away, but not before he saw the blush sweep up her throat or her flattered smile.

There was a time when he would have felt a fool for speaking such flirtatious nonsense to a woman, but it was easy to say such things to Jocelyn. Perhaps because he believed them. Each day she grew more relaxed, seeming to shed years right before his eyes, turning from a severe, disapproving chatelaine into this pretty, lighthearted girl.

But such a boon did not come without its price. It took all of his self-control not to throw her over his shoulder and take her to his, nay *their* chambers, and be done with this torture.

With unseeing eyes, he stared down at the staff he held. He'd only himself to blame for the plight he found himself in. He'd been its architect. He'd wanted to calm Jocelyn's fears, to reassure her that they would lie together only when she willed it so.

Well, he'd succeeded in convincing her. He'd succeeded so well, in fact, that here it was nearly two weeks later and he'd still not tasted his wife's charms. As for the lust he'd been at such pains to deny, it ate at him like acid.

Simply put, his wife's friendliness was going to drive him mad. He looked up as she whirled once more, shyly preening as she smoothed the soft wool over her hips. It was like her. She valued things, from the alewife's skills to the way the light fell on the budding rowan tree.

She'd given her life for this place, these people, and never asked anything back. How could he fail to admire her? And there, between admiration and lust, lay a fertile bed for love. Yes, he'd grown to love his wife and growing in love, grew even greater in desire.

It was a hell of a circle.

Now, if he could just trust her not to kill him—

"My lord!" Keveran burst into the chamber unannounced, fear breaking his voice. Nicholas stood up, and set down the staff, his hand reaching for the battered sword that was never far from his person.

At once, Jocelyn went to the lad, austerity and purpose falling like a curtain over her features, hiding the girl she'd been a moment before. "What is it, Keveran?" she asked.

"Sir Guy is coming!" the youngster blurted out.

"Aye?" asked Nicholas calmly. "What of it? He is welcome as our neighbor—"

"It isn't neighborly what he's coming to do. He's coming to challenge you to another joust. This time to the death!"

Jocelyn turned her head quickly toward Nicholas, a question and an accusation clear in her expression.

"I haven't seen the young dog since I unseated him," Nicholas answered tersely. What did he have to do to make her believe that he wanted nothing but peace in his life?

"It's true, Lady. Guy Moore has been in Glastonbury licking his wounds. But my father says he hasn't healed them, he's only kept them open."

"This is ridiculous," Jocelyn said, straightening up and looking about angrily. "What does he hope to accomplish with your death?"

"The land. The manor. The fields. The mill." Nicholas looked at her. "You."

"He couldn't be such a fool to think I would accept him."

"Of course, he's a fool," Nicholas said in a dangerous voice. He picked up his sword. "No one else but a fool would challenge me. Keveran, when he arrives, fetch him hither. Then I will—"

"No," Jocelyn said.

Nicholas turned. His wife had moved away from the boy, and stood, tall and regal, in a pool of sunlight. "No."

He struggled to keep his fury in check, knowing how she loathed violence. He glanced at Keveran. "Begone, Keveran. Do as I say."

As soon as the boy had left he returned his attention to Jocelyn. She remained where she'd taken her stance, her face colorless and her eyes dark. "What say you nay to, my lady?"

"No joust. No fighting. It only begets more fighting."

"If I refuse to fight, others will soon know of it. Such refusal amongst men, Jocelyn, is an invitation to take what another owns, abuse what they do not want of it, and use what they do." He looked at her in telling silence.

She understood. She trembled but her gaze did not waver. He felt torn by conflicting desires, the one to comfort and deny what he knew must be done, the other to force her to concede that he was right, and see in his ability to protect her his worth, not his worthlessness.

"Do not meet with him, Nicholas," Jocelyn asked between stiff lips. "If you do, it will be the beginning of an unending line of men waiting outside my door to challenge you. And each day they come, you will grow more accustomed to their challenges, more accustomed to spilling their blood and more accustomed to having your own spilt."

Her lips quivered. Her eyes blazed behind a chrysalis of tears. "Well, I *won't* become accustomed to it! I never did!"

"You are wrong—"

"I *thought* I was wrong!" she broke in, trembling where she stood, her body tense. "I thought you would prove to be more than a man with a sword. But give a man a sword and sooner or later he'll wield it." She spoke derisively, her dark eyes flashing with contempt.

"You are like all the rest, all the godly knights lusting after battle, not content lest you have marred something, brutalized someone, defeated, cowed or beat another."

"Is that what you believe?" he asked, his voice dropping. The air between them crackled with the accumulated tension of the last weeks. All the desire, the hope, the longing seemed suddenly futile and wasted.

"What else *can* I think?" she countered fiercely. "With the first man to tip his sword in your direction, you rise like a dragon, all fire and fury, the promise of battle in your eyes and in your fisted hands. I'd rather—"

The remainder of her sentence was lost in the sound of clattering footsteps and shouts of warning from the outer hall. The door to the chamber crashed open and Guy Moore stood framed in the doorway.

Nicholas regarded him coldly. His golden hair streamed down upon his shoulders. A silver clasp glinted on his shoulder, pinning back the rich, dark red cloak and exposing the gold threads adorning his saffron-colored surcoat. His pale doeskin gloves were likewise enriched as were the cuffs of his leather boots.

The overweening pup had dressed the part of Saint George come to slay the dragon.

Well, he would not be disappointed. For Nicholas certainly felt the part of a beast watching the cave door, enraged at any challenge to the treasure he guarded. Why hadn't his bride even named him "beast"?

He looked at Moore and laughed, sudden bitter realization returning to him his once vaunted recklessness. She would *never* come to him of her own free will. And he would never force her. They would be forever thus, he standing without her chamber longing for entry, she guarding herself against his supposed nature.

Maybe she was right. Maybe, after all, he would never be more than a human destrier, a hulking dragon, making mayhem with fists and blade. But, by God, if that was all he was, it was something at which he excelled.

"What do you want, Moore?" he asked, stepping in front of Jocelyn.

The knight had the effrontery to let his gaze touch Jocelyn before bowing with bare civility. "And a good day to you, too," he sneered. "I see no one has bothered to mention that a knight should have more to recommend him than brute strength and animal cunning. Which all of Trecombe knows, sir, is the only way in which you unseated me."

If Moore thought to provoke him to a rage with such obvious taunts, he would be sorely disappointed. Nothing this pretty fribble called him could touch him. He'd already been pierced through by Jocelyn's words and the knowledge that he would never win her wary heart. And since he could not have her love, why then . . . what mattered anything else?

Nicholas snorted. "You know nothing of war or battle, boy. Pray thee you never will."

Guy flushed hotly. "I may not yet have been christened on a battlefield, but at least *my* honor did not die in some heathen's cell."

Nicholas regarded him flatly. "Go home to your mother's hearth and return to me when you've grown a beard."

"Like yours? Pah! You've come to England more heathen than native son. What other vileness did you learn from your captors—or were they your masters?" Moore stepped forward, his clean chin jutting belligerently. Nicholas stood silently. Behind him he heard Jocelyn hiss on a sharp indrawn breath.

"If you were worthy of being a knight, you would never have surrendered," Moore continued. "Thus, I can only assume that you are no knight, sir, but a jumped-up villein who Richard, in battle blindness, mistook for a man."

Nicholas turned his back on him. "Get out of here, Moore, before you have to be carried out."

"Not before you and Jocelyn hear me out."

At the sound of his wife's name on another man's lips, Nicholas's head swung back around. "You speak with a familiarity to which I take exception, boy. Henceforth, refer to my wife as *Lady* Jocelyn."

"Why?" the young knight asked. "I am far more familiar with the lady than you are, Sir No-Name."

The suggestive tone sparked the embers Nicholas had been trying so hard to keep banked. In one long stride, he was at Moore's side, his face inches from the lithe young knight's. "Go, boy," he said in a velvety rasp. "Now."

Moore met his gaze, his eyes wild with injured pride and greed. "I challenge you to a joust, Sir Nicholas, the winner of which shall have Cabot Manor and its holding." His gaze leapt to where Jocelyn stood, dutifully silent but trembling, her eyes hot and contemptuous. "And Jocelyn."

He smirked at Nicholas, confident in his jousting skills. Now that he knew the sort of tricks the barbarian utilized, he would easily overmatch him. He'd better weapons and finer steeds than this hairy brute had ever seen, let alone owned. "Three days hence."

He mistook his man. Nicholas had seen the leer cast upon his wife and it drove a spike of pain through an already open wound.

"A pox on your 'three days hence!'" With a savage snarl, he backhanded Moore, the violence of the blow hurling the young knight across the room.

"You want my wife?" he thundered striding across the room after the fallen man. "You dare come in here and leer at my *wife?*"

He seized Moore's embroidered surcoat and hauled him to his feet only to shove him away and stalk toward him again. Feverishly, Moore staggered back, barely able to keep his balance, hand groping at his side for his sword. When Nicholas was almost upon him, he found it and with a screech of steel wrenched it from its scabbard, bringing its tip to the center of Nicholas's broad chest.

Nicholas looked down at the point denting his tunic and sneered.

"I should kill you!" Moore howled. The brute's sneer became more pronounced. "If I kill you I'll be doing her a favor. She can't want you. She can't!"

A shadow crossed Nicholas's face, blunting the hard edge in his expression. Something dark and foreboding, deeper still than pain, bloomed into a hideous resolve.

"Perhaps not," he said, without looking at her, "but unless you release her with my death, she is mine and mine she'll stay until my dying breath."

He could not bring himself to see how Jocelyn received this timely reminder that with his death, she would be free. She need not even be party to it. She simply needed to stand by and witness his death. Then accuse the murderer and be free of both men.

With a sound of pain, he grabbed Moore's blade in his bare hand and shoved it aside while cuffing the young knight across the face, as one would a presumptuous brat.

"Last chance, boy. Go home." He struck him again. Moore staggered back under the seemingly casual smack. His lip broke, dribbling bright red blood down his chin. His brows lowered and his chest heaved. He started to bring the sword back up to Nicholas and, with a sound of contempt, Nicholas ripped it from his hand and tossed it aside.

"I warn you, sir," Guy panted. "Don't lay hand on me again or—"

Nicholas smote him across the face again. "Or what?"

"Please, Nicholas!" he heard Jocelyn.

Only her voice could have turned him aside. He looked

69

toward the sound of her voice and as he did, a short dagger appeared in Moore's hand from beneath his short cape. With a triumphant roar, he slashed at Nicholas. The blade cut across his tunic and sliced through his flesh.

With a gasp, Nicholas fell back but not before he'd seen the feral glint in Moore's pale eyes and the spittle at the corner of his mouth.

Be damned if the boy wouldn't do Jocelyn's work for her yet! Nicholas laughed, holding his arms wide, backing up and circling the panting young knight. The sword had spun beneath the table on the other side of the room. If he could just get to it, he might end this farce.

"Stop laughing!" Moore shouted, slashing wildly.

"Why? That you might kill me with an all due sense of gravity? Never." He sneered.

He'd humiliated the boy in front of his lady love and now Moore was nearly frantic with the need to repay him for that humiliation. That frenzy of hate was the only thing Nicholas had on his side. The boy was young, quick, trained, and had a dagger. And he was spilling precious blood by the moment.

"Don't you see the humor in it, boy?" he asked, backing toward the sword. "I survived a crusade, a spear in my side, a fetid Syrian dungeon, and a three thousand mile trek across hell, and here *you* are, a moment away from dispatching me with that little toadsticker. Well, you'd best do it quickly, Moore, lest I die of laughter first."

Moore plunged forth again, slashing Nicholas across the forearm before he could leap back. It was a shallow wound, but one which would soon grease his palm with blood, making it difficult to grip the sword. Should he get to it. He edged sideways, his gaze never leaving Moore's.

Suddenly, Moore darted forward, his dagger flailing as he broke between where Nicholas stood and where the sword lay.

"What sort of fool do you take me for, Sir No-Name?" he spat contemptuously. "And who is now trapped? Why, 'tis you! Ha!"

Moore sauntered forward and flipped the dagger over, holding it by its tip, preparatory to hurling it. Into his chest, Nicholas supposed.

"I should thank you," Moore said before addressing Jocelyn who stood behind him. "You'd best leave now, Jocelyn. You wouldn't want to see this—"

Crash! Out of the corner of his eye, Nicholas saw the guild master's staff come careening out of nowhere and catch Guy Moore flush to the side of his head. Like a poleaxed beef, the young knight crumpled where he'd stood.

Nicholas turned. Jocelyn stood beside him, her lips pursed, her eyes dark as she stared down at the fallen knight. "Oh, yes, I do," she said to the knight she knocked senseless.

Nicholas stared at her. She'd saved his life. She lifted her head. Tears spilled down her cheeks.

"Why?" he whispered, uncertain what he would do if he allowed himself to move.

The tears might flow unabated, but this was Jocelyn, not some tender, sentimental girl. Her lips tightened with exasperation.

"Why?" She threw down the staff in disgust. "Because I love you, you great hairy ox!"

And without awaiting his reply, she marched through the open door.

CHAPTER 6

"Witless ox. Blind knave. Dullard! Fool!" Jocelyn strode down the corridor leaving a litany of her husband's failings in her wake, the servants fleeing before her approach. Having begun in fear, her tears had continued in a glut of relief. They streamed down her face as she strode to her chambers and slammed the door shut behind her.

If he ever, *ever* put himself at such a disadvantage again, she would stab him herself! And what of those wounds? Had he sense enough to see them properly bound? Would someone make a compress for him. Perhaps she should . . . ? *No!*

She dashed a renewed flood of tears from her cheeks and sat down on the window seat, glaring out at Guy Moore's squire loading his barely conscious master onto his palfrey. If Guy Moore ever set foot on their land again, she would give order to have him shot.

When she had seen the paltry *boy* draw his dagger on her unarmed husband, her heart had stopped, and her breath had stilled in her chest. She'd tried to avert the scene, tried to convince Nicholas not to see Moore. But would he listen to her? No. So, she'd confronted him.

She hadn't anticipated his reaction, his shock and disgust. Then Moore had entered and provoked her husband more than any man she knew would have allowed. Still, Nicholas hadn't hurt him. Not even when Moore had held a sword to Nicholas's throat.

Restlessly, she rose and paced through her room, picking up and setting aside her needlework, uneasy with her thoughts. She had been wrong to accuse Nicholas of blood lust, wrong to judge him by her uncle's ghost, wrong to try to stay his hand when it had only been raised to protect her. He was no ravening beast, her husband, he was a man who would die for her, a man she wanted desperately to live *with* her. Because she was in love with him, Sir Nicholas No-Name.

As for killing him, she would as soon kill herself. Sooner. He was vital to her. Everything to her. Each morning she rose eager to hear his voice, to speak with him. Each night she trudged listlessly to her pallet, unhappy to be parted from him. She loved arguing with him, teaching him, listening to his tales, looking up and seeing his green eyes fixed with such solemn directness upon her.

What a fool she'd been. But no more, she thought fiercely. It was time she put away her fear and pride. If he was to walk in here in the next minute, she would greet him as her husband, her beloved—

The door crashed open and her beloved stood in the empty frame, his hands on his hips, bare above the waist save for a hastily tied bandage wrapped about his broad chest.

"I am the master of this fief," he said in the belligerent tones of one who expects an argument.

"Yes," she agreed, folding her hands in front of her and looking down.

"I am master of this manor," he went on, looking mildly surprised and a bit suspicious.

"Indeed, sir, you are," she replied calmly.

"I am master," he looked about for some likely thing to lay claim to and spied her wardrobe, "of that chest."

She bobbed her head in assent.

He frowned, but more in consternation than ill temper. He took a few steps into the room, looking about with a proprietary air. "Good. Then we are clear on this matter. I am the master. You are my lady."

"Yes." Her palms had grown moist contemplating the boldness she planned. But she'd never been a coward. Not true, she amended honestly. *He* had made her a coward. She feared losing him more than she feared death.

She took a deep breath and crossed the room until she stood directly in front of him. Resolutely, she placed her hand on the bandage covering his breast. "Are you badly wounded, sir?"

He went still the second she touched him, his gaze falling greedily upon the sight of her hand on his chest. Slowly, his gaze lifted to hers. "Nothing that would keep me from your bidding, my lady."

She smiled then, a little wobbly but a smile nonetheless, because he was not subtle, this husband of hers. His desire heated the air between them, his look scorched her, and yet, she was not afraid. She would never be afraid of him again. He would not trespass where he was not welcome. And because she had the power of consent or refusal, she luxuriated in that power. She could even tease this big, bold spouse of hers.

"And how dire do you judge your condition would have to be before you admitted you were not up to . . . to any *task* I might require of you?"

He broke into one of his rare and beautiful smiles. "Perhaps a minute or two past death, ma'am."

She laughed, finding an unexpected delight in such wordplay. "As I thought."

She walked her fingers carefully to the edge of the bandage and peeled the upper edge back, peering at his wound. "It is deep."

"I've had deeper."

"I would not cause you harm."

"Too late."

"How so, sir?" she asked, alarmed.

"I am returned from a foreign land, starving and in need of what you possess, and you withheld it from me."

"I did?"

"In truth," he replied somberly.

"Then I must make recompense." Her heart raced as the laughter in his eyes faded before her implied promise.

" 'Twould be honorable," he allowed softly.

She broke away, laughing nervously now that they had arrived at this point of making choices, of no returns. She turned, plucking at her gown's embroidered girdle. "So, what do I owe you, sir? Wine? Honeycakes?"

Suddenly she was swept up in his arms, held high against his broad chest, his brilliant, beautiful green eyes were boring into her. "I admit to wanting both, *needing* both," he said, "the intoxication of your embrace and the sweetness of your kisses."

"I see," she murmured faintly, linking her hands around his throat.

He smiled at her. "You said you loved me."

"I do."

"You know you have my heart."

"I know." And she did. Everything he had done since returning home—for, as God was her witness, this place never was her home until his presence made it so—bespoke his respect, his regard, and his love. He may have fallen in love with an ideal she represented but he had ended loving *her,*

75

both her assets and her shortcomings, her quick temper, her astute management, her economy, and her impulsiveness. "I know."

He was watching her carefully. She became attuned to the easy rise and fall of his breathing, the effortless way he held her, the scent of his warm skin. "Alas, my love comes housed in bones and flesh."

"Alas?" she asked, unlinking her hand and letting it drift along his collarbone to the base of his throat, where an increasingly erratic pulse pounded.

"Alas, because the flesh is weak, ma'am."

"This flesh does not feel weak to me."

"It is," he insisted, "It is—ah!" He closed his eyes as her fingers drifted in gentle exploration down his unbandaged chest to the flat copper nipple partially obscured by silky, dark hair. It was leathery and supple beneath her feathering touch but, she lowered her lips against it, also satiny and—

"Enough!" he burst out. She rolled her chin into his broad chest. The muscle contracted and swelled.

"Sweet Jesu, Jocelyn, are you purposefully striving to discover my limits?"

Delicious, wanton desire suffused her. Curiosity drove her. Love guided her. "I am touching you, sir, as a wife does her husband. Is not that what you mandated I do before you would—" she strove to find the perfect term for what she wanted, what he wanted, too, and found—"make love to me?"

In answer, he looked wildly around before spying her small pallet.

"Yes," she murmured, seeing the direction of his glance and, though the pallet looked small and mean on the flagstone floor, she did not doubt that it would seem an Ottoman's enclave if he took her there.

But he looked down at her and his expression warmed with pleasure. "Not here. You deserve better."

"The bed . . . ?" A tincture of distaste followed the suggestion, but it was just a bed, after all, not an emblem—

"It has been burned," he answered, the hard cast of his features relating clearer than his words the pain his remembered adultery caused him.

He turned with her still in his arms and pushed open the door, heading down the hall toward the stairway. He mounted it two steps at a time, and though she worried such exertion would cause his wounds to start bleeding again, though his heartbeat drummed thickly next to hers, his breathing scarcely changed.

At the top of the stair he turned toward the solar where he and Keveran were oft heard battling. He paused at the door and looked down at her. "My lady, I would propose that I have more to offer you than a sword arm."

She reached up and stroked his cheek above the black beard, looking deeply into his eyes. "I know that, Nicholas. Ire provoked words I knew even speaking them were nothing but malice. Forgive me. I know you are more than simply a powerful man, Nicholas. And I pray you think no less of me if I confess that I revel in your power, sir. For I admit that your strength pleases me. Your breadth excites me. Your power quickens my pulse. Indeed," she caught her lower lip between her teeth, "I would know that strength as wife as well as lady."

He lowered his head and placed upon her lips a kiss so gentle but intense that tears sprang to her eyes. She wrapped her arms tightly around his throat and kissed him hard in return. Vaguely, she heard the door open. He lifted his head and slowly she opened her eyes, cupping his cheek in her palm.

"Madame, I have made you a present."

He turned with her and she saw it. Indeed, how could she

not see it? It was a bed, a bed such as she had never seen before. Tall as it was wide and long as it was tall, it had been carved in a fantastical manner, the style both ornate and austere, foreign and familiar. The rich walnut gleamed in the morning light. The elegantly carved posts at each corner were as wide as, well, as wide as Nicholas's biceps—which were formidably wide, indeed.

It was fabulous. It was magnificent. It was the most lavish thing she had ever seen, from its thick feather mattress to the fine, bleached linens stretched over it.

"You made this?" she asked in amazement.

"I am not a nobleman, Jocelyn, but I am a freeman as was my father before me. He passed his skills on to me though scant heed did I give them. In my youth, I was hot tempered, bold and rash, all afire to seek glory and renown. So, I followed the path I thought most likely to lead me to them."

"Your father was a carpenter," she murmured admiringly, "as are you."

"So, 'twould seem, for I have never forgotten my father's legacy. It pleases you?" There was eagerness in his voice.

"Yes," she breathed ecstatically. "Oh, yes."

"Then, lady, let us christen it." He needed no word of assent. Her agreement was implicit in the kiss she settled on his lips as she twined her arms about his neck and pulled his dark, shaggy head down to meet her eager lips.

Quickly, he moved to the side of the bed and lowered her gently upon the thick feather mattress. Silently, he stripped her tunic from her and peeled away the thin chemise beneath. She astonished herself, so little heed did she give the faint call of modesty. She bathed in his admiration, assured by the care he took with her, his assiduous restraint, his gentle touch.

And when she lay, naked and flushed and warmed by his ardent regard and his reverent caress upon the linen coverlet, he stood up and stripped away the rest of his clothes, leaving her breathless with awe. He was as magnificent as the bed he'd made, just as bold and just as elegantly fashioned.

The golden tanned skin stopped in a sharply delineated line at his waist, the skin of his legs pale below. But the dark fur that covered his chest and narrowed into a thick line as it descended over the rippling belly spread out at the top of long, thickly muscled thighs. His sex jutted from that dark forest, thick and aggressive, and for a second her dreamy state dissolved as she realized the physical dimensions of this big man.

He read her alarm and smiled crookedly. "I am a most patient man, Jocelyn. I will not hurt you."

He needed to say no more to still her fears. He said he would not hurt her; thus she would not be hurt. She lifted her arms in welcome and with a sound of gratitude and love, he came to her, covering her slight body with his own, blanketing her beneath his heat, his masculinity, his sheer size. And she gloried in it.

He braced himself above her on his arms, and she speared her fingers through his cool, silky hair, pulling his head down. He trembled, holding himself just above her as his mouth descended on hers. His kiss was open-mouthed, his tongue ardent against her untutored lips, sliding luxuriantly along them.

She clung to him, raising herself up to press her breast against his rock hard chest, wanting him closer, nearer, struggling with a sensation alien and yet essential. She desired to absorb and be absorbed, to cleave so tightly that their two bodies became one.

His lower body sank against her. She felt the hard presence of his sex against her thigh, the warm weight of him between her legs. Her legs fell apart, her hips tilted instinctively and he lifted his head.

"Lay upon me," she whispered.

"I am too big."

"No," she argued, laughing. For her body conformed to his as if it was made for his weight and breadth, gladdened by his power and finding pleasure in his strength. "No."

She pulled at his broad shoulders and after a moment's hesitation, he eased himself down and suddenly rolled over, so that she lay atop him. He reached down and clasped her thigh, pulling it wide, so that she straddled him. At once she felt his member at the entry to her most intimate place.

His hand slipped between them, touching her deeply and intimately with a sure stroke that caused her breath to catch and her eyes to close. Again. Again . . . Her back bowed and her throat arched with each teasing promise of culmination. He slid his finger deep within her and her hips bucked in anticipation.

It was too much, too intense. Pleasure danced along her veins, sensation rippled through her body and yet . . . and yet, there was more. She sobbed in frustration. She could almost reach it, the crescendo of this profound and ancient rhythm. If only she knew how. If only he would help her.

"Please," she gasped.

He obliged. His hand withdrew, replaced by that thick masculine part of him she'd feared, but now seemed so essential a part of this. She pushed herself down on him, taking him into her body, filled with him, joining with him. She shuddered and the movement translated to him, breaking through the ungodly restraint he'd been exercising.

With a low sound, he thrust slowly, deeply into her body. She gasped with the sensation, new, stinging, and beautiful. He seated himself all the way to his root within her and slowly, terribly, withdrew, the thickness of him grating with nerve-destroying deliberation across that most sensitive nub. Then back again, a reverse slide of fullness.

Her head swam with need, her hips found the rhythm and next time he pushed into her, she met his thrust.

"Jocelyn!" He clasped her hips and pulled her down to meet him, his mouth traveling hungrily along her face, throat, and breasts.

She wanted. She needed. And he held the key, the answer, the promise. Deliberate, soul-eviscerating thrust, excruciating withdrawal, pure essence of pleasure tantalizing her, just beyond her reach, just . . .

Then she understood. He was being cautious for her sake. She did not want his caution. She *needed* his passion.

She planted her hands on his chest and sat up, seating him deliberately and forcefully deeper within. Beneath her palms, all the muscles in his belly clenched with the sudden unexpected movement. Once more he clasped her hips and rolled, this time pulling her beneath him, grabbing first one leg then the other wrapping them about his hips.

Then he began making love to her, roughly, urgently, his thrust deep and hard and fierce. She closed her eyes and just felt him, felt him take her, fill her, ride with her. And as he did, pleasure intensified into a hard, inward spiraling ball of sensation. He tensed, his head flung back and his teeth set in a grimace of unspeakable effort. With one final thrust, he ground against her, flinging his head back and at the same time . . . oh Lord!

"Please!" she cried out.

Her heels riding the hard buttocks, her mouth open in a soundless gasp of fulfillment, passion overtook her. Wave upon wave of physical ecstasy washed through her, sweeping her along in a sea of ecstasy, stroking each instant with physical rapture.

And when it was over and at long last sentient thought returned, she found herself once more in the sunlit room, lying on a deep, feather-soft mattress, her husband's warm body curved protectively against hers as his hands with the delicacy of an artist, traced a damp tendril on her temples.

Only one thing could have made her more content and he, who'd given her so much, gave her this, too.

"I love you, Jocelyn. God alone knows how very much I love you, but I intend to try to make you understand."

Chapter 7

One month later

Father Eidart bent over the row of little cabbages, weeded out a spindly specimen, straightened, and pressed his hands to his lower back. "I miss Keveran," he said glumly.

"I, too," said Father Timothy from across the garden. "Though I must admit, I thought we might have him back with us last week when Sir Nicholas declared his intention of making the lad his squire. Lady Jocelyn was fit to be tied."

"Aye," Father Eidart said, dusting the dirt from his hands. "She puts no value on knightly skills and is right fond of the boy. I thought for sure that rather than let the boy be endangered by Nicholas's plans for his future, she would—" He stopped suddenly and bent quickly to his weeding.

But Father Timothy knew what Eidart had meant to say and being a man, if not close to holiness, still farther from evil, he decided it was time they made a clean breast of this thing that had festered long enough.

"I am glad she hasn't killed him," he declared, drawing a surprised look from his fellow cleric. "It was wrong of us to even hint such. We shall tell her so at the first opportunity and then ask her pardon and *then* we shall confess to the bishop on our next pilgrimage."

With a sigh of intense relief, round little Father Eidart once more stood upright. His face was the picture of spiritual liberation.

"Oh, good!" he exclaimed. "I have felt horrible for weeks now, watching and wondering when and if the poison we fed that poor girl would take effect. Thank the Good Lord she is made of finer stuff than us. In fact, I think . . . I think. No. Never mind."

"What do you think?" Father Timothy asked.

Father Eidart squinted, unwilling to commit himself to making any declarations. "Well, she speaks quite freely to him and once I actually saw him pick her up whilst she was in the middle of some tirade and toss her over his shoulder and stalk off with her, but for all that, I think . . . I think . . . they are not unsuited."

Father Timothy, who had never had any experience with women, eyed Brother Eidart in amazement. "Really? Well, that would be nice but really . . . ? Jocelyn Cabot, a loving wife? Frankly, if I was Nicholas I would be here right now, begging us to say novenas for him in hopes of the Lord keeping him safe from her temper."

And with this both men fell into laughter. They were still laughing a minute later when they saw that very same Jocelyn stalking past the church on her way from town, a sharp razor in her hand and a thunderous look on her face.

"Good day, Lady Jocelyn!" Father Eidart hailed her.

She ignored him. Indeed, it would be hard to say whether she even heard him, intent as she was on her mission. The razor glinted with evil purpose in her hand and she muttered as she walked, her voice carrying to the startled priests.

"I can't take any more. And why should I? The great, hairy

barbarian. He hurts me and no thought to my pain. Thinks he can do as he likes and I will simply accept his edict? Ha! I swear, this *will* be the end of it!"

And she was gone.

For a long stunned moment, Father Eidart and Father Timothy stared at each other.

"Dear God!" Father Eidart whispered.

"Her immortal soul!" Father Timothy breathed.

"*Our* immortal souls!" Father Eidart countered.

"Ah!" both priests wailed and in a flurry of motion, exited through the small stone gate, pushing and shoving each other in their haste to avert a great and dire tragedy.

They clambered up the rocky path to the manor, only to see Jocelyn disappear inside minutes before they arrived panting and gasping at the door. They tried the handle but the door was locked. Frantically, they pounded on it and still it took a good five minutes before a servant finally answered.

They pushed their way in. "Your master!" Father Timothy demanded. "Where is he?"

The young man, a half-peeled onion still in his hand, looked around, confused by the appearance of the two frantic priests. "Upstairs. In The Bed Room."

"The Bed Room?" Father Eidart echoed in confusion.

The boy nodded. "The solar right at the top of the stairs. Where The Bed is."

Father Timothy ignored the lad's odd references and hurried along the great hall, scrambling up the stairs, Father Eidart close behind him. Having just recently been delivered from certain damnation, they weren't going to willingly let heaven slip from their grasp now.

Without hesitation, Father Timothy burst through the door.

"For the love of God, stop, my lady! Only think on your

immortal so—" Father Timothy trailed off, as Father Eidart piled into him from behind.

Jocelyn stood behind her husband, razor in hand, regarding them with an imperious crook of a brow. Her husband sat before her, his throat arched, half of his face shaved.

"Why look, Nicholas, the holy fathers have finally deigned to come calling," Jocelyn said dryly. "And what an odd manner they have chosen to announce themselves."

Father Eidart cringed guiltily. They hadn't come to visit the new lord since their, er, suggestion to Lady Jocelyn. Apparently the omission had been a topic in the household.

With a sardonic cock of his own dark brow, Nicholas took the linen towel from the table next to him and swiped at his face. He stood up. He really was enormous. And intimidating. Even with only half his beard on his face.

"Ah. The holy brothers. How good of you to come. You will forgive our dishabille. My wife has taken a notion into her head and I am paying the penalty."

"Ah!" Jocelyn gasped, affronted. "Just as my skin has paid the penalty of that beard for the past four—" She broke off, realizing the intimacy of the details she'd been about to divulge, and blushed.

Nicholas smiled calmly at Fathers Eidart and Timothy. "Now, what can I do for you, good brothers?"

Eidart, seeing that there was no cause for alarm, would have willingly bowed his way out of this rather too private tableau but Timothy, bent on expiation, had bravely stepped forward. "We have come to see how it goes between you and this good lady," he said. Eidart groaned.

Nicholas regarded the cleric with the lazy, if suspect, good-will of a well-fed cat watching a mouse. "Oh, it goes well." He turned to Jocelyn. "Wouldn't you say it goes well, sweetling?"

Jocelyn nodded but her expression remained sardonic.

"Come, Jocelyn," Nicholas said in a cajoling tone. "We mustn't bear grudges against God's appointed ones."

"Humph."

"Yes," Father Eidart agreed miserably. "You mustn't."

"Humph."

"She'll come 'round eventually," Nicholas assured them pleasantly. "She simply has a very protective streak and she," he leaned forward and whispered conspiratorially, "rather takes it amiss that you seek my death."

"But we don't!" Father Eidart blurted out. "Not anymore!"

At this, Sir Nicholas looked mildly gratified. Lady Jocelyn looked skeptical.

"Really!" Father Timothy added his voice. "We have considered the matter and are convinced we erred. In fact, we came here to avert a calamity we feared we had fomented."

"Ah!" Nicholas said, gesturing expansively. "That explains the bursting in here, then?"

They nodded vigorously.

He turned to Jocelyn who'd crossed her arms over her breasts and whose skepticism had turned into a sort of cool disapproval.

"See, darling? No reason to be bitter." He smiled magnanimously at the clerics. "And you won't ever again try to convince my wife to kill me, will you?"

They shook their heads, again, vigorously.

"Good. Then perhaps we can discuss this toe and it's box—"

"Toe? Box?" Father Timothy murmured before enlightenment dawned on him. "You refer to Saint Neot's toe and the reliquary? Yes, by all means, let us discuss—"

"Not yet." Jocelyn's voice cut through Father Eidart's enthusiastic agreement. She let her arms fall and stalked across the room. Sir Nicholas, seemingly content to let his wife have her head, settled back against the table, watching them with ill-concealed amusement. "We have to get some things clear between us first."

"Of course, My Lady," Father Timothy said, stuttering slightly and backing up. She stopped and eyed both clerics narrowly.

"Henceforth, you will direct all your parishioners to bring their business to Sir Nicholas."

"Yes, yes," both priests agreed, visions of a gem-encrusted reliquary and shriveled toe dancing in their imaginations.

"Because Sir Nicholas is master here now."

"Yes."

She swept her arm out toward the window. "This is the master's holding."

They nodded.

"This is the master's manor."

More nodding.

"That," she looked behind her, "is the master's bed." Both priests looked at the immense and disheveled bed behind the couple and quickly away.

She smiled then, for the first time since they entered, and her smile was for the man who stood regarding her with open admiration, love, and hunger on his dark—well, half dark—face. "And as Sir Nicholas is the master of my heart, I am certainly the master's lady."

Nicholas stood up, drawn to her by ties the priests could not see but felt as clearly as if they were physical things. When he was a few paces away, the lady reached out and clasped his hand and drew it slowly to place upon her belly. Her smile filled with tenderness.

"And this, my darling," she said, *"this* is the master's son."

nd that, my friends, is how the Masterson family got
its name." Laurel was proud of her recitation, proud
that she'd kept the tourists enthralled. Even the boy
stood beside the bed, rubbing the wood as if he could feel the
passage of time.

Everyone except the handyman, who now knelt on the
floor, quietly placing his tools in his kit.

That was a good place for Max Ashton. Kneeling. On the
floor. Preferably, far away from her.

"Because the first Masterson love affair ended so happily
and with so many progeny, the family built"—Laurel gestured
grandly—"their castle! If you look out either window, you can
see the ruins from here."

The tourists divided up and rushed to the windows.

"It's on a cliff overlooking the beach." Laurel followed them
and peered over their shoulders. "You can see that the keep—
that's the place where the family lived—has walls intact, but the
outer castle walls are almost completely grown over, the stones
carried away by the villagers as building material. Here and there,
there are rock columns jutting up like fingers pointing to the sky."

"Shouldn't an archeologist excavate?" Mrs. Plante asked.

Laurel shook her head. "The ruins are no different than a dozen other castles in England. It's only of interest to local historians, and that's because the Mastersons were *the* influential family in this area for almost eight hundred years." Laurel pointed to the portraits on the walls: the formal portrait of Lord Rawson Masterson, the more carefree portrait of Lord Sterling Masterson, and even the darkened, stylized sketch of Sir Nicholas, the founder of the family.

Brian covered up a yawn, but when his mom nudged him, he jumped and asked, "Then what happened to 'em?"

"I'm sad to say the line vanished from England in the early years of the twentieth century," Laurel answered.

Max clanged his wrenches together. "Bunch of losers," he muttered.

She knelt beside him and in an intense whisper, said, "Excuse me? What did you say? Did *you* accuse someone else of being a loser? A family of nobles? Of rulers? Because I have to say, Mr. Handyman, you've got the nerve."

Max stopped and turned his gaze to hers.

He looked . . . funny. Like he wanted to laugh, or yell, or . . . kiss her.

The blond American, Miss Ferguson, made a cooing noise.

So Laurel wasn't the only one who thought he looked . . . funny. Hastily, she scrambled to her feet and made a show of adjusting the large, eggplant-colored velvet comforter on the Masterson bed. "I had this made specially," she said to no one in particular. "The bed is too big to buy anything off the shelf."

Miss Ferguson seemed impervious to the undercurrents. "So the Mastersons no longer own the lands?"

"Nor the manor, either. The Barrys are my employers, and they recently sold everything to a new owner. That's why this is"—heavens, she almost couldn't say it—"the last tour." There. She'd managed to choke it out.

Miss Ferguson turned to the other ladies. "It's a good thing we got here when we did!"

"I should say so!" Mrs. Stradling replied.

Mrs. Plante nodded.

"Gosh, yes," Brian said in a deadpan voice. "I would have hated to miss a single museum in all of England."

Mrs. Ferguson rumpled his hair. "We'll go eat as soon as we get back to the hotel, and maybe find you a video game."

Brian pulled his head away, but he grinned and shuffled his feet. "Hey." He pointed at the fifteen-inch-tall, upright cross set atop the cherry tallboy. "Is that real gold?"

"St. Albion's cross is real gold, yes, but gold sheets pounded thin and shaped around a plaster cast. It's value is in its antiquity, not in the metal." Laurel reached up and lightly caressed the rounded edges of the gleaming ornate cross. "It's older than the bed. It's over a thousand years old."

"It should be in a museum," Miss Ferguson said.

Laurel subdued the urge to snap at her. As it was, her voice was a little brisker than normal. "It *is* in a museum, and more important, it's at home here. It's been in the Masterson possession since a monk presented Lord and Lady Masterson with the cross as a wedding gift."

Meghan stood on tiptoe to look at it. "It's so beautiful. The work is exquisite. Aren't you worried it will be stolen?"

John put his hands on her waist and pulled her easily against him. "I'll bet they have quite a burglar-proof system here, honey."

Laurel neither agreed nor disagreed. She'd come to be wary of discussions about locks and security. "Actually, St. Albion's cross is quite heavy, and it takes a large man to lift it off the tallboy."

Meghan turned in John's arms and looked adoringly into his face. "You could do it, darling."

His lips lowered toward hers. "Do . . . what?"

Laurel wanted to cover her eyes. Instead she looked away . . . right into Max's knowing eyes.

Oh, gads. She cleared her throat. Had he seen how much she envied the newlyweds that unabashed glow of love?

"Ick," Brian said. "They're at it again."

"Fascinating," Miss Ferguson murmured as she studied the young couple.

What had Laurel been talking about? "The castle. The castle was built on an outcropping on the coast because that was the best natural defense, and that defense was badly needed during the War of the Roses." She spoke too rapidly, but apparently the tourists readily accepted eccentricies in their tour guides, for no one seemed surprised by her abrupt segue.

"Ah. The War of the Roses. That was a difficult time." Mrs. Stradling nodded sadly. "Noble families had to build defenses to save themselves from the rampages of the armies."

This time nothing could stop Brian's jaw-cracking yawn.

Okay. Fine. The boy didn't like history. Neither did Max, although he had risen to his feet and was pretending to listen. They could keep each other entertained. Laurel confined her remarks to the *adults* in the group. "You ladies know your English history. You must be medieval scholars?"

The middle-aged American women smirked and shook their heads.

"Librarians?" Laurel guessed again.

Mrs. Plante beamed. "Not at all, dear. We're romance writers."

"Romance . . . writers?" Laurel could feel her face heating. The day just got worse and worse.

"Really?" Max sounded fascinated. "My mum reads

romances. She tells me I should read them, too." His beautiful, plush lips quirked in self-deprecating humor. "She says I would learn a few things about making a woman happy."

"Couldn't hurt," Laurel muttered.

"Your mother's right," Mrs. Plante said. "I know when my husband reads my novels, he—"

"Mom! I do not want to hear this." Brian covered his ears and began to hum loudly.

Everyone laughed, and Laurel relaxed.

Mrs. Stradling rapped on one of the colossal bedposts to get everyone's attention, then shook her fingers as if her knuckles hurt. "What I would like to know, is whether it is true there was much crime on this stretch of the coast?"

Startled, Laurel asked, "Crime?"

"Yes." Her brown eyes darted about as if anticipating an attack. "I heard that smugglers have lived and worked here for centuries."

"Oh." Laurel understood now. "Smugglers. The locals never truly considered smuggling a crime. Trecombe is so far from London, and in times of need it was necessary to make a living any way possible."

"I love smugglers," Mrs. Plante said to Miss Ferguson in an aside. "They're so romantic."

"Smugglers are *not* romantic," Laurel said emphatically. "They're thieves who are stealing England's heritage away, piece by piece, and they should be drawn and quartered!"

Max watched her as if enthralled by her vehemence.

She shot a sharp glance at him but it did little to quell his apparent amusement.

Mrs. Stradling leaned forward. "So there are still smugglers!"

Laurel's fiery indignation collapsed. "Yes, I'm afraid so, and they're almost impossible to catch."

"Were the Mastersons smugglers?" Meghan asked.

"Not at all." Her straight black hair was slipping out of its clip, and she wound it tighter and clipped it again. "The Mastersons were well known for their loyalty to the crown and for enforcing the law."

Max proved he was still listening. "The Mastersons were so gallant, they never got off their noble arses and did the work of smuggling, they just raked in the profits."

"They were law-abiding citizens." Laurel sat on the bed with a flounce. "And chivalrous to boot! Just yesterday, in my research, I found a story about a Masterson who came home from fighting for Her Majesty Queen Elizabeth the First to discover a scoundrel on the verge of abducting a maiden, and he saved her from certain dishonor. . . ."

The Bed Is Unmade . . .

TRECOMBE, CORNWALL CIRCA 1583

CHAPTER 1

Not until her kidnapping did Lady Helwin realize how badly security in Trecombe had disintegrated.

When she heard the hoofbeats galloping down the beach toward her, she turned—and smiled. Any woman who appreciated masculine beauty would have smiled. The beach stretched on in a smooth, unbroken line of silver sand and sheer cliffs, the wind blew off the sea, and Rion Masterson rode like a centaur, black cape and raven hair flying behind him, eyes glittering in the late afternoon sun, pleasure in the exhilarating ride emanating from every line of his fine form. A handsome figure of a man, an adventurer who had gone abroad to seek his fortune—and failed miserably.

Now he sought prosperity closer to home, and Helwin wanted to wish him luck—sarcastically, of course. She'd observed the newly returned nobleman many a time as he visited her uncle's house. She'd admired his grace, his wit, the skillful way he used his green eyes to tempt and seduce—not her, but her cousin Bertilda. She could have told him Bertilda might relish a dalliance with the dangerous lord of Castle

Masterson, but Bertilda vetted her suitors' finances with the cool eye of a cutpurse.

But Helwin could tell Rion nothing. She was not permitted to show her face to visitors. Out of sight, out of mind, had been Uncle Carroll's philosophy about Helwin, and thus far it seemed to be working. Except for the occasional careless inquiry from one of her father's old friends, no one cared about Helwin's fate. Helwin might as well resign herself to living out her life as a lonely spinster in her uncle's household.

But she could still enjoy a solitary walk on the beach, and she did thrill to the sight of handsome, daring Rion Masterson riding toward her . . . right toward her. Right *at* her, although surely by now he'd seen her.

She tried to move out of his path.

He swerved as if to follow her.

She waved her arms to call attention to herself.

He laughed, an open-mouthed, merry laugh that frightened her in its intensity.

Why was he riding at her so determinedly? Was he the kind of man who found pleasure in running down a helpless woman?

Or had someone—Uncle Carroll, even Bertilda—told him she would be here and offered him a reward for eliminating that annoying remembrance of former days?

Helwin caught her breath. Her heart skipped a beat, then leaped into a pounding frenzy. Bertilda. That witch Bertilda had insisted Helwin go for a late afternoon walk. She had insisted Helwin wear her purple velvet cape.

Bertilda had set her up!

Helwin fled, swerving to reach the boulders scattered at the bottom of the cliff. If she could make it that far, Rion wouldn't dare ride his precious war-horse through the rubble and take a chance of laming him.

She could make it. Surely she could make it.

The stallion thundered behind her. She could almost feel its hot breath on her neck. But she was safe . . . almost there . . . when the horse charged past her. She had only a moment of optimism, a bleak hope that Rion would ride on when, with an arm under her ribs, he scooped her up.

She opened her mouth to scream, but in a single smooth movement, he brought her up and over, flinging her face-down before him on the horse. The wind rushed out of her lungs, and she gasped, trying to get air.

"There you are, darling," he shouted. "You put on a good show, but I vow no one saw us. We'll be safe for the night."

What did he mean? What could he mean?

What had Bertilda done now?

The horse was warm, its gait smooth, but hanging head down hurt her belly, and watching the sand fly past produced a dreadful sensation of dizzy helplessness. She tried to struggle up on her elbows, to get her breath and tell him he'd made a horrible mistake.

He pushed her down, his hand in the middle of her back. "Just a few more minutes." His voice was warmed by the faint accent he'd acquired in his years abroad, and wretchedly amused. "Castle Masterson is directly ahead."

Indeed it was. She'd seen it from afar many a time. Perched on a broad, granite-hewn outcropping that thrust into the sea, Castle Masterson's gray battlements chewed at the sky with primitive stone teeth. The Masterson family had lived on this land ever since a noble crusader had arrived to save his lady-wife from the strategems of evil conspirators. Previously, Helwin had gazed on the castle and sighed for the romance of those former times.

Now she could think only of the narrow cliff path that crumbled away with every new storm, and how she did not wish to ride its length facedown on a horse like a bag of corn. Indeed, she didn't want to ride its length at all. "I don't know what you're doing," she shrieked. "But you're going to be sorry!"

"Hush, dear. Samson is a difficult beast and rears when he hears loud noises." Rion tossed the hem of her cape over her head to muffle her squawk of dismay and sped up. The horse slowed as they reached the bottom of the path, then labored as they began to climb.

Helwin fought with the flapping folds of the material and wondered bitterly if he took her threat seriously. For who would make him sorry? Not Uncle Carroll, with his cold eyes and handsome face. He wasn't home to notice if his only niece failed to return, and until he returned, there would be no rescue.

Then, of course, he would come after her, but only because— 'od's mercy! In brief glimpses below the hem of the cape, she saw the beach fall away as they climbed. Again she wanted to shriek in abject fear. But she didn't dare speak a word, for as they clambered up the narrow path, the beach retreated and the cliff hung straight over the ocean. Below her, the waves crashed on the jagged rocks. The setting sun turned the shadows to purple. One misstep would send them plunging to their deaths. And perhaps no one else held her to be of value, but she valued herself enough to make up for all of their indifference.

With a swift box on the ears and a hearty scolding, she'd correct Rion as soon as she set foot on the ground, and with any luck she'd be back in Smythwick Hall before Bertilda had had time to crow about her clever ruse. And Bertilda had reason to fear; she'd faced Helwin's fury only twice since Bertilda and her father had moved into Helwin's home, and both times Bertilda had come out much the worse.

So Helwin sagged onto the horse, letting it carry her along the narrow path to the top. But for all her compliance, she couldn't halt a gasp when Samson's front hoof slipped on the loose stones. The horse staggered. Pebbles spattered down the cliff face. "Whoa, my boy, whoa." Rion worked the reins, keeping Samson on the path with the patience and skill that had made him such a valuable mercenary.

And as they resumed their ascent, Helwin deliberated on how she would make Bertilda pay for this humiliation and peril.

When they reached the top, her head spun from hanging upside down and from the smothering depths of the cloak, her belly ached from being draped across Samson's back, and she barely heard the castle's postern gate open or the cackle of male mirth as Rion rode inside. "Did ye capture her, then?" a rough voice called.

"Aye, that I did. Everything went off without a misstep." He slipped from the horse before the beast had stopped moving. "I told you I'd turn our fortunes!"

Helwin shoved at the cloak and tried to kick herself free.

Rion dragged her off and flung her over his shoulder. "Be calm, my beauty." He gave her upraised bottom a gentle pat and pealed off a mighty laugh—a laugh which stopped abruptly when she clawed her nails into his back. "There'll be time enough for that later," he joked.

The men chortled.

But Helwin heard the note of irritation which tinged his voice. Good. She'd show him irritation—just as soon as she got rid of this cloak and stood on her own two feet.

A door opened. They entered the castle. They started up stairs.

She struggled with the clasp on her cloak. Dropped it to the floor. Looked down to see a dozen manservants and knights in the vestibule gaping at her. A few of them raised their goblets. A few staggered and sniggered.

"See, lads?" Rion called. "She can't wait for my attentions."

"Lord Masterson," she snapped.

Rion bounded up the stairs, jostling the breath out of her. He reached the level of the great hall, took a turn, went up another flight.

"Lord Masterson, you've made a mistake!"

He kicked a door open, stalked inside, and kicked the door shut.

The light had faded to dusk, but as he turned, she saw a whirl of furnishings: a clothes cupboard, a stand with a jug of wine and two glasses, a fireplace where flames licked at the logs. A massive walnut bed, with a heavy carved headboard, a great canopy and faintly exotic bedposts. A bed weighed down with history.

The Masterson bed.

Turning again, he tossed her on the fur-laden mattress. Before she'd sunk into the welter of feathers, he landed beside her.

"Listen to me, you dolt!"

"No time to talk, lass. If your plan is to work, we've got some compromising to do." Sliding his hands into her hair, he lowered his mouth to hers.

Temptation washed over her. In all her twenty-two years, she'd never been kissed. In sooth, she'd given up all hope of ever being kissed. Now, here she was, flat on her back in a man's bed.

And not just any man's bed. In Rion Masterson's bed, the man she'd watched court her cousin. The man she'd secretly dreamed of and lusted after. The man she'd wished would court her.

Now she didn't know whether to fight or, for one wicked

moment, taste the fruit of sin. After all, what harm could come of a brief yielding? She was a sensible woman. She would stop him before he went too far. And Rion's lips were marvelously opulent and skillful, the exact opposite of the brutish man he was. He kissed like a man enthralled with kissing, lingering over each soft touch as if he relished learning the contours of her mouth. Her upper lip. Her lower lip. The corners and, when he slid his tongue within—

She boxed his ears. "Oh, vile churl. Release me!"

He reeled backward, swearing.

She wound up for another blow.

Catching her clenched fists, he slammed them on the mattress beside her head.

Briefly, she caught a glimpse of his infuriated expression lit to demonic intensity by the fire's flames, and braced herself for a slap such as her uncle would bestow.

Instead, he took a long breath. He threw his leg over her legs, leaned his chest to hers. In the low, soothing voice he might have used for a fractious mare, he said, "You're an innocent. I understand that. But don't fear. Every maiden comes to this time, if she's lucky, and if she's truly lucky, she lands in my bed. I promise"—he nuzzled her neck—"I'll fulfill your every romantic dream."

In this light, he couldn't see her well. That was the problem. That, and a definite family resemblance between her and Bertilda marked her as his chosen prey. She strained away from him, away from his warm breath and tongue that traced, shockingly, the contours of her ear. "No!" she said. "I don't have any romantic dreams."

He chuckled indulgently. "Ah, sweetling, I know better."

She sucked in a shocked breath. *How* did he know better?

In a voice as warm and golden as heated honey, he said, "You whispered your dreams to me in the alcove in your father's gallery, remember? You told me to ignore your protestations, to override your fears, so we could be together always. And I live to obey you . . . Bertilda."

Bertilda. She would get even with that witch Bertilda. "But I'm not—"

He smothered her objection with a kiss. His eyes closed, his eyelashes a dark fringe on his skin. He smelled like soap, horse, and leather. He weighed heavily of a man's desire, and this time, when she tried to hit him, he restrained her with his arms braced on hers and his hands holding her head. Thrusting his tongue into her mouth, he sampled her as if she were a delicacy prepared just for him, and she . . . she liked it. The madness that swept him along pulled at her, too. She closed her eyes. Her senses bloomed in the darkness. Tentatively she accepted him, answered him, delicately sucked on his tongue.

He moaned, a deep blissful sound, and freed her hands.

Catching his shoulders in her grip, she kneaded them like a cat.

He shifted, lifted himself—and his fingers settled on her breast.

Her eyes sprang open in shock. How dare he? How dare . . . she dug her nails into him.

He ignored the pain, caressing her with slow circles of his thumb.

She dug her heels into the mattress and tried to scoot away.

He controlled her with his strength and pulled at the lacings of her bodice.

She hit at him, she flung her arms toward the headboard to pull herself away . . . and beneath the pillow, her hand landed on a short, smooth, heavy piece of wood. A cudgel. Ah, aye, a man like this had best sleep with a weapon.

She stopped struggling. Slowly, she lifted the cudgel behind his head.

Something of her tension must have transmitted itself to

him, for he looked up just as she brought the cudgel down. With a dreadful thud, the wood cracked across the back of his skull. He dropped, a dead weight, right on top of her.

She lay there, trembling. She hadn't killed him . . . had she? Taking a breath, she groped for the pulse in his neck. It throbbed strongly, and she sighed with relief. Of course she couldn't really hurt him. He had been a mercenary. It would take more than a blow from her to disable him for long.

With a grunt, she pushed at him, rolling him to one side.

He groaned.

She gasped and shoved him off onto the floor.

He landed with a thump that shook the floorboards.

From below she heard raucous laughter and shouts of encouragement, and any sense of elation she might have felt vanished before it formed. She needed to get out of here, but how? From the sounds that drifted up the stairs, Rion's men were celebrating their master's impending matrimonials and the acquisition of an heiress.

If they only knew . . .

Cudgel gripped tightly in her hand, she slipped off the bed and checked Rion again. He appeared to be hearty, if knocked cold and blessed with a large lump on the base of his skull. She prowled the chamber. She opened the door and peeked out. The master's bedroom was at the end of a wide gallery, and just over the railing was the great hall crowded with Rion's men. Silently she slipped back inside, shut the door and dropped the bar. She would wait until everyone fell asleep. Then she would go.

Rion woke to sunshine and the twittering of birds outside his window. His head ached abominably. He was cold. He was cramped. And when he opened his eyes, he realized he rested on the floor without rug or pillow. He must have drunk far too deep last night . . . although he couldn't quite remember last night. . . .

He sat up abruptly. The aches in his muscles made him groan, but he damned well did remember last night. He'd kidnapped Lady Bertilda, an admirable heiress, if a silly twit, and brought her to Castle Masterson. He'd carried her to his bedchamber, placed her on the bed, planted one very pleasant kiss on those luscious lips—and been knocked silly, probably by his own well wielded cudgel.

Who would have thought Lady Bertilda had the wit to find the weapon he kept always beneath his pillow? Or that she had the arm to land him such a blow? It almost gave him hope for their marriage.

Staggering to his feet, he crept toward the bed.

The woman slept sitting up, coverlet clasped about her hunched shoulders, weapon clasped in her hands as if she'd defend her virtue again.

He stared. He blinked. He rubbed his eyes and stared again. Then he shook her hard.

She came awake, blue eyes fierce, cudgel rising.

He dodged and demanded, "Who in the plague are you?"

CHAPTER 2

I f the female was intimidated, she hid it well. "I'm the woman you kidnapped by mistake."

"What in hell were you doing in Lady Bertilda's cloak?" Hope sparked in Rion as he observed the ragged hem of her brown, homespun gown. "Are you a servant? Did you steal it?"

"No, I'm her cousin, and I was tricked into wearing it."

For one moment, his heart sank. Then he rallied. "You lie. Lady Bertilda doesn't have a cousin."

"Indeed she does." The woman's silky blonde hair straggled out from her old-fashioned cap. "The daughter of the last earl of Smythwick, left inconveniently living after disease took her parents. Look." She patted the dimple in her stubborn chin and smiled with a chill fury that turned her blue eyes gray. "It's the Smythwick dimple."

As the truth sank in, he staggered backward. "No. It's impossible." He clutched his aching head. "How could Lady Bertilda have made such a blunder?"

The female laughed, a clear peal of unadulterated merriment. "You pitiable dolt! She didn't make a blunder. She insisted I wear the cloak because she hoped you'd pick me up and carry me off, thus ridding herself of an importunate, impoverished suitor and her incommodious cousin at the same time. You, my lord, have been used."

The female had a tongue like a stinging fly. "I am not just an impoverished suitor. I've worked hard to make that giddy-head fall in love with me." Damn. He hadn't meant to reveal his contempt for the silly Bertilda. Nor would he believe that Bertilda had been ahead of him all the time.

"She's a giddy-head, all right, except when it comes to wealth. Then she calculates a man's worth in the blink of her protruding, bug eyes."

No. He couldn't have blundered so badly. Except, when he looked at this woman, he saw the family resemblance right down to the pale, soft skin and narrow, aristocratic nose. "She doesn't have bug eyes"—perhaps just a little—"and you're not as pretty as Bertilda."

"I wonder where you got your reputation as a charmer." She pressed her finger to her cheek. "Ah, but that's right. You don't have to charm the poor cousin."

Bertilda was blessed with an oval face, narrow lips, and fine figure. This woman's jaw was square and stubborn, her lips wide and plush, and her figure . . . well, who could tell, huddled as she was in that blanket? But probably blowsy and bony, as was typical of the ugly relative left behind while others go into society. And she certainly did nothing to soothe a man's ego with her sarcasm and her blunt speaking. "You look like your uncle," he observed.

She sprang to her knees, cudgel raised. "And you look like a filthy swine."

"Ah." He rubbed his stubbled chin. "You don't like your uncle."

"Who does?" She settled down again. "He has all the appeal of a fish gutted three days ago. Especially about the eyes."

She surprised a laugh from him. "Aye, his eyes are rather . . . lifeless." In fact, when Lord Smythwick turned his gaze on Rion, Rion remembered the eyes of the older men he'd fought with—cold and ruthless clear to the soul. Lord Smythwick would stop at nothing to achieve whatever he desired.

Rion eased himself onto the bed.

The cudgel rose.

He stood again. "Are you legitimate?"

She raised her eyebrows. "Seeking a way out of this fine kettle of herring, are you? But that's not the way. I am legitimate."

"Then why haven't I seen you about the castle?"

"I'm legitimate, not welcome. I haven't been since Uncle Carroll and Bertilda moved in. A messy reminder of times past, you might say."

The sense of being trapped increased. "So your father was . . ."

"The previous earl. My father knew your father. In fact I met you years ago before your father sent you away to be taught your letters and trained for battle."

He stared at her so hard his eyes ached. "I don't remember."

"I wasn't yet out of the nursery."

He paced to the window. He stared across the hills, toward the elegant Elizabethan manor not ten miles from his own castle. How could this have happened? He had plotted his strategy so carefully, and he was an excellent strategist. If he had not been, he and his men would have been killed one hundred times over. Yet somehow, when dealing with females, the usual preparations proved inadequate.

He turned. He stared at Helwin. Somehow he'd been taken by surprise with an attack to his flank. Now he held a prisoner of the battle, but she was worse than useless—she was a liability.

He needed someone to blame. "You tricked Bertilda. You took her cloak—"

She held out her hand to stop him. "Oh, don't. I wouldn't have you on a pewter platter. What do I need with a recently returned mercenary who everyone knows is looking for an heiress so he can recoup his fortune?" She examined him, and by the curl of her lips, what she saw gave her no pleasure. "You must have been a very slothful mercenary."

Stung, he retorted, "I was a bloody good mercenary. Men paid well to have me and my troop fight in their battles, and my name was spoken in hushed tones around the enemies' campfires."

She appeared to be not at all impressed. "But you returned with nothing."

"I returned with a respectable fortune, but this place requires more than that. My honored father"—he was being derisive—"let the Masterson land slide so far it requires a damned bonanza to keep it going until . . ." Why was he explaining himself? And to this female of all people! "Don't bother your pretty head about it."

"You shouldn't have flown off in a rage like you did. Perhaps if you had stayed, your father wouldn't have gambled away the last of the fortune."

"My father never listened to a bit of sense in his entire life, and he certainly never listened to me!" He caught himself. The pretty head was a little too shrewd for his taste. "How do you know that?"

"I live here. Except for several trips to London with my father, I've always lived here. I know everything that goes on in the district." She plucked a piece of lint off her skirt. "And of course, everyone knows about your monetary difficulties, or you'd find a bride with no trouble. After all, you have a noble old title and a fine piece of ground."

"Of course." As she discussed the facts of his dismal life, Rion's spirits sank ever deeper. "I didn't expect to come home to paradise, but I didn't expect that Father would have thrown away everything the Mastersons have held for three hundred years." This time when he seated himself the cudgel stayed down.

"My uncle has discussed many times how he will take your land when you've starved or given up."

It was one thing to suspect his troubles provided the neighbors with a subject for speculation. It was another to have it confirmed. "So to please your uncle, you're in on the plan to ruin me?"

"I'm the one who is ruined, my lord," she reminded him. "I would have sneaked out last night and saved my reputation, but your men didn't stop their revelry until . . . well, I don't know when they stopped. I finally fell asleep." She contemplated him with faint scorn. "Are you always so lax with discipline?"

"The men fought many battles at my side. They deserve a little recreation."

"You've been home . . . what, four months?" She drew her finger along the headboard and showed him the dust. "That's enough recreation."

He'd been thinking the same thing, but he didn't know how to mend matters. Didn't know how to run a castle. When most men his age were learning how to care for their properties, he had been off in Spain and Prussia, fighting first for Her Majesty and then for himself. But to have this badly dressed shrew of a female tell him . . . well, that raised his hackles. "Who are you to tell me how to supervise my men?"

"I'm the woman who manages Smythwick Hall while my uncle and cousin go mincing off to Queen Elizabeth's court in hopes of catching Bertilda a noble suitor. Which, by the way, they have thus far failed to do." She bobbed her head. "I am Lady Helwin Smythwick."

"How suitable—Hellion."

She bent her lips in an obviously fake smile. "A play on my name. How clever." Edging away from him, she tossed back the rug, slid out of the bed—although she didn't release the cudgel—and uncoiled herself to her full height. "It's not my fault we're in this fix. I tried to tell you last night, but you were too intent on ruining me—"

His eyes widened.

"—Or rather, ruining Bertilda to listen." She shook out her skirts, then glanced at him, then looked hard. "My lord, are you all right?"

Helwin might be a shrew. She might be poor. She might be the wrong girl, but God's sheets, she was tall and slender, with elegant hands, a narrow waist, and a glorious pair of plump bubbies trussed into a tight, shabby gown. Her face, when she was not frowning, held an exotic allure, and as she strode to the table to use his comb, she moved with a sensuality that pulled at a man's senses. At his senses, and certain of his more unruly body parts.

With that thought, Rion gave up his last hope. He had indeed been gulled by the beauteous Bertilda. Helwin might not realize the threat she presented to Bertilda's self-confidence, but he did. Bertilda would do anything to get her cousin out of the house, and if she could destroy Helwin's reputation and her every hope of happiness when she did so, so much the better.

And if he did the right thing and wed Helwin, he would lose his castle and she would be destitute, a mercenary's wife, at the mercy of fate. His stirrings of desire must be dismissed. "So if I assume you're telling the truth—"

She placed her fists on her hips and glared.

"—And I don't want to marry you—"

"You need an heiress, and a fool of one."

"—And you don't want to marry me—"

"I want to marry a rough swashbuckler like you as little as you want to marry a destitute relation like me."

"Then we must come up with a solution to our problem."

She pulled her coif off of her head. Her blond braid tumbled down past her hips. "I listen with a uncomplaining ear."

"You were out walking on the beach last night and got trapped in a cave by the rising tide."

"I wouldn't be such a sprat, but all right." Efficiently she loosed the braid and set to work removing the tangles.

'Od's bodkin, a man could spread that length across his pillow and dream he was lost in moonlight. He swallowed. "You had to stay there all night, and this morning you walked home."

She nodded, but he could tell she wasn't satisfied. "The trouble is, someone is going to say that I was here. One of your men will talk, or one of your maids."

"I haven't hired any maids." If he had been around women, he wouldn't be so in awe of this female's beauty. She wasn't as comely as Bertilda. She wasn't.

"That explains much." Helwin looked pointedly at the trail of wood chips leading to the fireplace and at the pile of dirty laundry in the corner. "Believe me, gossip travels. If nothing else, Bertilda will tell everyone so they can admire her cleverness and titter at your gullibility."

"A pox on't! You're right." And he truly hated saying that.

"We need to confuse the issue. To admit that I've been here, but in no compromising way." Helwin drew the comb through the last of the silken locks. "I was trapped by the tide all night. I arrived here early this morning. You took me in, put me before a fire and fed me."

"Good of me."

"Very neighborly." Once again she braided her hair and tied it with a bit of ribbon. As she reset her coif, she said, "This morning, you take me home personally, you pull Bertilda to the side and ask where she was last evening. And we hope that she wasn't watching as you snatched me off the beach."

Helwin looked so pleased with herself, he hated to puncture her satisfaction, yet he had to. "There's only one problem with that plan."

She frowned. "What?"

"I can't lie."

"What?"

Her incredulity was not flattering. "It would be better if I said I was bad at lying. Perhaps I could look your uncle in the eye and tell him you arrived at Castle Masterson this morning—"

"My uncle is not—"

Rion ignored her. "—But I can't smile at that little tart Bertilda. Not now. Not after knowing how she has laughed at me. And, um, helped me to ruin you."

Helwin's sharp glance acknowledged his admission. "You lied when you courted her."

"What do you mean?"

"You told her you adored her, you thought her the sweetest, kindest, most beautiful woman in the country." Helwin smirked. "She told me."

Ah, how good to know a man's best efforts were the object of merriment. "Perhaps I believed it."

"You might not have realized it, but I've watched you."

"Really?" He lounged back on the bed and ran his gaze over her figure. "You watched me, did you? I trow you liked what you saw."

"Aye, forsooth, you're as handsome as a fine stallion and just as virile." She flapped her hand at him as if dislodging an irritating fly. "Although you did underestimate Bertilda, I judge you're not a stupid man."

He straightened. Helwin's compliments bit deeper than any trickery, but he supposed he deserved it. "When I was courting, I could lie because I was indifferent to her. Now I am not. Now I'm angry."

"Oh." Helwin tapped her toe. "I've had a lot of experience being pleasant to Bertilda when I wished to tear her hair out, but I do see your difficulty. Could you write a letter asking that . . . someone . . . at Smythwick Manor send a cart?" She eyed him oddly, as if she should say more but did not choose to. "You could say I sprained my ankle and can't sit a horse, and you have no appropriate transportation for a lady."

Clever lass. "I could do that."

"Very well." She placed the cudgel carefully on the pillow. "Shall we go down to break our fast?"

CHAPTER 3

Two dozen of Rion's men were gathered around the long table in the great hall, shoveling gruel into their mouths, and a dirtier, more surly group Helwin had never seen. Their heads drooped. They scratched and yawned. They all wore long, wicked knives at their belts, and each had a sword resting on the table at their right hand.

Near the head of the table one knight lifted his head as Rion and Helwin approached. With a grin that showed his brown teeth, he called, "Let's hear it for Lord Masterson, who has captured his lady and filled our coffers!"

A few of the men released a gravelly cheer.

A few held their heads and squinted their eyes as if in pain.

Rion slashed the air with his hand. "Sir Lathrop, slap a codpiece in your yap. I got the wrong lass."

The cheering sputtered to a stop and every eye turned to examine Helwin. She dipped them a curtsy. "I give you good morrow, gentleman."

"The wrong lass?" Sir Lathrop glared balefully at Helwin. "Then throw her out and get the right one."

"It's not that simple. Lady Helwin is Lady Bertilda's cousin."

Rion gestured toward Sir Lathrop. "Lady Helwin, may I present my head knight, Sir Lathrop."

Helwin eyed Sir Lathrop. His stringy brown hair hung around his neck, and an equally stringy brown beard made him look like a rug with a fringe. Food and drink crusted his garments.

The great hall was no better, recognizable as the castle's main living chamber by its size and its height, but filthy and almost empty of furniture. The long table was nothing more than planks on crude wooden legs, the benches were rough, and the walls were empty of any decoration except for a couple of ragged tapestries, well-used battle-axes, shields, and longbows and quivers full of arrows.

"Ye ruined the wrong woman?" Sir Lathrop sounded incredulous.

"No, I didn't ruin her."

"If you didn't lift her skirts, then send her back!" Sir Lathrop belched loudly.

"Charming," she said.

"Actually, she arrived only this morning after being trapped by the tide all night long."

One of the men, blond-haired and slack-jawed, guffawed.

Rion bent a hard stare at him. "John, understand me. Lord Smythwick is a powerful lord in this region. This is his niece. If word got out that she spent the night here, Lord Smythwick could insist I marry her. And why did I try to kidnap Lady Bertilda?"

"Because . . . um . . . she's an heiress and we need money."

"That's right." Rion picked the ladle off of the floor and filled a bowl from the cauldron bubbling beside the fire. "And what will happen if I'm forced to marry an impoverished female?"

Helwin could see John working it out in his mind. "We'll all be put out of the castle?"

"That's right." Rion swept the men with an all-encompassing glance. "So where did Lady Helwin spend the night?"

"On the beach trapped by the tide," they recited.

"Good." Rion handed Helwin the bowl.

She sniffed the bubbly gray sediment, then jumped back and held it away from her nose. "Lord Masterson, you need a new cook."

The men brayed with laughter and nudged each other.

A big bear of a warrior slammed his spoon to the table and stood, shoving his bench back and upending three of his compatriots. "Are ye complainin' about me cookin'?"

Helwin looked him over. He weighed easily eighteen stone and stood six and a half feet, and beneath his ragged shirt she could see rippling muscles tensed for a fight. A wise woman would back down.

Helwin was tired of backing down. She had spent her life backing down. "Not until I taste it." She dipped her tongue into the bowl and grimaced, then paced forward. When she stood right before him, she looked up into his face and said, "It's awful."

Rion swore.

The men close to Helwin and the bear shuffled backward.

The two of them glared at each other. Helwin held the hot bowl at ready, just in case he reached for her. Finally, just when she was ready to kick him in the shin and run, the bear burst into a shout of laughter, grabbed her, swung her around to face the others and hugged her shoulders. "This be one helluva woman. She'll teach th' master a thin' or two!"

Helwin sighed with relief. She'd passed muster and managed not to spill a drop of her gruel.

"I thank you, Barth." Rion freed Helwin from the bear's hug and shoved her toward the head of the table. "But she's the wrong woman."

"She's perfect fer ye, m'lord. Ye need a mouthy one." Barth seated himself again and picked up his spoon. "Once she learns t' like me cookin', she'll do."

Helwin looked at the short bench set for the master, and waited for one of the men to pull it back.

No one moved.

"Barth, I can do better than learn to like your cooking," she observed. "I can cook, and admirably, too."

With sudden gallantry, three men leaped to their feet and fought for the privilege of seating her. Rion shoved them aside, took her arm, and helped her settle on the hard bench. Then he seated himself close against her.

Up and down the table, Helwin saw raised eyebrows.

A dripping cup of ale was poured and passed to them, as well as a plate with a flat bread burned almost to charcoal.

Then a young man about her own age asked, "What do ye cook?"

"What do you like?" she countered.

"I wish you wouldn't tease my men." Rion's leg moved restlessly against hers. "As soon as we eat, I'm sending that letter to your uncle. You're not going to be here long enough to cook for them."

Heartfelt groans were followed by two mighty thumps as Barth, manners strained past bursting, shoved his benchmates onto the floor.

Helwin turned to Rion and found his face close—so close she recalled the exquisite kiss of the night before. Hastily, she lowered her gaze before he read her desire—or her guilt. "I assure you, my uncle will not bother to rush to my aid." *Because he's not home.* "I wager I'll be here through supper, at least. I've got time to set the men to cleaning and to prepare a hearty dinner of . . . what do you have?"

"What do ye mean, set the men to cleanin'?" Sir Lathrop

demanded. "These men are warriors, and *I'm* a knight. We don't clean."

Ah, Sir Lathrop. She had known immediately he would be the problem. "No, from what I can tell, you drink until you puke and eat your master out of hearth and home. It's time you earned your keep." She scraped at the toast, then nibbled on a corner. It was cold.

"Women." Sir Lathrop sneered. "Women are good for only one thing."

Helwin didn't pretend to misunderstand, but answered briskly, "Until you muck out the great hall, you won't get a woman here to do that one thing."

She watched as two of the men stood. One started clearing the table. One fetched a ragged broom. Obviously, with the right incentive, these men could be trained.

The young squire still loitered on his bench. "Cleaning is women's work."

Rion looked directly at him. "I can't afford maids. Without Bertilda and her fortune, I can't afford even your keeping, Terris."

Standing, Terris grabbed a bucket. "I'll go fetch water."

The other men rose reluctantly and gathered the bowls, rolled up the faded carpets, and swabbed at the dust-encrusted windows. All except Sir Lathrop, who stayed stubbornly on his bench and glared defiance at Helwin.

When Barth stood, she called, "Barth, may I prevail upon you to start a fire in the courtyard? Since Sir Lathrop doesn't wish to join in the duties of cleaning, perhaps we can prevail upon him to be the first to bathe himself."

Everyone in the great hall froze.

Swelling like a toad, Sir Lathrop rose to his feet. "Lord Masterson, I have long served you faithfully. I have saved your life in battle. And I will not stand for being treated so saucily by a female—and not even a female who is to be your wife, but one who, after spending the night with you, is little better than a trollop!"

Helwin's face flamed. If she were a man she would have smashed Sir Lathrop's face with her fist.

"Really?" Rion rose to his feet. "Even with my word that naught passed between us, still you deliver judgment on the fair Lady Helwin?"

Sir Lathrop's eyes shifted from side to side. He couldn't be more than thirty, yet he had the manner of a man who had given up on life. "You lied for her."

"Nay," Rion said softly. "I didn't." His hand shot out. He grabbed Sir Lathrop by the shirt and pulled him toward him. "You'll want to apologize to her for your misspoken words."

"Foolishness! I have been your lieutenant for twelve years, and no mere trollop—"

Rion's fist flashed out, knocking Sir Lathrop flat on his back. Before Sir Lathrop had recovered enough to do more than shake his head, Rion said, "She is right. You stink. Barth, assist Sir Lathrop out to the horse trough so he can bathe."

With a slow grin, Barth started after the scuttling Sir Lathrop. The other men laughed and jeered as Barth cornered Sir Lathrop, hoisted the struggling man onto his shoulders and headed out the door.

Helwin found herself treated with a sudden, overwhelming respect, and the housecleaning took on an enthusiasm it had previously lacked.

Well satisfied, she dusted off her fingers and rose. "Now, my lord—what foodstuffs do you have in your larder? I'm going to make your dinner."

CHAPTER 4

By the time Helwin had a stew bubbling in the pot, the shrieking and imprecations from outside had ceased. The men moved quickly about their work, and Rion, who had never imagined anyone could bully his ragtag group of soldiers, watched Helwin with increasing amazement. She was a whirlwind of energy, directing the cleaning, jesting with the men, singing as she whisked about the great hall setting all to rights.

Rion himself had not been set to any task—Helwin claimed nothing was required of the lord except that he sit on his noble arse—but for some reason he read a challenge into her words. He had wet a broom with soapy water, scrubbed at the floor and found himself joining the men in a rousing chorus of a soldier's song so risqué Helwin couldn't sing for laughing.

When she was smiling, she really had a pretty face. She'd never be as beautiful as her cousin, of course, but the slant of her blue eyes made her look sleepy, as if she'd just risen from bed after a good, long loving. And her figure was . . . magnificent. When she stood on a stool to strip a tapestry off the wall and almost toppled over, it was no wonder that four men were there to catch her. When John held her a bit too long, Rion shouted, "Put the woman down and get to work, you loafer, before I assign you to muck out the stables!"

Hastily, John placed her on her feet, and Rion ignored the grins exchanged by his men. They'd taken a liking to Helwin, and that was fine, but they might as well stop with their imaginings. He had to find a real heiress to wed, and fast.

When Sir Lathrop's damp, sullen figure appeared at the top of the stairs, the laughter and singing stopped. Silence filled the great hall as everyone's gaze shifted from Helwin to Sir Lathrop to Rion. Rion himself tensed; since their return from battle, Sir Lathrop had gotten above himself. If he was still defiant, Rion would have to throw him out—and he needed Sir Lathrop. A man in his position needed a warrior to protect his back.

Helwin stopped stirring the stew. "Sir Lathrop, since you're the first to look respectable, I would beg that you go to the village and seek out a dear old woman named Winetta. She was my wet nurse, and on my command she will send maids to assist with the cleaning. Bring them here."

For one long moment, Sir Lathrop stared at Helwin as if she were insane.

He hesitated long enough to convince the other men he would refuse, and like lads with their first chance at courting, they jumped up and down and waved their arms. "Send me," they chorused. "No, send me!"

Sir Lathrop stalked into the great hall, shoving his compatriots aside. "I'll do it," he snarled. "I can handle an old wet nurse, and with my instruction, she'll get us the best women."

"Indeed, I depend on you." Helwin sounded respectful, but the small smile that played around her mouth worried Rion.

Sir Lathrop didn't seem to notice. "I'll get a real cook, too."

"Ask for Bessie," Helwin instructed. "She is very skilled."

Rion sidled over to her. "Sir Lathrop is surely not our best choice. He's angry, and if he chooses to tell the truth of your sojourn here, you're ruined."

She nodded. "In this matter, I depend on his loyalty to you."

"Aye." She was right. If Sir Lathrop chose to smirch her in a fit of pique, he might as well do so right away. Rion hated to say it, but he had to add, "I can't pay the women."

"They'll work for you as lord of Castle Masterson." Helwin smiled openly at him. "They remember you with affection from your boyhood, and they've wondered why you haven't sent for them."

He wondered if Helwin suffered from deafness. "I can't pay them."

"You can take it out of their rent in the autumn."

"Unless I marry Bertilda, I won't survive until the autumn."

"Then we'll find you another heiress." She laid her hand on his arm. "I promise you, all will be well."

For no reason other than the fact she'd reassured him, he believed all would be well—which was madness.

Where was Lord Smythwick? Rion needed Helwin out of here before she drove him insane. In fact—he stroked his stubbled chin—mayhap that was the plan. Mayhap that explained why, despite Rion's note informing him of Helwin's situation, Lord Smythwick hadn't sent for her. Mayhap Lord Smythwick had tricked Rion and placed his niece in Rion's castle to destroy Rion with unwarranted hope. Rion had been a mercenary; he well understood the disasters that followed a man who hoped for no reason. Aye, he had reason to be suspicious. He would keep aloof from this cunning wench and keep an eye on her schemes.

"Now the other men can take their baths," she announced.

Terris groaned.

Rion turned on him. "Do you require Barth's assistance?"

Terris glanced at the giant warrior hovering in the doorway. "No! No, I can bathe myself."

"Before you go to the village, Sir Lathrop, mayhap you will allow me to trim your hair." Helwin sounded respectful and concerned as she set a tall stool before the fire.

Sir Lathrop's eyes shifted from side to side as he tried to decide if he would be ridiculed for obeying her suggestion or forced if he refused.

In a brisker tone, she said, "As you like, of course, Sir Lathrop. The village women are naturally timid, but they'll follow Winetta regardless of your fearsome appearance."

With a scowl, Sir Lathrop walked to the stool and sat down.

Helwin snapped her fingers. Terris produced a comb and scissors. Helwin draped Sir Lathrop's shoulders with an old piece of cloth.

Rion found himself fascinated by the sight of his most cantankerous warrior squirming like a lad as Helwin combed out the tangles. She kept up a low-toned chatter as she worked, and once Sir Lathrop almost smiled. Almost, but that was more than Rion had seen since they'd arrived back in England in the spring and found his father dead, the estate impoverished, and their prospects devastated. It was a difficult thing for a man to work hard all his life and find no reward for his good faith. Rion suspected bitterness soured Sir Lathrop, for it had begun to sour Rion, also.

Now this woman came along, the wrong woman, and in a matter of hours she had turned his castle into a place of warmth, laughter, and song, with willing men who worked for the glimpse of hope Helwin provided. He didn't understand. They knew what he knew—that unless a miracle happened, they would all be roaming the countryside looking for positions as knights-in-arms or even returning to the Continent to fight and die on foreign soil. He could do nothing, and he was their leader. Ah, aye. Bitterness. The taste stayed on his tongue.

"There you are, Sir Lathrop!" Helwin removed the cloth and shook out the loose brown hair. "What a comely head you've been hiding. I know women who would fight for hair as beautiful as yours."

Sir Lathrop snorted. "Women are nothing but vain and selfish creatures."

Helwin dusted at his shoulders. "One looks on all God's creations and wonders what He was thinking."

Sir Lathrop sharply scrutinized her. "Humph." He stalked toward the door.

"I expect to see you running when you get back," Helwin called, "a bevy of village women after you!"

"Humph." He stomped out.

Rion saw the grins that swept the great hall, and shouted, "Get back to work, men, else the women will take one look and flee." He turned back to his bucket and broom, and found Barth and Terris blocking his way.

"M'lord, I've fought wi' ye fer ten years, through freezing weather an' mud t' our knees an' heat so intense our stalks hung t' our knees." Barth paused and stared at Rion expectantly.

Rion didn't know what Barth expected, but he assured the big man, "You've been a worthy servant and a great warrior."

"I want t' settle now." Barth gestured about. "We all want t' settle now."

Rion's chest tightened. He knew the men were tired of wandering, tired of fighting for one puny Teutonic lord or another. When he'd failed to win Bertilda, he'd failed to secure their future. "I know."

"Me point is, given a chance wi' a woman, there wasn't one

ye couldn't debauch t' her pleasure an' yers. So tell me th' truth"—Barth nudged Rion so hard he stumbled sideways—"ye did toss up Lady Helwin's skirts, didn't ye?"

Terris crowded close, and his face shone with trust. "We get t' . . . we have t' keep her, don't we?"

Rion didn't know what to say. Did they think, if he had debauched Helwin, that he could keep her as his leman?

He glanced at Helwin. Ah, that was a tempting thought. Yet his lust must be the result of a long abstinence from feminine companionship. For no other reason would he want a woman whose only attributes were a fine bust, a narrow waist, a mouth made for laughing—and for kissing. But he couldn't keep her. She was a lady, and a lady who'd been badly used by fate. She deserved better. "We don't get to keep her," he said.

Barth stomped his foot and the crockery rattled. "If ye debauched her, ye can keep her!"

"Lady Helwin knocked me out with my own cudgel before I could do more than kiss her."

Both Terris and Barth grinned.

"Nay." Clearly, Terris didn't believe it.

"Aye." Rion showed the bump that rose on the back of his head.

Terris's grin faded.

Barth's did not. "Just as I said. She's th' perfect woman fer ye."

Rion flushed. "Nay, she's not. She's a shrew and a meddler."

Barth paced toward Rion, pushing him into a corner. "Aye, an' a handsome miss who would warm yer bed!"

"An' she can cook." Terris followed.

Trapped by two insistent men and his own thoughts, Rion glanced in desperation toward the door. Where was Helwin's uncle, anyway? Why hadn't he sent a cart to take her away?

CHAPTER 5

As the afternoon progressed, Rion asked for what was surely the millionth time, "Where is your uncle? Why hasn't he come for you?"

"I suppose he doesn't care if he gets me back." Helwin rolled up her sleeves, and scrubbed the table with sand and a brush. "He has forbidden me to look at him. I make him uncomfortable."

Rion could imagine. Those clear blue eyes easily conveyed her scorn. "Then why doesn't he marry you off?"

In fact, those blue eyes conveyed scorn right now. "Because nobody wants an impoverished twenty-two-year-old spinster, my lord. *You* don't."

She was wrong about that. He did want her, wanted her badly. The taste of her lingered on his lips.

Damn, he shouldn't have thought about last night's kiss. He should put it directly from his mind. Her fresh breath. Her startled response. The way her breast fit in his hand for the one moment before she knocked him out cold . . . what a woman.

Rion was desperate to get rid of her. "Lord Smythwick

should marry you off to some lustful, deaf old fool who would never hear you nagging. If I ever again speak to him, I'll suggest that very solution." And Rion would laugh, laugh! at Helwin's vexation.

Her eyes flashed. "You do that, my lord. I'm sure he'll give your advice the consideration it merits." She lifted her head. "Listen!"

From outside, Rion heard the chatter of women's voices intermixed with the occasional low-pitched comment from Sir Lathrop.

"The maids are here!" All around the great hall, rags, brooms and mops dropped as the men ran to the narrow windows. Pushing open the shutters, they leaned out and stared down at the courtyard . . . and marveled. "She's a pretty one." "Look at the one with the red hair!" And, "Look at Sir Lathrop with that beautiful woman! He's following her like he's bewitched."

Rion glanced at Helwin. She was cleaning the sand from the table now, but that enigmatic smile played about her mouth again. "Winetta?" he asked.

"Aye."

"I thought you said your wet-nurse was a dear old woman."

"Winetta is a dear woman, and old means different things to different people." She grinned at him, inviting him in on the jest. "I didn't want to make Sir Lathrop nervous. After all, she's a recent widow."

Merriment rose in his belly. "You crafty little vixen. You set him up!"

"I think you'll find his disposition much improved."

Rion laughed. He couldn't help it. But at the same time, he was aware of a wary dismay. Was Helwin going to mend all that was wrong with his household in one short afternoon?

After a last twinkle in his direction, she called to his knights, "Gentlemen, the maids will be here soon."

To Rion's amazement, they hurried over to line up in front of her as if she were a general.

"We'll eat as soon as they arrive. You should wash your hands."

"But we just bathed," Terris objected.

The men, some still damp and all newly shorn, nodded in agreement.

"You've been cleaning, and your hands are dirty."

"You might as well do as she says," Rion said. "We've been gone from England for so long, most of you don't remember, but take my word for it—women are finicky about things like this."

As the men fought to line up at the washbasin, Rion found himself exchanging a smile with Helwin. Together, they could handle any challenges that arose in this household . . . if they married. But they couldn't. It was impossible. Turning, he plunged toward the outer door.

"Where are you going, my lord?" she cried.

"I haven't bathed." And he wanted to watch for her uncle.

"But there's no one to heat water for you!"

"Cold water will do very well."

By the time Rion stepped back into the great hall, toweling his hair, the village women had spread throughout the great hall. Their lighter voices blended with the rumbling voices of the men, and Rion marveled at the difference in his knights' behavior. No one spat on the floor. No one scratched at his codpiece. No one fought or shouted, and for the first time since they'd returned to England, they were smiling. His mercenaries had been transformed into gentlemen. Of course, their clothes were still dirty and most of them could use a shave, but Rion had no doubt that, too, would come.

There weren't enough women—perhaps one for every two men—but the competition urged his men onto heights of courtesy and good behavior.

The female who stood next to Sir Lathrop spotted Rion first. The top of her head scarcely reached Sir Lathrop's shoulder and her hair showed a dusting of gray, but as the men had said, Winetta was a handsome widow indeed. "Here is our dear lord," she called.

The chatter stopped and at once, the women turned to him and in unison, they curtsied.

Ah, how he had missed the presence of women in his castle! The rustle of their skirts, the sound of their laughter. And he recollected this woman, in a vague sort of way, as a memory from his past. His gaze traveled the great hall. He remembered quite of few of the maids. They'd changed, but so had he. New memories intruded, experiences had changed them, but the common link of land and heritage united them. They remembered. So must he.

His gaze shifted to Helwin, standing beside the bubbling pot. The way she looked, with her smiling eyes and her generous mouth. The scent of her body, rich and warm.

Bowing to the women, he said, "Welcome to Castle Masterson."

Winetta stepped forward. "My lord, we pray you look favorably upon our efforts in your service."

Now he felt awkward, unsure of how to answer. If only his father had been less of a turd and more of a teacher, Rion would know how to greet the village women who had come on faith to work for him. "I vow I will."

Helwin clapped her hands and brought everyone to attention. With a gesture toward the head of the table, she said, "My lord, if you would take your place, we can eat."

He smiled at her. Who wouldn't? She had labored long this day, yet her blue eyes sparkled as if she were enjoying herself. He made his way to the head of the table and seated himself.

Winetta organized the women into a battalion of servers, shooed Helwin toward him, and within moments a steaming bowl of stew was placed before each man. There weren't enough bowls; they would have to share with the women. Rion saw how the men's fingers twitched as they held their spoons; they'd not eaten decent food for far too long. But they waited until the women had seated themselves before securing a seat, fighting to sit next to a wench.

Rion's stomach growled as he inhaled the wonderful aroma. He picked up his own spoon.

And Helwin laid a restraining hand on his arm. "Shouldn't we say grace?"

The chatter stopped. The men looked astonished, then apprehensive.

Rion and the Lord had been at odds for too many years for him to think of thanking God, but he didn't dare say so. Somehow he thought Helwin would turn that sharp, reprimanding tongue on him. She'd frown all the way through dinner, and ruin a fabulous feast. And, after all, hadn't the Lord blessed him with a few hours of Helwin? That was surely something to be thankful for. Bowing his head, he said, "You do it."

Her grace was mercifully brief and appreciative of the food and the company, and the women—and most of the men— echoed her "amen" with fervent endorsement. Aye, the men were thanking God for more than the food. They were grateful for the plump, feminine bodies seated next to them, and for the possibility to tumble those plump, feminine bodies at some not too distant date. They had had their fill of wandering about Europe, and they wanted to settle, to breed, to be citizens and not fearsome invaders. They wanted wives. They wanted love.

Rion wanted . . . he scowled. He had to wed an heiress, regardless of how hunchbacked or evil-eyed she might be. His men had followed him through battle and famine. Now he was responsible for making their dreams come true. He had no right to dream as they did—and he would not, for Helwin sat beside him, and Helwin could never be his.

"Is the stew not to your liking, my lord?" Helwin asked.

"What?"

"You're not eating."

"Oh." He dipped in his spoon. The stew was hot and rich, made with a haunch of venison he'd shot but yesterday and the shriveled vegetables from his cellar. "You *can* cook."

A dimple quivered in Helwin's cheek. "You don't have to sound so surprised."

Gruffly, he said, "Most ladies can't."

"They can if they have no one to cook for them." She lifted one shoulder in a shrug. "When Uncle Carroll goes to London, he takes the French chef."

Winetta reached under the table and brought forth a cloth bag. "My lord, I bring gifts from the village baker." She pulled out a dozen round loaves of bread. "He begs you to forgive yesterday's loaves, but he had no other baked."

Rion heard his men's intake of breath. They'd baked flat loaves on hot stones before the fire, and hadn't had real risen bread in far too long. "I am most grateful to the baker."

"I'll tell him." Winetta smiled. "He's my father."

For most of his life, Rion had been responsible for himself and his men, and no one had given him anything except a blow with a sword. Now these women, who hadn't seen him in years, acted as if they were honored to serve him. As Winetta sliced the bread and the conversations around the table resumed, Rion leaned his head close to Helwin's. "Why are they so kind?"

"They know my uncle covets your land and your prestige, and if he should win your land, things will go ill for the villagers. Uncle Carroll has a well-earned reputation for ruthlessness and parsimony."

"How do they know I won't be worse?"

"You're their ancestral liege."

"So was my father, and he was a drunken, gambling lout."

"You and your men have been watched, my lord, and gossiped about in the village." She took a bite of stew and chewed with thoughtful deliberation. "Anyway, better the devil you know than the devil you don't."

Stung, he replied, "For that exact reason, I wonder if I should wed *you*." Pish! He shouldn't have said that. That was ungrateful, after all of her labor, and surly, for she hadn't sought the dilemma in which she found herself.

Her eyes flashed, and she drew away from him. "I will not be wed because I'm the lesser of two evils, and live with a man so addle-witted he believes me the inferior of my cousin Bertilda." She looked him over as if he were an ox on the auction block. "Although if by chance our plan goes somehow awry and I do get stuck with you, I could comfort myself that you're not repulsive. You have good teeth and you're not pockmarked."

"I thank you, my lady shrew. With praise like that, I will indeed suffer a mighty conceit."

She tossed her head, and when straggling tendrils of blond hair fell around her face, she poked them back under her coif. "Now *that* you do suffer already."

He couldn't stand it. He couldn't sit next to her, eat the food she prepared, listen to her verbally thrash him, and still want to drag her upstairs to bed and see which of them would win the next wrestling match. He had to get rid of her. Standing, he grabbed her hand and pulled her to her feet. "That's it! If your uncle will not send for you, I'll take you back. Now. At once!"

CHAPTER 6

Helwin tried to cling to her dignity, but dignity was in short supply as Rion dragged her out of the great hall. He'd lost his patience, and she didn't know why.

All right, she did. She'd spoken without a care for his tender male pride, but of all the men she'd ever met, she had thought Rion the least conceited. Apparently she was wrong.

So she would apologize. "My lord, I'm sorry I said you weren't repulsive."

Casting a blistering glance over his shoulder, he started down the stairs.

She bit her lip. That hadn't come out right, but in the last few years, she'd lost the art of compromise. Nay, more than that. She had learned to deal with her lot by the liberal use of sarcasm, and now she tried desperately to remember the simple skill of civility. "My lord, any woman would be pleased to rest her gaze on your countenance."

"Except you?" He slammed through the door and strode across the courtyard toward the stables.

She skipped along at his side. "No, I tolerate your face exceedingly well."

He stopped. "Tolerate?"

"Enjoy." He looked down at her, unmoving, and so encouraged she continued, "Relish, even. You look not like a silly popinjay, but like a man, seasoned in warfare and ready to defend what is his." And she hoped he didn't realize how attractive that was to a woman, especially a woman who had been without affection or security for far too many years. "You are tall, you are well-formed, you have all your teeth and they're straight and white."

He still held her wrist, and he squeezed it gently. "Go on."

"I like your hair, so thick and black, and your eyes are . . ." She faltered. He really did have beautiful eyes, green as a forest pool and surrounded by lashes so long and curled she envied him them. Right now he watched her so intently, a blush rose in her cheeks and she found herself unable to hold his gaze. She glanced down, then peeked up at him to see what he was doing.

Expressionless, he stared at her. "What about my eyes?"

"You have two," she mumbled. "And I like them very much."

"I thank you. Is there anything else you want to tell me?"

She scuffled her toe in the dirt. "Nay."

"Then come or I won't get you back to your uncle's before dark." He started toward the stables again.

Incredulous, she stumbled along behind him. "But . . . I flattered you! Isn't that what you wanted?"

He gave a brief, hard laugh. "I enjoyed it very much, but I'm still going to take you back."

Infuriated, humiliated, she doubled up her fist and punched him in the arm. Then she ducked.

He flinched and shoved open the stable door.

He wasn't going to hit her back. She glanced back at the castle keep. The women and the knights were crowded around the windows, watching solemnly as their lord dragged his badly chosen guest out the door. The castle was dirty, old-fashioned and impoverished, but, oh, how she wanted to stay here for at least a little while longer! "I'll say whatever you want. Just tell me what you want me to say."

He led his stallion from its stall. "I don't care what you say. You're going back."

Desperately she groped for a reason why she must stay. "You need someone to supervise the maids."

"You said Winetta would do that." He strapped the saddle on the horse.

"A meal. I could cook you and your men a meal."

"You said Bessie was a cook." He mounted the horse, guided it to the mounting block, then leaned down and offered her his hand. "You're going back."

In despair, she stared at the hand, then up at him. He watched her with dark determination, a formidable warrior who had made his living by his wits and learned well how to enforce his will. Now he made it clear—she'd done her job too well. He didn't need her.

She had nowhere to run, no refuge to seek. Since the loss of her parents, she'd had to do as she was told. She'd had no power, no happiness, and now the brief moments of freedom had come to an end. In mingled despair and resignation, she put her hand in his, nimbly mounted the block, and climbed on the stallion before him.

The animal moved restively beneath their double weight. Rion wrapped his arms around her and settled her back against him. The warmth of the beast and the warmth of the man should have made the ride a pleasure, but instead she wanted to weep. Weep at losing these brief moments of freedom. Weep with knowing she would never see Rion again, or spar with him until the blood raced in her veins and she remembered what it was to live without fear. Nay, more than that. To live with hope, with laughter, with anticipation.

Yet she would not weep. She was Lady Helwin. She stiffened her spine, lifted her chin, and moved with the gait of the horse as they rode out of the gate and toward her uncle's home.

As the miles passed, the road rose until they reached the top of the highest hill in the area. There, Rion pulled the horse to a halt. To the left, she could see the place where she had lived her whole life. She should look on it with affection, but for too many years it had been her uncle's home, an orderly stone rectangle with well-lit windows set at regular intervals, fashionably restrained gables and finials, and a sumptuous green lawn sweeping away toward a well-designed garden.

To the right, Castle Masterson rose above the cliffs in savage primitive majesty. Crumbling towers thrust skyward, scarcely a candle shone from the narrow windows of the dark stone keep, and part of the outer wall collapsed toward the ocean. Compared to Smythwick Manor, Castle Masterson was a grim, dark, antiquated hovel. Yet she knew well where she would rather be.

Desolation turned her pride to dust. Turning in the saddle, she grasped Rion's shirt. "Please, my lord, don't send me back. I beg of you. Please."

He stared down at her. His lips parted. His head dropped toward her. For one moment, she thought he would kiss her. Instead he said, "I'll not have you spend the night at Castle Masterson. Tomorrow everyone in the district would know, and I would indeed be forced to wed you—a mistake I could ill afford."

His words stabbed at her, but she took heart because he hadn't blankly refused her. Eager and hopeless, she said, "The village women are there. Winetta was my wet-nurse. She can serve as a chaperone. Please, Lord Masterson, don't make me go back."

"Where is your uncle?"

In London. "He's never wanted to bother with me. Don't you see? He won't force you to marry me. He doesn't even care that I'm gone." She, Helwin, who had never begged for anything, begged now. Because it was important. More important than maintaining her optimistic façade. "In my uncle's house, I'm an unwelcome burden. The last lord's daughter. Despised by the servants and ignored by the guests. There I'm less than a person. A mere ghost who drifts the corridors and who, someday, will vanish. With you, Lord Rion, I'm real again."

His lips flattened, his nostrils flared, his eyebrows turned upward in devilish disdain. She thought he was going to say no, and she braced herself for this final rejection.

"Hellion." He cupped her chin in his hand and lifted her face to his. He kissed her as if driven by a fury of desire and despair.

She kissed him back with the same fervor, opening her lips to him, touching her tongue to his, inciting and incited. She ran her hands over every part of him she could reach, straining to press herself against him as if he were the safe haven she had sought for so many years.

He wrapped one arm around her, lifting her, trying to fit her to him when there was no way they could manage on a war-horse made restive by crazed riders.

The westering sunshine beat against her eyelids, her back hurt from being twisted around, and she wanted nothing so much as to stay here, just like this, in his arms forever.

Lifting his head, he glared into her eyes. "My Lady Hellion!"

And, gloriously, wonderfully, miraculously, he turned his

steed toward Castle Masterson, and urged it to a gallop. The wind tore at Helwin's hair as they raced down the hill and along the ocean cliffs. Rion leaned forward, pressing his chest to her back. She inhaled the clean scent of the sea breeze. The wind brought tears to her eyes . . . or was it more than the wind? She only knew she had been granted one additional night of happiness, and she would relish each moment, storing away the memories.

CHAPTER 7

A week! It's been almost a sennight, and nothing." Terris spoke to the little group huddled into the corner of the great hall.

Winetta scowled. "If he spent just one hour in her bed, she'd have him eating out of the palm of her hand."

"One hour?" Sir Lathrop hooted with laughter. "Lord Rion never spent just an hour with a woman. If he joined Lady Helwin in bed, she wouldn't have a chance to rest for two days—but she'd never get the smile off her face."

"Really?" Winetta cooed, and ran her hand up Sir Lathrop's arm. "Is he so much of a man, then?"

Lifting her hand to his lips, Sir Lathrop kissed it and gazed at her soulfully. "Like me, he well knows how to pleasure a woman."

Barth slapped his knee and hooted with laughter.

Sir Lathrop glared at him, then glanced about with crafty care. "I've never seen Lord Rion lust so desperately before. He watches her like a stallion watches a new mare, practically pawing the ground."

"Yet she sleeps alone every night in the Masterson bed." Barth sighed weightily.

"Surely he'll break," Terris said.

"I tell ye, I know th' master." Barth's lugubrious face drooped like a hound's. "He's decided he can't have her an' nothing will breach his defense."

"Nothing?" Winetta grinned. *"I have a plan."*

"A bonfire! We're having a bonfire on the beach!" Barth danced a lumbering jig that shook the floorboards and rattled the crockery.

Elated at the chance for a holiday, Helwin laughed at him. "Save your cavorting and pack the dishes."

He nodded his great head, picked up a pot and dropped it.

At once, Mercia, young, beautiful, and adoring, rushed to help him. The two stood together, laughing and so obviously in love, Helwin's eyes filled with tears.

She blinked them quickly away. Stupid to be jealous of another's happiness, when she had so much to be thankful for.

She'd never had such a wonderful sennight in her life. She refused to look ahead to that inevitable day when she would have to return to the manor. Eventually Uncle Carroll would return and reluctantly decide he must bring her back under his dominion—he could hardly not—and send for her. But for now, she cooked, she cleaned, she laughed with the maids and jested with the men. And always, always she was aware of Rion, watching her from afar.

He scarcely spoke to her, even at dinner. He avoided contact with her as much as possible. Yet every time she looked up, there he was. Staring. Brooding.

Lusting.

He was a man. If he truly lusted, he would give in to his desires and crawl into the huge Masterson bed with her. Yet for the past seven nights, she had slumbered alone in the

Masterson bedchamber while he slept heaven knew where.

If he did crawl into the bed with her, what would she do? Reject him, or welcome him? She didn't know. She only knew she also lusted. Lusted after his sculpted body, his serious mouth, his heavy-lidded eyes.

Oh, she liked him, too. Liked the way he thanked the maids when they served him. Admired his dignity as financial disaster loomed ever closer. Positively adored his occasional dry comment and his captivating stories. She could listen to him for the rest of her life. But it was the sound of his warm, deep voice that brought her body to attention, made her nipples bead and a dampness form between her thighs. The mere sight of his firm buttocks pressed firmly on an unbroken horse made her damp with longing. There was no escaping the truth. She, Lady Helwin Smythwick, the woman who had so prided herself on her character and intelligence—she was superficial and inclined to admire the physical.

Sir Lathrop stopped on his way out the door, arms laden with rugs. "'Tis a beautiful, clear, cool morning. A great day for anything you'd want to do."

"And I want to go to the beach." Since Winetta had come into the castle, even the detestable Sir Lathrop had grown mellow.

So every morning, Helwin thanked God she was still at Castle Masterson and embraced every moment, every activity, every word and laugh and sigh.

Today would be wonderful. They were going to the beach, all of them. Winetta had suggested a merrymaking as a reward for the men and the maids. The castle sparkled, the garden was tended, the stables mucked out. If good will and hard work could save Castle Masterson, all would have been well.

Of course, it was not. The harvest wouldn't begin for another two months, and Rion needed to buy corn for his villagers if they were to survive until then. He couldn't. He had no coins hidden in his coffers. But Helwin hadn't been to such a revelry since she was eight years old, so for today she refused to worry.

Had Rion gone ahead? She hadn't seen him since the morning. Surely he did intend to go and make merry with the rest of them.

She *wanted* him to go. She wanted to look on him for as long as she could, because she knew... she knew that if Uncle Carroll didn't send for her soon ... she would have to return of her own will. She would slip back into the household routine and perhaps someone would say, "Where have you been, Helwin?" Or perhaps no one had missed her. Bertilda would smirk, her fish eyes glinting with malicious pleasure, never realizing that when Helwin got the chance, she would put itch powder in Bertilda's best wig and pins in her corset.

The castle was emptying rapidly, and she checked to make sure the food had been packed, the casks and baskets carried away.

"My lady." From the gallery above, Winetta beckoned. "I have something to show you."

Helwin controlled her impatience. "Can't it wait? They'll start the beach fire soon and I want to be there."

"Please, my lady, come and look."

Helwin heaved a sigh and climbed the stairs. Winetta stood at the door of the Masterson bedchamber, her broad face alight with anticipation. Helwin stepped in the room, and a lovely sight met her eyes. A large wooden tub, filled with steaming water, stood next to the fireplace alive with flame. Linen towels were laid across the firescreen, and the scent of mulled wine wafted from a pot over the fire. A tray of bread, cheese, and dried fruit sat on the table by the bed, its furs turned-down and waiting with fresh linens and a scattering of crimson rose petals. She hadn't been so indulged in years, but . . . but . . . "For me? Now? I mean, when the celebration's starting?"

"Come on, my lady, let me help you unfasten your gown." Winetta pulled her toward the tub. "I thought, after this hectic week, you'd like a chance to be alone, and what better way but a bath while everyone's gone?" As she burbled over with enthusiasm, she tugged and pulled at Helwin's cap, at her bodice, at her skirt and petticoats. She pinned Helwin's hair ever more closely to her head, and said, "You can come right down when you're done. We're going to make a night of it on the beach. There'll be no one in the castle to bother ye. Take all the time ye want."

"All right." Helwin found herself standing beside the tub, nude and confused. But she would bathe, if that made her old nurse happy, and go down to the beach within the hour. "I thank you for your thoughtfulness."

"I've wanted to do something for you for a long time." Winetta pulled a tall, folding screen between the tub and the door. "Something you could treasure forever." With a curtsy, she slipped away, latching the door behind her.

Helwin stared at the door and murmured, "I don't know about forever. It's just a bath." She stuck her toe in the water. A perfect temperature. Sinking into the tub, she grabbed the soap. She would wash as quickly as possible and . . . she moaned as the heat from the water sank into her bones.

Ah, she had forgotten how a bath relaxed every muscle, every nerve. Herbs bobbed on the surface of the water: mint and rosemary, fresh and delightful. Forgetting the bonfire, she leaned her head against the back of the tub and breathed in the steamy scents. She folded her legs under her, sank down almost to her chin, and abandoned herself to luxury. She paddled the water to create waves. She stared, eyes heavy-lidded, at the sunshine streaming through the window. Lifting one leg, she pointed her toe and wondered how it would be if Rion was with her, sliding his hand up her thigh . . . she slid her own hand up her thigh, imagining how it would be, how his eyes would flash with desire, how he'd kneel before the tub and beg for her hand in marriage, and all the while he would be silently demanding she welcome him into her body. And she would . . . Helwin heard the latch click. Her head swung in the direction of the door.

In a voice oily with satisfaction, Sir Lathrop said, "Right this way, my lord. I think you'll be satisfied with my arrangements."

She froze, staring at the screen, the water sliding down her calf toward the tub.

Then—*satisfied with his arrangements!* What did Lathrop mean, *Satisfied with his arrangements?*

More important, who was Lathrop addressing when he said, *My lord?*

Very quietly, she glanced frantically about for a drape. He must mean—

Rion sounded brisk. "I don't know what you have done, Lathrop, but it had better be good. You haven't given me a chance to dress, and the bonfire on the beach has already started."

Rion! She heard his bare feet moving on the wooden floor. *A towel, where was a towel?*

"I, for one, am determined to eat the whole of the bread pudding Lady Helwin made, and will take it ill if you—" He came around the screen clad in only close-fitting trousers and a loose, white linen shirt, observed Helwin, and halted, color draining from his face.

The two of them stared at each other, ashen-faced, each caught in the midst of their own personal imaginings.

"Did you plan this?" he asked.

She shook her head.

The click as the door closed sounded loud in the room. The key grated as it turned in the lock.

Rion whirled, his shoulder knocking against the screen. It wavered and toppled. He hit the door at a run. He tried the door handle—fruitlessly. He pounded on the panels with his fists. He yelled, "Let me out, Lathrop, you traitor. Let me out if you value your life!"

There was no answer. Sir Lathrop was gone. Winetta was gone.

Rion and Helwin were alone.

CHAPTER 8

In despair, Rion thumped his forehead onto the door. Helwin spied the towel on the nightstand. Smoothly, she rose from the tub, stepped out and reached for it.

Rion faced her. His restrained watchfulness had vanished, and wanton, open, unrestrained lust had taken its place. His eyes were hot, his face intent. He looked like a starving man presented with a steaming loaf of bread. Was it possible she had doubted that he wanted her? He did. He sought to escape because he wanted her—too much.

Never in all her life had a man viewed her unclothed. She wanted to cover herself with her hands, to cower behind the tub . . . to flaunt herself and see, even more, the fire of his gaze turn to fever. Deep in her belly, desire reawoke and wrapped her in its heated coils. "Turn around." Her voice wavered. "I'm not decent."

"Fabulously decent." His gaze followed the stream of water as it slid between her breasts and down her belly to nestle in the golden nest of curls between her legs. "Marvelously decent. So decent I can think of nothing else, day and night." He laughed, a great, deep, hearty laugh of masculine satisfaction, a laugh that expanded his marvelous chest.

Heaven have mercy, because he wouldn't.

He paced toward her.

She swallowed and lunged for the towel.

He lunged, too, and reached the towel a moment before she did. "Let me assist you," he said.

"You can't. It's not right. You shouldn't. I shouldn't . . ." She backed up, sliding first one foot, then the other, in a slow shuffle toward the window. Away from sin. But sin, oh God, sin closed in on her, towel in his strong hands, and she wanted to embrace him.

Embrace sin. What kind of woman was she?

"I didn't want this," he said as he followed after her. "Every day, I've tried to avoid this. But I am at the breaking point. Did you know I'm at the breaking point?"

"Nay." The sheen of water that covered her made her shiver and brought a rash of goosebumps to her flesh.

"*They* did." The jerk of his head indicated the devious Winetta and her cohort Sir Lathrop. "*They* knew. That's why they locked us in, those scheming matchmakers. Because I want you so badly, I can't sleep. I can't eat. I can barely speak. All my thoughts are consumed with taking you in my arms and pleasuring you until you scream with delight."

"Oh, dear." She bumped her hip on the table.

"Would you like that?"

Far too much. "Never."

"Liar." Reaching out, he caught her in the towel. "Let me show you. Let me . . ." His hands, wrapped in the folds of the towel, caressed her chin. She stared at him, her breath coming in small pants as he stared down at her, observing her mingled fright and excitement. "You've never done this before." He caressed her lips with the linen's rough texture. "You're untouched."

"Of course I am," she said indignantly. "I'm unmarried!"

He smiled as if she'd said something funny, his lips a tender curve of amusement. The towel slipped over her shoulders, down her arms. The material dragged over her nipples, already erect with the chill, and she shuddered with yearning. He wrapped his arms around her waist, pulling her close against him. As their bodies touched, she gasped to discover his heat, so close and overwhelming. He held her as if she were a jewel he treasured—securely, yet tenderly. His fingers glided across her back and lingered to massage her bare buttocks. He smelled like soap and rosemary—so he'd had a bath, too, and briefly she wondered how Winetta and Sir Lathrop had tricked him. Then, as the towel rubbed up and down her spine in a long, slow caress, that thought slid away.

"Are you warmer, now?" he asked.

She gripped his upper arms, holding on for dear life. He backed her toward the bedside table. She leaned against it.

He said he was at his breaking point. Well, so was she. She had wanted his strength to protect her. She had wanted to defend him against the cruel merriment of her cousin, against the careless disregard of her uncle. And in this last week, every moment, waking and sleeping, she had been obsessive with desire for him. She knew, in some savage corner of her soul, that in bed with this man she would give and receive ecstasy until all of themselves had burned away, leaving two souls fused into one.

He dragged that towel, that wicked instrument of indulgence, over her hips, down her thighs . . . he nudged her knees apart and knelt between them.

Wanton. She felt wanton and daring. Fear made her want to close her legs. Longing made her want to open them further.

She wrestled with temptation.

He dried her down to her toes. Then he looked up at her.

God, he was handsome. Sunlight streamed in the window, illuminating each carved contour of his gorgeous face. His dark hair swept his shoulders, so dark it shone with blue highlights. His eyes glinted clear and green, wicked with intention, and he devoured her with his gaze, lingering on her breasts, gliding down to the indent of her navel, traveling the curve of her hip to the apex of her thighs. Slowly, he reached for her, grazing the curly underbrush of golden hair with a tender touch that made her shiver and tense. His fingers wandered between her legs.

She gasped, and gasped again.

He grew bolder, more familiar.

She clutched the edge of the table, holding on as if it were the only solid reality in her changing world.

He opened her, and he stared at those parts which were usually concealed.

"Don't." She blushed, a heated, furious blush that slid up her belly all the way to her forehead, and she tried to cover herself with her hands.

He brushed them aside. "Beautiful. I knew you would be beautiful, and you are."

His beautiful, velvety lips parted slightly . . .

Too late, she realized his intention. She tugged at his hair, but he rose to his knees and placed his mouth there, at the spot that his fingers had bared. His tongue lapped at her, found her sensitive nub and drew it forth with a gentle suction.

She threw her head back in an agony of delight. Moans fought their way up her throat and escaped in low, frantic sighs. Her knees trembled and she thought . . . she feared she dampened his tongue with her excitement.

All the while he suckled her, his hand cupped her bottom, pressing her in a slow, firm rhythm that made her want to move her hips in his direction. Dimly, she knew what he was doing. He was teaching her how to respond to him—primally, savagely, without thought or logic. Because this response between the two of them had nothing to do with sense and everything to do with instinct.

The roughness of his tongue continued its torture, and her moans grew louder, breaking from her in a constant, unthinking tide. Her body surged in his direction, gathering power from him, until her flagging discipline failed. Pleasure shuddered through her, convulsing her against his mouth. And he kept control of her, thrusting his tongue inside her until she thought she would die of bliss. Her legs trembled, her fingers dug into the table behind her. She tried to escape—it was too much. But he held her and fed on her until sheer exhaustion brought her to a halt.

He stood, and stood too close. Facing her, he stripped out of his clothing. First he discarded his loose linen shirt, and his chest was everything she imagined. Rippling with muscle, covered with a mat of black hair that grew in an inverted triangle and pointed to . . .

His canions, those trousers whose contents she had admired so surreptitiously—when he discarded those, she closed her eyes.

"No, don't close your eyes. Look." He took her chin in his fingers and shook it slightly. "Look what you do to me. I've spent the whole damned week pointing at everyone and bumping into furniture—"

She couldn't help it. She giggled.

"I can't bear to wear my garments because the mere touch of material makes me ache for you more." He stared at her broodingly. "Laugh if you like, my lady Hellion. I'll have my revenge."

She sobered, and she looked. He had narrow hips made to separate a woman's legs, and thighs muscled and bold for riding. Yet it was that which pointed and bumped that made her eyes widen and her breath catch. Pale, except for the purple veins just beneath the silky smooth skin. His cock . . . her fingers touched the cap, skimming around and around in fascinated discovery. Large, more than she had ever imagined—and she had imagined far too often.

Where she got the nerve, she could never afterward tell, but she spread her arms wide. "Take your revenge."

He didn't need another invitation. He picked her up, and wrapped her legs around his waist. He laid her on the bed sideways, so her feet dangled off the edge of the mattress, and he stood on the floor between her legs.

The sheets were cool beneath her back. The mattress cracked with the sound of straw as it sank beneath her weight. The crushed rose petals gave up their sweet scent, and she wanted to hold this moment to remember forever. Such perfection surely only came once in a lifetime.

Holding her thighs hooked over his elbows, he ran his fingertips up and down her flesh. "So delicate," he whispered. "So dainty and yet so strong. You're everything I've ever dreamed of, and I've done nothing but dream this whole week. By God you're going to pay."

He climbed up, one knee on the mattress under her buttock, which freed his hand, and one foot on the floor. As he touched between her open legs, he stared into her eyes, and if she imagined his gruff speech meant he had lost patience, she was wrong. He stroked her as he might pleasure himself, with slow sweeps of his fingers along her feminine nub, milking her of pleasure in the most erotic manner possible.

Pleasure crashed on her like a wave, taking her under to drown in euphoria. His every movement brought her closer to climax once more. She closed her eyes, flung her head back, moaning, feeling too much.

His finger slipped inside her, and massaged her inner passage. Her body responded, dampening his hand, and still she wanted more.

She got it.

No. Wait. No longer his finger.

The size . . . this was discomfort. This *burned*. This was him. Her eyes sprang open.

He hovered over her, one hand braced near her head, watching her hungrily. "Take me," he commanded. "All of me."

She wanted to say something sarcastic. Something foolish, for he wanted her to accept him as badly as he wanted her body. So she turned her head and pressed a kiss on his arm, and tried to relax . . . anything to make his entry easier.

It wasn't easy. He was too big, and unwilling tears trickled out of the corners of her eyes. She breathed carefully, trying to adjust to the tension of his entry.

He knew. Oh, he knew. He observed her as he thrust forward, steadily taking possession of virgin territory. When he had seated himself to the hilt and his hips shuddered under the need to thrust, he stopped and held himself carefully above her. "Take me," he said again.

So he needed the words. "Please," she whispered, "I want you," and she lifted her legs to embrace his hips.

He smiled, a wicked slash of experience. "Oh, sweetheart. I vow you will want me until the day we die." He lowered himself on her and kissed her. His lips caressed hers with love's lightest touch, and when she parted them, his tongue slid between and possessed her mouth as he had possessed her body.

She wrapped her arms around his neck.

Everything began to feel . . . better. Each breath no longer hitched with anguish, but grew long and soft as she absorbed his passion. While his cock twitched within her and his need was upon him, he was indulging her. He reached between them, adjusting and opening her so that he pressed against her when he moved.

Leisurely, gently, he drew out. Her body gave him up reluctantly, and when his eyes closed with an expression of such exquisite gratification, she was flattered. Then he pushed back in, just as slowly, and she wanted to cry with the sweetness of it. He pressed his body against hers, and she forgot pain and remembered only . . . pleasure.

This time when he withdrew and thrust again, she lifted her hips toward him.

He moaned.

Her toes curled. The thrust of him inside her warmed her, melted her around him. She felt swollen, damp, and overflowing with sensation as he sank into her body. Gradually the sensation of tightness, of wanting too much, of needing . . . something . . . again grew within her.

He still moved deliberately, each lunge timed for her delight. But more quickly now. "I adore you," he whispered hoarsely. "You're perfect."

Her hips rolled beneath him. Heat climbed from her belly to her head, driving out thought and reason. That marvelous, breathtaking release was overtaking her. "Rion," she cried. "Dear God, Rion!" She hovered on the edge of oblivion, far from the ache, from the here and the now and into some netherworld where only she and Rion existed. Existed as one.

He plunged at her, powerful and insistent. The sheets beneath her bunched and wrinkled. One pillow fell from the bed. The steamy scent of rosemary and mint filled the room, and the rose petals whispered of their bliss.

Orgasm overtook her, sweeping her along to dark pleasure . . . or was it Rion who swept her along? She didn't know.

They were no longer two people, but one, united in pleasure. Convulsions shook her, her womb contracted over and over, massaging him, taking him, all of him, just as he demanded.

Deep inside her, she felt warmth and fullness as he spilled his seed inside her.

Spilled? Nay, he was thrusting it deep within, demanding she hold it for him, and give it back as progeny.

His baby. His child.

They were one.

"You did what?" Nostrils flared, Lord Smythwick stared first at the note in his hand, then at his daughter.

Bertilda, his only offspring, his darling daughter . . . this stupid child, released the affected giggle she cultivated for her suitors. "I told Lord Masterson to meet me on the beach and he could have me for the night. I knew full well he would send to you demanding my hand in marriage. Then I insisted Helwin wear my cloak." Bertilda giggled again. "I watched from the top of the cliff, and the dolt picked her up and carried her away to his castle."

Smythwick's hand snaked out and slapped the girl right across the cheek. "Do you know what you've done?"

Eyes wide, Bertilda staggered back, hand to her burning face.

"Nay, of course you don't, you silly cow. My God, we're ruined."

"What's wrong? I thought you'd be happy. You hate Helwin."

"I don't hate Helwin. She isn't worth my spit." He tapped the paper against his knee. "How long did you say she'd been gone?"

"Almost a week."

"Are they married yet?"

"Nay, there's been no word of that."

"You had better hope they're not." There had to be a way out of this. Surely somehow he could turn this to his advantage.

If only Queen Elizabeth didn't constantly ask about her dear departed Edwin's daughter, Lord Smythwick would have solved the problem years ago. But his hands had been tied by her concern . . . a slow, horrid smile curved his narrow lips.

"My lord father?" Bertilda's voice quavered unbecomingly, and she trembled with that repulsive shuddering that had affected her dear, departed mother when he came to her bed.

"Have you told anyone what you've foolishly done?"

"Nay, I saved that for you."

"Good. For I would hate to have to rid us of anyone you confided in."

Bertilda shook her head as if she couldn't stop. "What may I do to correct my mistake?"

"Nothing." He turned his cold blue eyes on her, and she shrank back. "You are to do nothing, do you understand me? Don't tell anyone what you have done. Don't tell anyone about this letter. I will handle everything."

CHAPTER 9

Helwin woke to early morning sunshine and Rion eating a cherry off of her stomach. She watched him roll the cherries around with his lips, grazing her skin more than seemed likely for a man as gifted with his mouth as Rion had proved to be. The morning stubble on his chin scraped her soft skin only once, and she wished she could wake to such a treat every morning.

This man, this dread warrior, looked boyishly appealing with his dark hair falling over his forehead and a frown of concentration on his features.

She giggled softly, then caught her breath when he looked up. He gazed at her as if she had given him the money to save his home and a new horse, too.

"Good morning." Her voice was husky. They had made love so many times yesterday afternoon and last night, her voice was husky from moaning and occasionally screaming, and her skin was sensitive to even the slightest breeze through the open window. "Couldn't you find a plate?"

"Why use a plate when the container can be as tasty as the meal?" He bit into a cherry and lifted it toward her mouth, dribbling crimson juice all the way up her body. Tenderly he placed the cherry between her lips, then propped his head on his hand as he watched her chew. Taking the pit, he tossed it in a bowl and made a tsking noise. "Oh, dear. Look at this." His finger slid along the dots of red that speckled her belly and her chest, then in slow, sensuous motions, he licked her clean.

By the time he had finished, she was digging her heels into the mattress and whimpering. The way he used his tongue made her tingle with heat and shiver with cold at the same time. She wanted to jump on top of him and ride him again; she didn't dare, for this morning she was sore and so tired she didn't know if her thighs would lift her. But her body seemed an entity apart from her mind and without a smidgeon of good sense, and she wanted him.

He lifted his head reluctantly. "We have to rise and walk . . . no, crawl downstairs."

She didn't want to go out and face reality, so she ran her fingers through his hair and hugged him close against her. "The door's locked."

"Not anymore. Sometime in the night, one of those treacherous vipers we call our minions released us from our prison." He caught her hand and kissed her palm. "I hope they didn't press their ears to the door."

She blushed all the way from her toes to her hairline. "You really should learn to be a little quieter."

He wiggled up to the pillow and smiled down at her. "I can't. Not when I've had a siren who, all night long, tried to see how long she can pleasure herself with my body. I'm drained dry."

But he pressed himself against her hip, letting her feel the length of his erection, the heat, the splendor. The man was inexorable, and she still couldn't believe she had taken that inside herself . . . and enjoyed it.

More prosaically, he said, "Besides, the bed squeaks."

"We're lucky it didn't collapse," she answered tartly.

He laughed aloud and patted the mattress. "This is the Masterson bed, my sweet, built by the first earl of Masterson with his own hands. Nothing that is of Masterson making ever collapses."

"I noticed." She sent a flirtatious glance down his body.

Easing himself down on top of her, he kissed her lips and said the one phrase that could make her heart sing. The one phrase she'd been waiting to hear all her life. "I love you."

Then he ruined everything. "I love you so much, and I can't have you."

She was gone.

Rion sat at the table in the great hall, stared at the goblet of ale in his hand, and brooded. Helwin had gone back to her uncle's, and that was just as it should be. She shouldn't be tied to a man who had nothing but a sagging castle and no prospects. She should remain safe under her uncle's roof.

If she didn't, Rion would marry her and lose even the sagging castle. He would once again travel the roads of Europe as a mercenary—and she would go with him.

He'd seen what happened to women who joined a mercenary troop to be with their man. They grew old before their time. They bore children in dirty tents and died of childbed fever. If they lived, eventually, their men died on the battlefield and they were forced to become camp followers.

He couldn't bear to have Helwin suffer with such a life. He'd done the right thing by sending her away.

And after all, she'd gone without a single expression of regret. She'd collected her cloak briskly, said good-bye to his men and the village women, and hurried—some might say bolted—out the door.

He glared around him, looking for someone to trounce. But the men had ridden out to exercise the horses, the cowards, and the maids worked cautiously around him, trying to avoid attracting his attention.

Damn Helwin. Couldn't she just once have turned and gazed longingly at him?

He'd *told* her he loved her. Didn't she realize how great an admission that was? He'd never said that to a woman in his life, but he told her because . . . well . . . he did. Feisty, intelligent, organized . . . luscious, wanton, giving . . . how could he not love a woman like that?

Couldn't she have cried as she trudged down the road?

He could have cried. He was losing his companion, his lady, the one woman he could ever love, and in her place he would have to find an heiress. Ugly, old, meek, dreary—it made no difference. He had to wed an heiress, or his lands and his people would be forfeit. Surely Helwin understood that.

Couldn't she at least have thrown him a kiss?

But better that she didn't, for then he would have gone and swept her into his arms and refused to let her go.

No. No. He wouldn't do that to her. He couldn't give in, for if he didn't marry an heiress, he would lose Castle Masterson. He would be damned if, after three hundred years of Masterson occupation, he became the one lord who couldn't hang on to his land.

Lifting the goblet, he drained it. He was the most cursed of men, he, who had been the greatest warrior Europe had ever seen . . . he, whose very name had made the opposition tremble . . . in peace, he had proved to be an unlucky failure.

The goblet clattered on the table as a thought struck him. Perhaps there was another way. Perhaps, with the help of his men and the villagers, he could bring prosperity to his people by . . .

"My lord!" Young Mercia came running into the great hall,

her face red with exertion. "M'lord, I did as ye commanded. I followed her!"

Rion glared at the maid. "And?"

Panting, Mercia held her side as if she had a stitch. "On th' south road . . . a man . . . rode out o' the wood . . . an' captured her. She fought. He left . . . her shoe an' her hat . . . in th' dirt."

Inevitably, Rion was suspicious. "If you're trying to trick me to make me follow her—"

"M'lord, I vow . . . what I say is true." Sharp-eyed Winetta handed Mercia a drink, and the girl took a gulp. "Th' odd thing . . . is that that man . . . was dressed like . . . ye."

The other maids gathered around, and Winetta burst out, "'Tis her uncle! The earl of Smythwick has waited long fer a chance to harm me babe."

Rion still doubted the tale, but he found himself on his feet, buckling his sword around his waist. "Why wouldn't his lordship have killed her before? I'm sure Helwin has many times made him wish to kill her."

Winetta wrung her hands. "Because Her Majesty, Queen Elizabeth, made it clear she held him accountable for Helwin's good health."

Rion stopped and stared at Winetta. "Do you know this in fact?"

"Aye. When her father died, before Lord Smythwick dismissed me, I saw the messenger which came from Her Majesty, and I heard the royal proclamation. I saw the look His Lordship gave Helwin—he hates her with all his shriveled heart, and he would do her a harm if he could. But ye kidnapped her off the beach, m'lord, and if she tried to escape from ye—"

"I wanted her out a week ago!"

"—And she dies under yer detention—"

Before Rion even fully understood, he was sprinting out the door. "Send someone after my men!" he shouted.

"At the curve o' th' road about half-way int' th' woods!" Mercia called.

What Winetta had said made a horrible sense. That explained why Lord Smythwick hadn't sent for Helwin. Like some giant, malignant spider, he, or rather his minion, had been lurking outside Castle Masterson waiting for Helwin to exit so Lord Smythwick could eliminate her from his life . . . and blame it on Rion.

Heaven knew, with that sharp tongue and wicked humor, she was aggravating enough that most men would wish they could toss her out of their lives—but that wasn't a good enough reason to kill the lass!

He saddled his horse and galloped down the south road. The memory of her rose in his mind, her mouth richly smiling, her nipples peeking out from the waves of her hair. He spurred his horse to greater speed.

Dust rose in a cloud behind him. The horse's mane flew in Rion's face, and the wind whipped past his ears. As he neared the wood he slowed, looking for signs of Helwin.

He found them, just as Mercia had described. Helwin's shoe and her hat were crumpled in the grass beside the road, and a clasp bearing his crest was tossed to the ground a little farther on. The tracks led toward the sea cliffs, and driven by a dreadful urgency, he spurred his horse onward.

Topping the hill overlooking the cliff road, he saw them. A man dressed in a cape and a hat like Rion's, wrestling with Helwin. A dreadful silence enveloped them as the villain tried to toss her off the cliffs and onto the wave-soaked rocks below. Helwin didn't scream, but struggled mightily as he pushed her ever closer to the precipice.

Howling with rage, Rion drew his sword and spurred his war-horse forward.

CHAPTER 10

At the sight of Rion, Helwin gave a shriek that shattered the silence, but the shriek she released was more of a triumphant shout than a scream of fear.

Her attacker looked up. He released her and staggered backward. He tried to reach his saddlebag and draw his own sword.

And Helwin, damn the woman, picked up a stout branch and knocked the villain out cold with a blow to the back of the head.

Rion could have screamed himself. He had wanted to kill the man who had attacked his woman. But he couldn't murder an unarmed, senseless man. "Damn you, Helwin," he roared as he pulled up beside her. "You should have let me handle this!"

"Why?" She almost danced with rage. The sun glinted off of her loose, blond hair, and her eyes snapped blue sparks. "You're not the one who was kidnapped—again!—and this time almost killed."

Dismounting, sword in hand, he wrapped his arm around her shoulders. "Are you hurt?"

"I'm fine." She pointed at the man on the ground. "Kill him!"

Rion liked her bloodthirsty demand. This was no milk-and-toast maiden who jumped at the sight of her shadow. She would make a fine bride for a mercenary warrior. "I'll take him to the village magistrate." With his foot, Rion turned the fellow over. "Do you know him?"

"I do. He's one of Uncle Carroll's men."

The news struck him like a blow. "So it's true. Your uncle is trying to kill you."

"Aye, the wretched knave!"

Rion hated to make such a decision, but he had no choice. "We'll leave this blackguard here and ride back to Castle Masterson as fast as we can go."

And accompanied by a thunder of hooves, Lord Smythwick rode over the hill. "I don't believe you will, Lord Masterson."

Of course. Lord Smythwick had come to personally make sure the foul deed was done.

He sat on his snowy-white gelding, surrounded by a dozen liveried men decorated with gold braid and armed with swords.

Rion placed himself in front of Helwin, raised his sword to fighting position, and directed, "Helwin, mount the horse and ride for my castle."

"I will not."

Without removing his gaze from Smythwick's sneering face, Rion said in his quietest, deadliest tone, "If we live to see the sunset, my dear girl, I swear I will beat you once a day whether you need it or not."

Stout branch in hand, she stood shoulder to shoulder with him. "If we live to see the sunset, I swear I will go as far away from you as I can go."

Sometimes the lass was not as bright as she seemed. "You . . . will . . . not. We're getting married."

"You have to marry an *heiress."*

"I love you, and I'm going to marry you, you stupid wench, and God help us both."

"Too bad we'll never live through this."

"At least one of us can. Get on that horse and ride."

This man, this warrior, was willing to give his life for her. But perhaps . . . that was what warriors did.

More amazing to Helwin was—he wanted to marry her. He wanted her more than money or respectability or even his heritage. He would abandon them all out of love for her. He really did love her.

Her gaze shifted to her Uncle Carroll, and her rage grew cold. She would not allow Uncle Carroll to destroy Rion on the very eve of her happiness. Stepping forward, she called, "Uncle? Is this your idea of a discreet little killing?"

Rion caught her arm and held her in place by his side.

Uncle Carroll rode toward them, close enough to speak but not close enough to be in range of Rion's sword. He looked down at her in apparent benevolence. "I don't know what you mean, dear niece. I simply want to kill the man who kidnapped you." In his most unctuous voice, he said, "Come over here and let me protect you."

She stared up into her uncle's dead-fish eyes. "What have I ever done to make you think I'm as stupid as Bertilda?"

His thin face flushed until two bright spots of red burned on his cheekbones. In a deadly whisper, he said, "You are exactly like your father." He rode back to the top of the hill, and in a voice so cold it broke icicles, he called, "Aye, Masterson, Her Majesty will be grieved to hear that you killed the daughter of one of her beloved courtiers, but she will be very, very pleased with me for killing you afterward."

Rion mounted the horse and reached his arm down.

Still holding her branch—a feeble weapon, but the best she

could find—Helwin grasped his hand and let him pull her up behind him.

He instructed, "Hold onto my waist and whatever you do, don't let go."

She wrapped her arms around him and felt his heartbeat thundering through his back. Stretching up to speak in his ear, she promised, "I will never let you go."

A chuckle shuddered through his body. "I depend on that." He sounded remarkably cool now that the moment was upon them. "If you're going to use that stick, push them away with it and parry their blows. Don't try to hit them—you'll expose your midsection."

She was shaking, trembling with fear as she realized her last moments were upon her.

Uncle Carroll lifted his arm and let it fall.

His men shouted and spurred their horses into a gallop.

And over the hill behind Rion and Helwin came the roar of two dozen mercenaries. As Rion held his horse still, the ragged mercenaries thundered past them toward Uncle Carroll's men, shrieking their rage. The gold-braided, liveried soldiers took one look, turned heel and fled.

At the top of the hill, Uncle Carroll sat immobile, frozen with rage and frustration—until a single arrow flew through the air. It pierced his shoulder. He screamed and dropped the reins. His horse pranced restively, then raced away, Uncle Carroll clamped into the saddle and tugging furtively at the arrow.

The men cheered and circled around Rion and Helwin.

Barth twanged his bow.

Terris lifted his sword above his head.

Rion leaned over and slapped at them as they paraded past. "Good men. All of you. You always arrive in time."

Helwin waved her stick at them. "Just in time."

Sir Lathrop grinned at her. "Oo, she's going to hurt us with her twig."

"Indeed, I would not." She dropped the stick. "I owe you my life, and more important, Lord Masterson's life. For that, I thank you all."

Sir Lathrop tipped his disreputable cap at her. "We had to do it. You're *our* mistress, now."

The other men murmured agreement, and Helwin found herself blinking back tears.

Rion turned the horse toward Castle Masterson. "Now we should return quickly home. I fear that little arrow will only infuriate Lord Smythwick."

"Let's ride," Sir Lathrop shouted.

The horse stretched out his legs, flying across the landscape in an attempt to outrun trouble. Helwin held on for dear life, loving the feel of Rion in her arms, knowing she had the right to hold him thus for the rest of her life. Never had she imagined a kidnapping would free her from bondage and bring her to such pleasure.

Rion must have felt the same way, for he shouted, "I've got you now, my lady Hellion, and I'm going to keep you."

But she knew how his feelings must be mixed, and she asked, "Are you happy?"

"I'm damned happy." They rode hard, his men staying close at their backs. "Don't I sound happy?"

He didn't. He sounded furious, and only a woman who loved him would understand that he must mourn the sacrifice he had made of his heritage.

"I've got a plan," he shouted. "I'm going to become a smuggler."

Startled, she repeated, "A smuggler? Why would you want to be a smuggler?"

"I don't want to be a smuggler, but I want you and I want

my lands and people, and that's the way I will keep them both. There've been smugglers here since the Conquest—I'll ask the villagers for help and all will come out well." Reaching back, he patted her knee. "I'll take care of you."

Torn between amusement and horror, Helwin said, "The queen won't like it."

"So we'll make sure the queen never finds out."

"There is another way." She picked her words carefully. "Uncle Carroll never bothers with anything he thinks is below his notice."

Castle Masterson came into sight and the ride slowed.

The horse's hooves clomped as they rode onto the stone of the courtyard. She continued, "So why do you think he would bother with me?"

"Because the queen said you must be kept alive." Rion slid out of the saddle and reached up for her.

She slipped down into his arms and stood, holding him in place with her grasp and her steady gaze. "True, and she occasionally sends a friend of my father's to make sure I still live. But Uncle Carroll hates me virulently, and he should not, for surely my existence is unimportant—except for one reason."

She had Rion's complete attention. "What is that?"

"A few years ago, while Uncle Carroll and his family visited the court, I went in search of that reason. I found it in his study. The title and the land for the earl of Smythwick was entitled to the eldest son, of course, and passed on my father's death to Uncle Carroll. But the fortune came from my mother, and that fortune has been inherited by . . . me."

Rion squinted at her. "You're an heiress?"

"A very great heiress."

"The entire Smythwick fortune . . . ?"

"Is mine. Mine . . . and my husband's."

Rion stared at her. Stared so long that she blushed and scuffed her foot. "I thought you'd be glad."

He shook his head. He gave an incredulous snort. He chuckled, and shook his head again, all the while never taking his eyes off of her. Throwing his head back, he laughed loud and long. Laughed as he had that day when he picked her up off the beach. Laughed like a man who had only to reach out his hand to satisfy his greatest craving.

Picking her up, he swung her around and around until the courtyard spun, and she held his shoulders and shrieked. When he stopped laughing and set her down, he didn't let her go—but he didn't laugh anymore, either. Sternly, he said, "You are an heiress and you made me suffer the torment of the damned while you went haring off to get yourself killed?"

She looked fixedly at his throat while she confessed, "I was going to come back. I can only love a man who would put his duty to his men and his people before his desire—and you do, and I do."

He turned her chin up with his thumb. "You love me?"

"Well . . . aye." Silly fellow. "Of course I love you."

He sighed as if a great weight had been lifted off his shoulders. "How was I supposed to know *that*? You didn't say it. Moreover, as soon as *I* said it you leaped out of bed and fled."

"I . . . I was sulking."

"For an intelligent woman, you're a fool."

She wrapped her fingers in his doublet and jerked him closer. "You are not always so brilliant yourself."

"Smart enough to take you and keep you." He yelled at the huddle of men on their horses and the maids watching from the door. "Send for the minister. I don't care that the banns aren't called. This is an emergency. We need to be married before Smythwick comes back with an army."

The cheer that went up from male and female sent a glow of pleasure through Helwin and made Rion grin.

Sir Lathrop snapped his fingers and directed the men to defense and as messengers. Winetta set the maids to work.

Helwin smoothed her hands down Rion's arms and peeked up at him through her lashes. "The clergyman won't be here for at least an hour. Do you think we have time to . . . relax . . . in your marvelous bed?"

"Aye, we do." Picking her up, he swung her over his shoulder, just as he had done the first day he brought her to Castle Masterson. "We have all the time in the world."

"Hey! These marks look like they were made by hand-cuffs," Brian said.

The comment brought an immediate halt to all other conversations. Everyone in the room, including Max, turned their attention to the teenage boy. Including his mother, Mrs. Plante.

Max Ashton edged closer to the bed, inspecting the marks Brian pointed to. A series of ring-like gouges scored the surface of the post on the left side of the headboard. The marks were deeper along the inner face of the post than they were on the outer, as if someone had tried to drag the thing with a chain.

"Probably how they moved the beastie," he offered.

Mrs. Stradling gave him a fond, if oddly pitying smile. "I doubt it. It wouldn't make any sense to try and drag something this size from one corner," she said. "There are no corresponding marks on the posts at the foot."

"Oh."

"Someone was chained to the bed." With the astute vulgarity of the very young, Brian immediately tumbled to the crudest interpretation.

Mrs. Plante smiled proudly at her offspring while the other two Americans, Miss Ferguson and Mrs. Stradling, nodded. Laurel, in no hurry to have the day end, sat down on the edge of the bed and let them speculate.

"Sounds a little far-fetched, if you ask me. Like something from one of those old pirate movies," John said. "Things like that don't happen in real life."

"Oh, I don't know," Mrs. Stradling popped the Ray-Bans off from the top of her head and began polishing them on the hem of her shirt. "I mean, a bed this size would be perfect for keeping someone in his or her place."

"That's true," said Max Ashton, who had apparently at some point erroneously believed that he had been asked to join the group. "Are there marks on the post on the other side of the headboard?"

Brian, finally having found something in the manor that interested him scooted around to the other side. He peered closely at the post before returning a disappointed, "Nope. No marks here. Blast."

Max smiled indulgently at the boy. He had, Laurel conceded, a very nice smile. "Don't look so glum, mate. Maybe the owner of the bed tried to spare it by cushioning the chains and this side slipped out."

"Do you think?"

"Could happen."

"I imagine it would be most uncomfortable being handcuffed to the two posts," Mrs. Plante, the most earnest of the lot, said in a troubled voice. "But from the looks of the marks on this post I'd say it's doable."

"Impossible," Laurel disagreed. "What with the marks being where they are," she added.

"And why's that?" Max asked, crossing his arms over his chest.

How had Max Ashton suddenly gained such prominence in this little group? Laurel wondered. Perhaps it was time she regained control—

"Tell you what, Miss Whitney," Max Ashton said. Her head shot up and she found herself looking into a pair of devilishly dancing eyes. "Be a sport and scoot to the middle of the bed. The folks here would like a demo."

He was mocking her. *Daring* her. She almost told him just where he could take his suggestion but then realized that her group—her *last* tour group—was watching her with innocent certainty that she'd be game and play along.

Oh, she'd play all right.

"Of course, I would comply, Mr. Ashton, but don't you think it a little, well, unkind to any remaining Masterson males, wherever they might be, to suggest that a *lady* was chained here? Look around." She waved her hand at the portraits lining the wall. Although they were dimmed by hearth smoke and time and in need of cleaning, anyone could tell that the male faces looking down at them were from a handsome and well-made line. "Do you think a Masterson would *need* to chain a lady here?" She met Max's eyes with a challenging lift of her brow.

"Nuh-uh. No-way, no-how." Mrs. Stradling's sudden appreciative comment broke the tension.

"Exactly," Laurel said. "For the purposes of verisimilitude, I suggest we use a male volunteer. How 'bout you, Mr. Ashton? You look like someone who might have been chained up in a former life."

"Only by error," he said.

"Whose? Your accusers' for getting the wrong man or yours for not slipping away quickly enough?"

"I'm not the sort that slips away. Not in this life or any other," Max said with a touch of tenseness. Then, abruptly, he shook off his darkening mood and moved on all fours to the center of the bed where he turned around, sat down against the piles of pillows, and threw open his long, muscular arms.

"At your service," he said glibly, his eyes glittering.

"Right." She hadn't really thought he'd do it and now the tour group was waiting expectantly. Well, she'd prove she was just as sporting as he was.

Resolutely, she got on her hands and knees and moved the short distance to where he waited. Once there, she looked around, spied the satin bed pull, and with a flick of her wrist dislodged it from the hook that joined it to an interior system of cables leading to the servants' hall. "Thank you for being such a trooper, Mr. Ashton."

She deftly secured the satin cord around the post and then looped it around his wrist. The action necessitated that she move closer to him. She half-expected him to . . . do something. She wasn't sure what, but her muscles tensed as if she stood in imminent danger as she secured his wrist.

In contrast, Max looked utterly relaxed. He caught her eye and smiled lazily. This hadn't worked out as she'd expected. She was the one who felt nervy and embarrassed while Max Ashton looked like being tied to a bed was nothing new for him.

Maybe it wasn't.

After she secured his other wrist to the second post she scooted away from him. "Well, there, now you can see why the prisoner wasn't chained like Mr. Ashton," she mumbled. "If they had been, the gouges would be quite a bit lower on the post, unless the prisoner was actually standing on the pillows and then they'd be higher."

"Thank you. That makes it all very clear, indeed," Mrs. Plante said, looking decidedly amused.

"You know," said Miss Ferguson, her nose inches away from

the bedpost as she studied the wood, "there actually do seem to be two sets of marks here. The deep ones higher up and another set, faint but there, low. Whatever do you suppose that means?"

Max, who'd apparently had enough of being tied up, pulled off his satin bonds and rolled to his feet. "More than one prisoner?"

"A series of prisoners," Brian breathed. Laurel could almost see the idea forming in his fertile, teenage boy imagination. "Maybe some bugger of a Masterson kept the local hotties chained up here as his sex slaves?"

Bugger of a Masterson?

"I doubt it." Laurel regarded the young man with something less than warmth.

"Why?" Brian demanded, unwilling to let go of his fantasy.

"Trecombe is a very small, very tightly knit community. There are families here that trace their ancestry back to the Domesday Book. If some mad Masterson—and I am by no means disallowing the possibility of a dissolute, odious Masterson—stole a local girl, don't you think there would have been some legend attached to the event?"

Brian looked sullen. The American ladies looked deflated. Only Meghan, the new bride, perked up. "Not if she found she fancied being a sex slave. Could be the affair turned into a love match and ended in a nice chapel wedding. And you know what locals are in that case: All's well that end's well."

The Americans laughed while John regarded his wife thoughtfully. Meghan, however, missed the look and turned to Laurel for support. "It could happen, couldn't it?"

Laurel smiled. "I hate to pop anyone's bubble, but actually we have an explanation for those marks, how they were made, and by whom and, again sorry to disappoint, but there was no love slavery involved."

"Come now, Brian," she cajoled the crestfallen boy, "don't look so woebegone. The real story is very dramatic, too. You see, as I mentioned earlier, the coast 'round here was once a prime spot for smugglers to put in with their contraband. Lots of little caves and inlets.

"Those marks there were made by Ned Masterson, the captain in charge of cleaning up the town, so to speak. Legend has it that he chained the leader of the smugglers here, as the bed was the heaviest thing in the house, while he rode off and routed the rest of the band."

"You're sure?" Apparently Brian preferred the love-slave notion.

"Fairly sure. It's a local story but they most often have their basis in fact."

"Wasn't a female smuggler by any chance?"

"Not unless she was strong as an ox," Max Ashton said.

"Why's that?"

"Well, son," Max said with a kindliness Laurel wouldn't have suspected him capable of, "look at how deep the gouges are. Whoever had flung himself against the chain was either very strong or very, very angry and while I've met my share of irate women"—he ignored Laurel's *sotto voce* "I bet"—"I've never met one *that* strong."

"You know what I'd like to know?" Mrs. Stradling suddenly asked. "I'd love to know what this Ned Masterson was like. I mean think of what *he* must have been like if he could overcome a man strong enough to move this bed. . . ."

The Lady Makes Her Bed

MASTERSON MANOR, 1815

CHAPTER 1

Stopping to gloat proved Philippa Jones's undoing.

If she had simply manacled Ned Masterson—*Captain* Ned Masterson—to his infamous bed and left, all would have gone according to plan. But no, Philippa Jones who, as everyone in Trecombe could attest, was as incapable of hiding her feelings as a rabid dog is incapable of keeping from frothing at the mouth, would never pass up the opportunity to enjoy the downfall of her enemy and her onetime lover, the despicable, deceitful, and treacherously attractive *Captain* Ned Masterson.

Especially since disaster had been so nearly averted. Indeed, only happenstance had led her to uncover his latest stratagem. She and her brother John, orphaned gentlefolk that they were, had been invited to the Masterson Manor house party by Ned's widowed Cousin Merry who'd recently arrived to act as his hostess.

Obviously it had been a mistake, because the affair between Ned and her had ended months ago and it had most definitely *not* been amicable. Apparently no one had bothered to mention this to Cousin Merry who'd sent them a hand-written invitation.

John had, of course, thought it spectacularly amusing and had insisted that they accept. She resisted, telling him how stupid it would be to place himself under even closer scrutiny by their host. Especially when that host suspected him—and not without warrant, Philippa feared—of being a smuggler. And most especially when that host had recently been revealed to be an agent of the Crown, sent here specifically to purge the coast of smugglers.

But John, on whom she'd not yet gathered enough proof to confront him about his nefarious activities, had affected not to understand her fears, countering with an appeal to her pride. If they accepted the invitation, all of Trecombe would see that she wasn't pining after Ned Masterson. The idea that anyone thought she was languishing was, of course, intolerable.

And so, here they were.

It had been a disaster. She'd been aware of Ned every instant of every interminable day, could have answered at any moment the question of where he was, to whom he was speaking, and what he was wearing. Worse, she felt his gaze tracking her just as closely. The proximity, the tension simmering between them, the accusation she could not yet make, conspired to make her miserable. She tried to hide it, to mask her pain for the sake of pride, but every now and again she felt the overwhelming urge to escape the charade.

She had done so that afternoon, leaving the card party to find a brief respite. On her way to the solarium, she'd been passing the library when two words had erupted from the other side of the closed door, spoken by a voice she'd have known anywhere.

"John Jones!"

She'd stopped. Yes, the door had been shut. True, she was a guest in this house. But that was her brother's name being spat with such venom. She'd snuggled her ear up against the paneled door and held her breath.

". . . first light at the caves Jones marked. And this time we'll take the slippery bastard," Ned's lieutenant, a man named Bragg, said.

"Finally," Captain Masterson replied. "Wait for me in the old kirkyard. Unless I hear something that changes my plans, I'll meet you there an hour before dawn."

"Aye, Cap'n."

"You're *certain* that the bastard will be there?" Captain Masterson's voice, low, threatening.

"Absolutely."

"Good. Because I *need* an end to this, Bragg, before I do someone a very serious harm."

Amazingly, Bragg sounded like he laughed but then it turned into a choked sort of coughing sound. "Name of this person wouldn't happen to be 'Jones' now would it?"

"Damn your impudence. Get the hell out of here, Bragg, and remember what I said."

Eyes wide, Philippa backed off and hurried away. She hadn't realized the extent of Masterson's animosity. He kept his feelings masked most of the time. Oh, not that he didn't swear and stomp around and all, but she would never have guessed he contained such anger.

Needless to say, she hadn't returned to the card party. She didn't waste time pondering her course. She knew her course. She *always* knew her course and it *always* was one charted from the heart. Clearly, she had to save John from the law.

Therefore, that afternoon she'd pinched the manacles and chain she'd noticed in the stables one day a few months ago when her visits had been regular and more convivial, *before* she'd accidentally intercepted a letter that revealed *Lord* Masterson also happened to be *Captain* Masterson, sent here with the express purpose of "ferreting out an iniquitous den of smugglers." Within an hour of that discovery she'd broken it off with Ned.

When he'd come calling, she'd left him cooling his boot heels in her great aunt's parlor while she'd fled out the back door and gone tearing along the cliff paths on her half-wild mount, trying to outdistance her anger and hurt. But that was months past. She was over him.

In hindsight, the appearance of those manacles in the nearly empty stables had a sinister air, one that would shortly become ironic air. She'd also taken a small, stalwart-looking padlock.

She'd avoided any conversation with her taciturn host that evening by passing the time flirting outrageously with brawny Hal Minton, a neighbor who chanced often to be near when she wanted most to avoid Ned. Then, after all the other guests had gone to bed, Philippa had snuck into Ned's bedroom, the manacles and chain carefully muffled in a shawl.

She'd held her breath when she saw the faint glow from his bedchamber, praying that he hadn't stayed up reading all night before going on his predawn raid. He must have planned and worked toward tomorrow's undertaking for over a year, the same year he'd spent manipulating the sister of his intended prey in order to get closer to him.

Her heart stomped in her chest. Even for her, this was bold work. Only her fear for John compelled her. He was her only living relative except for dear, doddery Aunt Grace who acted as their guardian—at least, when she remembered to do so.

And a frankly poor job she'd made of it, too, Philippa now thought with unaccustomed rancor, otherwise she wouldn't have stood there, staring with far too familiar an eye at the broad and beautifully muscled expanse of Ned Masterson's naked chest.

Naked.

The fire burned brightly in the hearth, lustering his pale skin saffron, casting shadows over the molded swells and ridges in that impressive, elegant torso. She'd seen this chest before. Touched it. No, honesty compelled her to admit. She'd caressed it. And enjoyed doing so.

She knew his body to be hard and dense, his skin smooth and clear, his fragrance earthy and male. Knew it as only a lover can. Her will wavered before this unanticipated and unwelcome distraction.

Why did he have to lie down atop his sheets half-undressed in a cold room?

Why? she thought with unreasoning anger. Because why would pragmatic Ned Masterson bother to undress when he planned to rise within a few hours? He'd taken off his shirt so as not to wrinkle it, but the buff-colored trousers couldn't wrinkle, not molded so tightly to his thighs and calves. As for being chilled . . . the day Ned Masterson kowtowed to a human frailty like being cold, the moon would fall from the sky.

No, in this and in all things, he was the quintessential tactician, taking the most direct route to his objective. Even when that route meant riding havoc over a woman's heart.

At least he'd removed his boots before lying down on the ancient, massive Masterson bed. His blond head was turned, the firelight polishing it's angelic color to a bright, refined gold. He slept on his back, his arms—as sculpted as Michelangelo's David—flung wide, even in his slumber exposing his heart with arrogant disregard for his safety.

His trousers fit snuggly about narrow hips, his chest was smooth and bare until low on his flat belly where a silky cloud of fine dark hair started, growing increasingly thicker as it disappeared beneath his waistband.

A blush rose in Philippa's cheeks. Once . . . Though they'd never . . . Not that she hadn't wanted . . .

She pressed her eyelids together, marshaling her treacherous thoughts before opening them and easing the muffled chain and manacles down onto the corner of the bed. She'd already taken too long. Gingerly, she took the manacles from the shawl and looped the chain around the thick bedpost and had just padlocked it into place when she heard him shift.

She spun around and he opened his eyes.

CHAPTER 2

His eyes were green in color and clear as cathedral glass, shadowed by thick dark lashes. It was absurd that one so fair should have brows and lashes so nearly black. As at variance as his sensualist's mouth, the dueling scar tracing a thin line on cheek, and his bright hair. "Pip."

He spoke her name like it was the answer to a question he'd been dreaming about, a whispered benediction and haunting imponderable. For a second, pleasure bloomed in his eyes.

"Pip?"

Oh, dear.

With as much casualness as she could muster, she sank down on the edge of the bed, obstructing his view of the bed-post. Behind her back, she groped for the shawl and, finding it, piled it atop the manacles while trying desperately to think of something to say.

"Ned."

He went very still, pleasure dissolving from his expression, leaving suspicion and an ineffable sense of vulnerability. Ridiculous. Ned Masterson was the least vulnerable man of her acquaintance.

He scowled, his gaze roving over her face as he pushed up to his elbows and braced on his forearms, his abdomen bunching as he did so. When he moved, muscle and sinew articulated in a refined shift and slide, a tautening and release of tension and energy. How she loved the way Ned Masterson moved.

"Philippa, why are you here?"

She could still flee. If she left now, she might be able to find the cave where John was unloading his contraband. But there were dozens of caves and miles of coast. The only other option was to stay and . . . and do what must be done, what she wanted to do, had wanted to do since she'd met him, this bright, wicked Lucifer.

"What are you—"

"No. No questions." She placed two fingers lightly across his lips. The touch lingered. She swallowed. She was breathing too hard and he'd gone very still, his eyes locked with hers, questioning.

She'd never been any good at dissembling. She was a terrible liar. And though she'd tried these past four months to be cordial and cool, she was well aware she'd been blistering and derisive.

She had been angry. She still was. But she didn't have to pretend the excitement she felt. Or the longing. Because as stupid and unpleasant and *wrong* as it was, she felt all those things for this man.

And if deep inside she recoiled from the idea of using Ned's undeniable attraction to her for her own advantage, well then, hadn't he done the same thing to her?

She wouldn't think. Not anymore. The manacles still waited on the corner of the bed. He still studied her warily.

She leaned forward and kissed him.

She wasn't prepared for how intoxicating that kiss would

be. How evisceratingly sweet. Their lips met, clung a second, pressed deeper. She sighed and melted toward him.

Abruptly, he seized her upper arms, sitting up and pushing her away, even though his mouth followed hers, belying the implied refutation. Her head swam at suddenly being torn from something so potent. She sagged in his grip, her head dipping forward, her eyes shut, overwhelmed and betrayed by her reaction.

"What are you doing here, Philippa?" Ned demanded harshly, his hands tightening into a bruising grip.

She looked up, her breath unsteady. "I'm here because of you."

She didn't need to lie. It was more of the truth than she wanted it to be.

Whatever restraint he'd been executing over himself broke. He dragged her forward, settling her across his lap and following her down, one hand splayed behind her head the other looped around her waist.

He kissed her, his tongue sweeping across her lips with deft certainty of his welcome. And he *was* welcome, damn him. He stroked the satin sleek lining of her cheeks and sucked gently on her tongue. She kissed him back, drank his passion with the desperation of the famished.

She'd forgotten the taste of him, the rich hunger he roused. His aggression drew a primitive response from her, their tongues meeting in an undisguised pseudo-coupling.

Her thoughts swirled away in a maelstrom of sensation. A few more minutes and every other consideration would be burnt away in the blast furnace of their desire. She struggled upright, pushing him with all her might. It was like shoving rock under which ran a river of lava. His lips broke free from hers and she pushed once more and finally he allowed her to topple him flat on his back. But he didn't let go of her arms.

His green gaze glinted. His chest heaved like a bellows. His expression hardened as he looked up at her. "What are you playing at, Pip?"

Two feet above his bright blond head, a baser metal shone.

"Ever since you came to Trecombe, you've had the advantage in this game you've played between us," she answered hoarsely, thinking of how he'd kept his true purpose here from her, and used their relationship to further his own ends. "You've had the whip hand."

His smile was wary, a shade bitter. "Have I? I could have sworn it was the other way around. In fact, I distinctly recall feeling the flail of your tongue more than once in recent months."

She sniffed at the blatant diversion. "It annoyed you. It didn't *disturb* you. It didn't keep you from doing what you—" She stopped in time, having almost given the game away. But for once, she would be as devious as him. "My manner may have caused you some minor social discomfort. A man like you would hate being slighted by a woman."

At that the muscles beneath her palms jumped and the hard line of his jaw tensed. His nostrils flared and the hands around her upper arms clenched before he forcibly relaxed them.

"'Some minor social discomfort?'" he echoed in a terrifyingly soft voice. "Is that what I feel when you flaunt Minton in front of me like your newest prize? *Him,* of all men? Oh, yes, I grant you, it has been . . . *uncomfortable.*"

Minton? What had Minton to do with anything?

But she hadn't time to ponder the question long because he sneered. "As has been the cut you give me at every possible turn, never once offering me a reason why. Don't you think that I feel—" He closed his eyes as though the sight of her was insufferable.

When he opened them again, his smile caused her to shrink back in his grip. He did not allow it.

"What do you know of 'a man like me,' Pip, my black beauty?" he asked in that terrible, cool voice made worse by its contrast with his bright, burning gaze.

"Nothing," she proclaimed. "Nor do I want to."

His eyelids flickered shut again. For a moment, she could have sworn pain trespassed over his elegant, severe features and caused the odd timbre in his deep voice.

"Then, tell me, darling, what sins have I been punished for these past four months? For, faith, I burn to hear them named."

She tried to pull away and he shook her, a little roughly, but with great control.

"Name my crimes, Pip," he commanded, "lest I name yours. Then tell me what my punishment is to be, because, as you can see, I am eager to pay whatever penalty you impose."

Her anger, ever intemperate and fierce, rose to meet this mocking invitation. She struggled to keep from condemning him with what she knew, because it was her nature to be direct, to confront openly that which threatened or hurt. Had no one else been at risk, she would have. But fear for John kept her from speaking. It was probably the only thing that could have. Instead, she told him a different truth.

"You've dominated in everything you've ever done. Decided what you wanted and taken it. You used my, my . . ." she searched for a word, "affection for your own ends."

"I do not recall your begging off," he answered hoarsely. "Though I do recall you begging."

She gasped.

"And, my darling, my beauty, if you still truly believe that in those sweet interludes *I* achieved my *end,* then Minton is either a eunuch or you are abysmally unobservant."

Her mouth flattened. He just made her actions easier.

"You wanted to know your crimes. I have told them to you."

"I pleasured you."

"You *took*. You used."

"I took *your* pleasure. I *used* my body to give you pleasure."

She turned her head. She could not argue with what he said and she could not reveal her knowledge of his perfidy. "We see this differently. Is that any wonder?"

"No." His face became shuttered. "And this is why you are here? To kiss me, upbraid me, arouse me and then leave me wanting? I would have thought you'd like to practice another form of torture, Pip, for I swear, I do not know how you can refine upon that which you already do so well."

She did not answer him but instead reached up and grabbed his wrists, yanking at them roughly until he released her upper arms. She did not let his wrist go, but pulled his hands up and over his head, shoving them against the cool, starched counterpane. In doing so, she had to lie on top of him, the bared upper swells of her bosom flattened against his naked chest. His heat soaked her with carnal awareness.

His eyes narrowed over banked fires, dangerous fires.

"I will lead this time, Captain. You will follow."

She'd made a mistake. She saw it in his expression the minute she'd addressed him by his rank—a rank no one was supposed to know. She did the only thing she could do that was certain to distract him. She lowered her mouth to his.

At once, his head and shoulders lifted off the mattress, meeting her mouth's descent. He twisted his hands as though to break from her grip but she jammed them back and he let her.

She slid forward, resting still more fully on him. His long legs sprawled on either side of hers and she was suddenly acutely aware of his state of arousal. The thick ridge of his organ rubbed against her hip and the urge to respond in kind nearly overwhelmed her.

Somehow she ignored her body's demand, stretching her arms and locking his wrists above his head. He made a sound deep in his throat, a sound of hunger and predation and she felt her resolve skitter away before the primal sound, retreating from any thought beyond the next kiss, the sculpted body supporting her, the fragrance of masculine arousal. He permeated her every sense, drugging her, toppling her from her momentary ascendancy.

Not yet. God, not yet . . .

She reached up and groped for the manacle while his mouth slanted hungrily across hers. Then, with the last shreds of her fleeing will, she slipped it around his wrist. And clicked it shut.

CHAPTER 3

Ned heard. He tore his mouth from hers and bolted upright as she flung herself to the far side of the bed. He surged after her, brought up short at the end of the chain.

With a snarl, he turned and saw what held him. His left wrist was bound tightly by a steel bracelet, the matching manacle swinging free. He jerked the chain once, savagely, while she inched toward the end of the bed. But at once, he realized her intent. He leapt across the bed, blocking her path to the door.

She stopped at the bottom corner of the bed, eyeing the length of the chain shackling him to the post. If she kept her back to the wall, he couldn't possibly reach her. She swallowed, marshaling her courage.

He didn't say a word. She could not help but admire that monumental self-restraint. But his eyes spoke. For one eternal instant their gazes locked, his brilliant with loathing and betrayal.

She edged away from his glare, even though he could go no farther than a few feet from the head of the bed. Before she realized how trepidation had driven her, she bumped into the back wall. He smiled. It was not a pleasant smile.

"Pip, my dark, betraying, beautiful Pip," he purred, stalking down the length of the bed, "that was *such* a mistake."

She lifted her chin, her fear fading before his taunt. He was the most arrogant man she'd met. Once, it had even been part of his attraction: his supreme self-confidence, the assuredness with which he moved, spoke . . . made love.

"Brave words from a man chained to his own bed," she said.

"Bloody hell!" Her words snatched away his composure. He flung himself against the chain and the weight of the mammoth bed, his arm raised as if to strike. His progress came to an abrupt end, his arm caught on a level with his shoulder, the bicep bulging, the manacle cutting into his wrist, while its mate jangled angrily.

"Don't," she said crossly. "You'll hurt yourself."

Instead of being grateful for her concern, her words only seemed to enrage him further. He grabbed the chain in both hands, yanked over his shoulders and surged against the weight of the bed. Every muscle in his chest and arms jumped into sharp, quivering relief as he strained against it.

"Stop it!" she cried. "You can't possibly think you'll be able to move that bed?"

His lips curled back as he heaved forward, his throat, arms, and chest cording with veins and his face suffused with blood. And the bed, the huge, solid walnut bed, eight feet wide and eight feet long, with posts the span of a woman's waist and as tall as a man, heaped with mattresses and topped with a heavy wooden canopy, groaned.

And moved four inches. Then six.

She stared at him angrily. "Fine, you pigheaded fool! You've managed to drag it a few inches. But you can't think you can keep this up—"

She didn't finish because he suddenly stopped straining on the chain. With a gesture of contempt, he let it drop from his shoulder.

"I hope you're satisfied," she said haughtily. "All that sweating and exerting, your wrists are scraped and bleeding and what have you proved? That the bed is heavy? We already *knew* that."

He regarded her with tiger eyes. "I can think of more interesting ways to sweat and exert, if you're game."

"You're being deliberately crude just to provoke me."

"Tit for tat, sweetheart."

She tossed her head. "I won't be provoked. You are an arrogant, conscienceless manipulator who is only angry that the tables have been turned on him."

The green eyes flashed. "Brave words from a woman trapped in a gentleman's bedroom. Though," he snapped his heels together, and bowed with exquisite grace, sweeping his free arm toward the door, "I beg you, *do* challenge that assumption."

Her eyes widened in horror. *That* is what he'd been doing! Dragging the bed just enough so that he could reach her if she tried to slip past him. Even with her shoulders pressed tightly to the wall, she wasn't sure she could elude his grasp.

But . . . she might.

She bit down on her lower lip, trying to gauge his reach, the chain, and his distance from the wall, and came to the unnerving conclusion that he'd stopped purposely right where he was, knowing that she wouldn't be sure if he could reach her, but daring her to try. Baiting her.

As he'd baited John.

"You are despicable."

"Now who is acting sullen because her plans have been thwarted? Besides, what's your hurry, Philippa?" he asked. "Expected elsewhere?"

It was worth a shot. If she could convince him that all his effort simply delayed the inevitable, he might let her go. He was a practical man, she thought bitterly. "Yes. I am. I'll be looked for soon."

His eyes blazed. "Damn him!"

Maybe this *would* work. "So, don't you think it would be best if you just rolled over to the other side of your bed and let me pass?"

"And exactly *why* would that be best?"

"Because you wouldn't want to be caught like that. Especially by . . ." By who? Which would be a worse bruise to that monumental ego? A woman or a man finding him chained? A man. ". . . by him."

"I don't give a bloody damn if he sees me." He took two long, earth-eating strides down the bed's side, until he was forced to stop, his hand stretched tight behind his back. He leaned toward her. "But what of when he sees you here?" he countered. "What if he brings others? What if they see you?"

She snorted. "What of it? Trapped in a room with a man chained to his bed? Somehow, I think my reputation will survive. After all, it survived *you.*"

"Ah!" He didn't move but the sound that tore from his throat sent her hurrying to the opposite side of the bed. And that gratified him.

"I will never let you go, Philippa. Not tonight. Not in the future."

"Why?" she asked coldly. "Because I am an accessory? Try to convict me. Since I haven't done anything, you can't prove I have."

His smile was grim. "This has nothing to do with the law, Pip. This is between you and me. *I* will never let you go. *Me.*"

His words frightened her and, if truth were told, in some horrifying way, excited her. He was the only man she'd ever met who could control her to any degree. Even as she railed against his powerful personality, there were times she craved his dominance. He would not allow her to go too far, not without being there to protect her from her own passionate nature.

But that time was past. In the future she would only be courted by tractable, tame men. She would learn to guard her tongue and consider her action. In short, she would become a tame hearth tabby rather than the wildcat all of Trecombe named her.

"When did you discover who I was and what I was doing here, I wonder?" he asked, recalling her to the present situation. "Was it before we ever kissed? In fact, was it really a bet as to who would be the first to meet the Masterson heir that led you to my door that first night, or was it *his* design?"

"Oh, no," she shook her head and her hair flew about her shoulders in angry denial. "I am not the one adept at subterfuge."

"No. You have other talents." Blatantly, he looked down at the thick bulge in his trousers. She averted her head sharply and he laughed without humor.

"You know what you are, Philippa?" he asked, prowling up and down like some big, chained cat.

She didn't answer.

He smiled, almost tenderly. "You're the worst kind of cheat. You're a tease."

Her head flew back as if he'd slapped her. "I am not."

He braced his arms wide on the edge of the bed and leaned over it. His chest leapt into sharply delineated detail. His stomach corrugated with muscle. His biceps bulged, revealing a tension belied by the throaty purr of his deep voice. "What else do you call a woman who makes promises she does not deliver on?"

"I promised nothing."

"Not in words," he allowed. "But every touch, every stroke of your tongue, every shift of your hips, made promises. Vows."

He might sound as if he'd calmed down, but his eyes followed her, tracking her ruthlessly.

She took a step back, determined not to pay any attention to his words . . . or his eyes.

"You don't scare me."

He laughed grimly and straightened. Casually, he wrapped one big hand around the bedpost and slouched against it. "Then you're not only a tease, you're a fool. Because right now, darling, *I* scare me."

"I don't have to listen to this."

"But you do. Unless, you want to take a shot at it . . . ?" he suggested, nodding toward the door. She vacillated. "Go on, darlin', give it your best go. Or is this, like the rest of our relationship, to be hallmarked by your refusal to *finish* what you *start?*"

"Stop talking to me that way!"

"Make me." His lips barely moved.

"I am saving someone I love from you. Even *you* should be able to understand that. You have no right to be angry with me."

"No right?" he mused quietly. "Oh, darling. I beg to differ. You entice me with your body, you play me for a fool, you use my weakness for you to chain me here and then, after arousing me to the point of agony, you manacle me to this cursed bed, unsated, heavy with want, and humiliated beyond endurance."

His knuckles turned white with the stranglehold he had on the bedpost but his voice remained soft, even calm, and was all the more frightening for it.

"Forgive my presumption in arguing with a lady, but damn you, Madame, I do, indeed, think I have earned the right to be angry."

CHAPTER 4

A s for the 'someone you love,'" Ned sneered the words
as though he'd found them coy, "to hell with him. To
bloody hell with him. If he was half the man you take
him for, he wouldn't be hiding behind your skirts. And if you
were half the woman you pretend to be, you'd let me go finish
my business with him."

"Yes," Philippa shot back sarcastically. "*That* is a fabulous
plan. You destroy the only man left on this green earth who
means anything to me and I stand back and allow it to happen
without so much as a sigh of discontent. What sort of woman
would I be *then,* Ned? *Less* than half. A dribble of a woman."

His expression grew stony, his eyes like jasper shards. "Do
not call me by my Christian name."

"Why?" she demanded, hands on hips. He'd whispered love
words to her, stroked her with lips and hands, and now she was
forbidden to use his Christian name? After all they'd done and
so nearly done?

She was angry, furious, but it had always been like this
between them, a tinder of emotions awaiting ignition. Once
she had yearned for that fire, been willing to step into the very

heart of conflagration that erupted around them whenever they touched, spoke . . . did anything. Now she simply wanted him to burn. She was already a cinder.

"You never took exception to my use of your name before. Or is it only when a woman is nearly undressed and lying beneath you that she has permission to speak your hallowed name?" she spat out derisively.

He trembled, the sleek elongated muscles shivering to life beneath the clear pale skin. "No. Yes."

She turned away and closed her eyes in spite of herself, aching with hurt.

"Yes," he continued, his voice a low thrum, coiling in her head, "only when you're beneath me. *You.*

"Fool that I am, I don't want to hear you speak my name with contempt. I don't want you supplanting the voice in my mind. I want the memory of you panting my name, your throat arched for my kiss, the syllable quavering with neediness. Neediness only I could satisfy. Tell me, Pip, damn you, tell me, who satisfies you now?"

She blanched. He could not believe that she'd done this with other men. But of course he would. She'd acted the wanton with him and thus, wanton she was and always would be. Still, it wounded her that he thought she would immediately seek to replace him and gratify desires he'd evoked with the first convenient candidate.

"You are no gentleman, sir," she said coldly.

He laughed. "And don't try to tell me you weren't damn glad of it. A gentleman couldn't have done to you what I did, Pip. He wouldn't have the imagination. Or the skill."

He was intolerable. And this conversation was at an end.

"Fine, *Captain* Masterson, I won't call you by your name."

But having discovered a way to torment her, he wasn't going to give it up. He leaned against the post, crossing his legs nonchalantly at the ankles, ignoring the jangle of the chains as he crossed his arms over his chest. He might have been a young buck, lounging outside his club in Mayfair. He regarded her with lazy interest. "Not that you weren't a prize pupil, Pip. You were. But I see you've added some new tricks to your repertoire."

"I don't know what you mean."

The slight smile on his lips abruptly dissolved and when he spoke again his tone was rough and accusatory. "Who taught you to accommodate a man's body so lushly, to open your mouth so deliciously? To suckle a man's tongue?"

How dare he!

"You!" she shouted furiously. "You and you and you. If I am expert, *you* are my tutor. Are you proud of your student? Would you like a further demonstration of what I learned at your hands?"

For a second something stark appeared on his face. "God. Come, Pip. Let me go and when I return we'll finish this matter."

But she heard only his threat to John. Let this creature with his sculpted body and his savage eyes have her brother? Never. "No!"

"Coward."

"I'm not going to be baited by you." She averted her face.

"Pity. Does he really mean that much to you?" He spoke so easily, so conversationally, yet the look in his eyes promised violence and the muscles in his body stood out even more sharply. She only wished that she could ignore his nakedness, the dangerous masculine beauty of it, the coiled strength in his lean, pale torso.

But John was all the family she had left. "Yes."

He regarded her stone-faced, a tic jumping in the side of his throat. "How sweet. And here I'd thought what we—" He broke off abruptly. "I could have sworn there was a day that you felt something for me. When did that end?"

She wheeled around and faced him. "The same day I realized that you'd used me to get to him."

"I didn't."

She laughed bitterly. "Excuse me for doubting you, Captain, but to my overly suspicious mind it seems too convenient, this sudden decision of yours to see your inheritance, the hitherto neglected Masterson Manor. And how timely your courtship of me!"

"Courtship," he repeated. "Is that what we were doing? It seems an insipid term for what we enjoyed."

She flushed. "I am just country-bred gentry. If I prefer to think you were courting me rather than simply seducing me, you must excuse my gross naïveté. I misunderstood your purpose."

If she pricked his conscience, he gave no sign. "I never seduced you. You're a virgin, still. Or were." She did not honor that with a reply and his face turned dusky with anger.

"So, we were both deceived, Pip," he continued. "Because I mistook you for a woman who would only give yourself to a man you loved."

"Then you were not mistaken," she replied haughtily, head raised and eyes flashing.

For some reason she could divine, her words bled the color from his face. His gaze looked stricken. "So," he said softly, as if to himself. "So. I see."

He looked up, shook his head as if clearing a blow. "Brava, Pip. Just when was it that you realized how important he was to you? Before or after I came?"

Philippa hesitated, frustrated by the absurd bent of the conversation. "What does it matter?"

"It matters to me."

He sounded so terrible, and while she wanted him to suffer, she could find no satisfaction in refusing to speak.

"I have always loved him but . . ." she hesitated, seeing Ned raising his chin fractionally, a soldier facing the flog, "but I never appreciated how important he was to me or what I would be willing to do for him until I realized you were planning to send him to rot in some stinking hole."

For some reason, her words seemed to relieve him. "You heeded nobility's call. Of course, you would," he murmured. "Tell me, my dark angel, if I had been a murdering, thieving coward instead of the man sent to stop him, would you have taken my part, too?"

She eyed him coldly. "But you aren't. And you seem to have missed an important part of the picture, Captain. *You* aren't my—"

"I know!" he broke across her statement that John was her brother before she could finish it. But he'd understood. "I'm not."

He turned his back to her. A broad back, but so pared and lean that the ribs showed in his sides. "It won't matter you know," he said after a moment. "I'll get him eventually."

"Not tonight," she vowed.

"What difference does a night or two or even a week make, Pip?" he asked. "He is what he is. He'll not change."

"No!" she said. "No. I'll convince him to quit this. He listens to me sometimes. We'll leave here. Maybe go to London. Or somewhere on the continent. He's not stupid just—"

"Just vicious. Oh, haven't you seen that side of him, darling?" He turned back around. "He cut a fifteen-year-old's finger off to make sure the boy understood the gravity of the pledge he'd been forced to take. Or didn't he tell you that?"

Calm swept over her, washing away the rising tide of panic. For a moment, she'd wanted to let him go and plead with him to stop her brother from the course he'd chosen. She'd almost trusted him to be merciful. His character, fierce and proud, had yet always seemed just.

Now, she regarded him scornfully. Clearly, he would say anything to get her to release him. But in this instance, he'd misjudged her. He'd lied and she knew it.

John was reckless and hotheaded but he was not cruel and nothing Ned Masterson said, no matter how convincingly, could make her believe it.

"Give me the key, Pip," he urged her, fatigue creeping into his voice. "He'll never change. Not even you can change a man like that."

"No, Captain Masterson. Not now. Not any time soon."

"For God's sake, woman, I am trying to save people's lives."

So many lies. Such a beautiful liar. But she knew him now. He'd revealed himself with that ridiculous tale about John. He'd lied to her before, he'd lied to her again, and sooner or later, because he was a very, very good liar and she was not, he might even persuade her into believing one of his lies. Because she'd believed them before.

She backed toward the window. Outside the thunder rolled in on a dark bank of clouds that was slowly eclipsing the star-bright night.

"Pip . . ."

She threw open the window and leaned out, her arms braced on the casement. The rising wind caught her hair and lashed it across her face. She closed her eyes and lifted her face to the elements as spray pelleted her forehead and cheeks and stung her lips. Far below, the dark ribbon of the river churned swift and angry. "A storm's coming."

"Philippa." She heard the sound of the chain clatter against the post and when he called her again, his voice was raised in urgency. "Philippa!"

She looked down longingly. But, creature of the cliffs and moors that she was, even she could not descend the wall of the manor at night in a storm.

"Phillipa, don't! For God's sake!" Behind her the bed groaned. She turned. He stood at the end of the chain, his pale skin white as frost, bright blood beneath the steel bracelet, his eyes burning like the heart of an emerald, the bed a half foot closer to where she stood.

She didn't care. She *wouldn't* care. "You always could get 'round me, Ned Masterson. But you'll not talk me into letting you go. I swear it."

CHAPTER 5

The wind whipped Philippa's hair into a gorgon crown of inky black locks. With her face flushed with victory and the chill night air coloring her lips and brightening her eyes, she looked just like she had the night he'd met her nearly a year ago.

One of Philippa's friends had bet her that she wouldn't be the first to meet the lord of Masterson Manor. Philippa had never backed down from a challenge in her life. Within the hour, she'd ridden from town, arriving in a rainstorm at his doorstep. He'd come out of the library and found her standing in a pool of water in the hall, shaking the silver droplets from her black hair, her cloak sodden, her boots mud-spattered but her eyes triumphant and amused.

She'd taken his breath away. She always had.

"Philippa. Close the window." She turned her head and looked down. She glanced back at him, her eyes glowed with dark intensity, her lips parted on a spontaneous smile, heady with the euphoria of daredevilry.

She was going to try to climb down the façade.

"No!" Reflexively, he lunged toward her again, hyperextending his arm behind him, nearly breaking it. She glanced once more with a certain piquant longing at the wind-lashed wall beneath her and with an annoyed twist of her lips, jerked the windows shut.

He relaxed, aware that he'd nearly given himself away. Again. For an intelligent and intuitive woman, she was ridiculously ignorant where he was concerned. How could she not know he loved her? But she didn't.

And he wasn't about to tell her.

How could he? She'd use that knowledge to break him just as she was using her knowledge of his desire for her to try to break him. And of late, she'd come damn close.

She ran untamed and undisciplined, as likely to speak her mind as a bird is to sing, tethered to respectable behavior only by the thinnest of cords and that held by an elderly, half-deaf aunt. She knew nothing of guile, little of inhibitions, less of pretensions. Indeed, as of this night every man and woman for ten miles 'round knew Philippa Jones loathed him. Because she was as passionate in love as she was in enmity. He'd tasted both.

She had wanted him once. She wanted him still. There was no possible way she could have feigned her reaction to that kiss. But wanting and loving were not the same. Particularly, not in the lexicon of a wild creature like Philippa Jones. Though once he had thought . . .

Was it so few months back that she'd desired him and been so breathtakingly obvious in that desire? She'd conveyed it each time they'd met by her dilated eyes, her parted lips, and the veil of delight that cloaked her skin. And if desire hadn't had time to ripen into love, she was young. He could wait for her heart to awaken.

But then she'd discovered he'd kept the truth of why he'd come to Trecombe from her. And having been deceived in one matter, she refused to believe he hadn't deceived her in all others.

Even now, regardless of the price it had cost him, objectively he knew he'd had no choice. Because as easy to read as she was, as obvious in her affections, he hadn't dared risk telling her the identity of the man he pursued. Only recently had he discovered it was the man she'd "loved forever," Hal Minton.

But she hadn't come to realize she loved Minton, he thought, until after she'd discovered his "treachery." It was like her to fall in love with someone she considered an outsider. She'd probably built Minton up into some misunderstood folk hero. The truth was that Hal Minton was two-faced, self-serving, and mean-spirited. But he'd been born and bred on the Cornish coast. And Philippa's loyalties ran deep.

Damn her, for her unreasoning heart, which mistook loyalty for love. Anger and frustration hummed in his blood, mixing powerfully with the lust she'd awakened. From the first, he'd wanted to conquer his wild Cornish lass without breaking her spirit.

She stood before the window, the storm building on the horizon a dramatic backdrop for her beauty, elemental and wild. She raised one slanting brow challengingly. Philippa: his promise and his blight, the most exasperating wench he'd ever been plagued by.

At that moment, he could have gladly throttled her.

He'd had about as much of her cold contempt as he was going to take. She'd started this and by God, she wouldn't leave this room until it was either ended or she was stepping over his dead body.

"Now what are you going to do?" he asked.

She shrugged elaborately. "Wait until the maids come. Then leave. Unless you plan to assault me in front of them?"

She was deliberately provoking him. She shouldn't be playing these games with him. Not now. Not after all the other games she'd played with him throughout the last four months.

She cast him a roguish look. "Lord of the manor though you be, Ned Masterson, this isn't the thirteenth century. No one lives or dies by your sufferance."

"I would some did," he growled.

"Are you referring to me?" She batted her eyelashes and despite his fury he felt a familiar twist of desire and amusement, the potent brew she'd always managed to conjure within him.

And now she'd added searing pain to the brew, because she loved another. She laughed with another. She fought with another. She allowed another's hand to stroke her and watch, bewitched, while she relinquished herself to pleasure.

He had never been a jealous man. He had always measured his responses carefully. But now, jealousy fair consumed him. His imagination drove him with a flail made all the more excruciating because of it's acuity. He recalled with acid-bright clarity every murmur, ever kiss, every smile.

"Too bad," she went blithely on, unaware of the havoc she wrought by spinning gracefully at the foot of his bed, well out of his reach, as pleased with herself as a kitten with a mouse. Her swirling skirts caught and released the light, the liquid glow of the fire molded itself to her body as though she'd been turned on a master craftsman's lathe.

She'd thought she'd outmaneuvered him. It would almost be a pity to disabuse her of that notion.

He sat down on the bloody Masterson bed. If only the oaf who'd carved the great monstrosity had been a bit surer of himself—for clearly with a bed of this size and bulk there was some matter of compensation going on here—he'd have been able to drag it across the room. A foot was all he'd managed. Still, it might prove enough.

He lay down on his back, crossed his arms under his head, and stared thoughtfully at the ceiling.

"What are you doing?" she asked suspiciously.

"Relaxing," he said with great patience. He glanced at her. "No sense in being more uncomfortable than necessary while awaiting my men."

"What do you mean?" she asked. She hovered near the foot of the bed, silhouetted in a radiant outline by the hearth light, her features blurred by shadow, her voice sharp.

"My darling girl, you don't imagine that my men will simply sit on their horses for hours waiting for me to appear and then, when I don't show up, sigh and say 'Oh, well, there's a night then,' and go home?"

Actually, that was pretty much exactly what they would do lest someone take command. His men were too well-versed in the vagaries of their profession to assume every job proceeded like clockwork. Especially this one. In point of fact, it was late enough now that the operation to apprehend the smugglers might have been scuttled.

But Pip didn't know that. And just because one project had to be abandoned, didn't mean another couldn't be undertaken. He could see her luscious lower lip thrust out in vexation.

"No need for you to be uncomfortable whilst we wait." He patted the bed beside him. "Best settle in for the nonce."

"You're lying. You're a liar."

"Tch. Your aunt would be devastated to hear you speak in such a manner to your elders."

Even in the murky light, he could see her measuring the distance between where he lay and the wall. She clearly did not like the odds.

"I'll scream," she stated. "Someone will come and then I'll be free and you—"

"And I will track you to the gates of hell itself before I let you go," he promised with sudden, suppressed violence. Then he smiled, shrugging indolently. "Besides, as you said, there's a storm without and my ancestors built their walls thick and their doors thicker still. Apparently, they, too, had things they didn't want overheard."

"Let me go." The taint of panic appeared for the first time in her voice. "Please. I have to try to find him."

He jerked upright and swung his legs off the bed, standing slowly. He could not pretend indolence. Not when she flagrantly reminded him of her new lover. Next she'd be pleading for his life and that . . . no, he did not think he could stand that.

"In answer to your request, no. I will not let you go. Not now." *Not ever. Not by choice.*

For a long minute, she did not speak. But her chin rose and her shoulders straightened. "Are you *threatening* me?"

She took being threatened no better than he. She had always been his match in temper and spirit. Damn her.

"Yes," he smiled. "And if you are wise, my delicious, sinful little tease, you will pay heed that threat."

He could tell from the expression on her face that she'd had enough, he'd pushed her to her limit.

He understood her so well, each vulnerability, each quality, what she lived by, what she would die for. He had never known a woman as well as he knew her. In his very *soul,* he knew her.

And that, even more than the romantic picture she'd built around Hal Minton, was probably in truth why she'd made an end with him, he thought. Such intimacy would be immensely threatening to a wild creature such as her.

Too bad. He intended to have her back, at whatever price, however long it took.

She moved toward him, and stopped just inches out of his reach. He watched her, barely masking his eagerness. A few more inches.

"You are so easy to manipulate, Philippa. You must acquire more mystique if you are to be a success at your chosen profession."

"And what profession, pray tell, is that?"

"A dead man's doxy."

CHAPTER 6

Ned was right. Philippa had no impulse control.

Her hand shot out, just as he'd anticipated and just as he'd planned, he caught it before she struck him. But she was fierce, his Philippa, and not one to give in. Not without a fight.

She hit him hard with her other hand, so surprising him with the unexpected savagery of her assault that her blow landed against his chest. Her eyes blazed with triumph. "Let me go!" she demanded. "Let go of me and fight me, you coward."

He stared at her, amazed. She undoubtedly knew that he would never hit her, just as she must know there was no possibility of her winning any fight between them. He had all of the advantages. Not only was he taller, with a longer reach than she, and stronger, but he was very, very conversant with rough-and-tumble brawls. In all probability, Philippa had never hit anything in her life.

But, she was beyond reasoning. She glared at him, panting, her one wrist locked in his clasp, the other clenched at her side.

"You want to hit me," he said.

"You have no idea how much."

He gave a short, exasperated bark of laughter. After all, she'd recently demonstrated a newfound talent for manipulating him. This could be a means of getting away from him. But he didn't think so. Her gaze was too intent, too blackly condemning.

He dropped her wrist and took one step back, his arms at his side. "Fine. Hit me."

She didn't wait for a second invitation. She lifted both hands at once and began swinging wildly at him, with such ferocity—and no form, at all—that often her balled fists met something other than his blocking forearms.

He absorbed the blows. He absorbed everything she sent him. All the months of anger and frustration and the betrayal poured out of her, realized in a flurry of flying fists. On and on she struck at him, because though she was no brawler, her wild rides on the rugged Cornish coast had toned her body, pared from it all laxity.

She'd stamina and she'd desire and she used both, pummeling away at him. And so it went, long minutes broken only by her occasional sob of frustration as he blocked each of her wild blows, diverting her energy, slapping aside her assault. Still, she refused to stop, refused to lower her arms. And finally, at long last, when her face was damp with sweat and her hair hung wildly about her shoulders and her arms were so tired she could barely raise them, he could stand no more.

"Philippa . . ." he said, frowning as he warded a feeble hit. "stop."

"No!" she rasped suddenly lunging forward inside his arms and pummeling at his chest. "No!"

"Easy," he said, startled by her vehemence. She ignored him, setting her forehead against his chest and beating at his sides and back and finally, seeing no other recourse he wrapped his arms around her and held her tight.

"No!" she grated out. "No! No! It's not fair!"

Helplessness bred fear. She was too wrought up. She'd exhaust herself. Do herself harm. "What the bloody hell do you think you're doing?" He shook her. "What do you want?"

"To hurt you!" she cried out, raising her face to his. Her voice broke. "I can't hurt you. I never could. It's not fair."

"You can't hurt me?" he echoed disbelievingly. "Is that what this is about? You want to *hurt* me?"

She'd cut his heart out, wrung pain from him he'd never imagined possible, trampled on his pride, destroyed his peace of mind, *fucked* with his ability to do his job and *she couldn't hurt him?*

"You've gone too far, Philippa." His voice was as cold as his rage was white hot. It had ever been a barometer of his emotions, at distinct variance with what he felt. It was frigid now.

He yanked her around, spinning her effortlessly, and lashing his free arm around her waist. His manacled hand clamped around her throat. She struggled for just a moment, for though she was foolish, she was not stupid and she understood that the hand about her throat was a threat.

She stilled, her back against his naked chest. Her heart thundered. Even through the thin material of her dress, he could feel its pounding. Her shoulder blades cut into his pectorals with each draw and release of her agitated breath. She was afraid of him. Good.

"You haven't any idea, do you? You've no concept of what you've done to me. Well, sweet darkness, you can rest easy for I swear to you, you hurt me," he rasped, his lips inches from the velvet cockle of her ear. "Now, give me the key."

"Take it."

Things were moving too fast. Every act committed now

unalterable, each word irrevocable. No time to think, plan, only time to act on instinct, and perhaps something less dependable, less reliable. Emotion.

Her whispered challenge caught him off guard. He hesitated. She'd excited him with her words and her body that was as lithe and supple as a spring willow, a feminine mystery. But not completely so. Not to him. He'd trespassed there and had craved a return until he ached.

He'd played with her, drawn a line along the velvety curve of her hip. His palms had weighed the slight, soft abundance of her breast. He'd tasted her. And it was the sensory memory of her that roused him and caused him to hold himself away from her.

She undid him.

"Don't play with me, Philippa."

She let her head fall back against his shoulder and gazed up at him unafraid and unreadable. Philippa, his open book, *unreadable*. It should have made him laugh but he could not even find a smile. He had no idea what was going on behind those dark, luminous eyes. Treachery? Simple lust? Some odd, desperate combination of both?

His grip around her throat relaxed. But his breathing grew deeper, harsher and her head, resting on the shallow indentation between shoulder and chest muscle, rode each inhalation.

"You won't like my games," he assured her under his breath.

"I might."

Was she daring him? He slipped his hand up her throat, capturing her jaw. He pressed his lips against her temple, fanning her closed eyelids with his breath. "We'll see."

Before she could react, he spun her around, put his hands on her shoulders and shoved her, toppling her on the bed. He followed her down, imprisoning her beneath his body, his arms braced on either side of her, his hips heavy and insistent over hers. Even through the layers of her skirt she would feel him.

She squeezed her eyes shut. He grappled her wrists together and pulled them over her head, trapping them in an intractable grip, just as she'd done to him.

"Open your eyes," he commanded. "Open your eyes!"

Her eyes flew open at his fierce tone. The minute they did, their gazes locked in contention, hers blazing with unspoken recrimination, his with anger and anguish.

"Do you see me?" His voice had turned into a harsh whisper. "Do you?"

"Yes!" she replied, just as vehemently.

"Do you *feel* me?" His lower body moved against her and she gasped.

"Yes," he whispered, answering for her.

His lips drew back in equal parts self-derision and desire, needing her to acknowledge *what* she was doing and *who* she was doing it with. "My name. Say my name."

"I don't know what you mean," she said. With his free hand he raked the heavy hair back from her face, clutched a handful of the dark stuff and pulled her head back, exposing her throat. Her heart thundered beneath him.

"My name."

"Are you going to hurt me?" she asked, still not afraid.

"Hurt you?" he asked, honestly amused. His head dropped alongside her throat. His lips glided over her flesh, assaulting her in ways against which she had no defense.

She'd always been ruled by sense and sensation far more than sensibility. Her body heeded the sensual call. Her eyelids shut, and she caught her lower lip beneath the pearl white ridge of her teeth.

"I would that I could, Philippa, and pay you back in kind

for the hell you've put me through. But you'd need to feel something other than lust for me to do that. So, I have other plans for you."

"Ned—"

"So you do know who has you."

"Yes."

"You wanted this. For me to force you," he accused her.

"No."

"Yes," he said. "You wanted me to control this. Because you're afraid of it. I'd never have pegged you as a coward, Pip."

"No." She shook her head violently, twice, the dark hair whipping across her pale face. "No, you're wrong. I know what I'm doing. What I've done. But I hate not being strong enough to say no." Her eyes blazed up at his. "And if *I'm* not strong enough to say 'no,' I'll be damned if you are."

He laughed acrimoniously. "That, darling, is the most obtuse bit of reasoning I have ever heard."

She flushed brightly at his laughter. "Let me go. At least let me go back to the other side of the room."

He laughed again. "But I haven't found the key yet."

"I don't have it."

"And I no longer care."

She bucked beneath him and he kissed her. For an instant, she resisted and then she was kissing him, kissing him with a hunger he'd thought he'd never know again. He released her wrists, slipped his arms under her and lifted her up into his embrace.

Her arms closed around his shoulders. Her fingers raked through his hair. Her tongue thrust deeply in his mouth, sounds—sweet Jesu!—sounds of desperate want and whimpering pleasure rose from deep in her throat.

He drank passion from her mouth like a drunk imbibes mead, sweet, honeyed, intoxicating. He burned with the need to bury himself within her, to finally take this to its ultimate ends, to finish this madness and complete the dance they'd begun so many months ago. To complete himself. In her.

He thrust his chained hand between their bodies, dragging the metal over her belly as he grappled with her skirt, fisting the thin, material in his hand and dragging it up over her thighs. Suddenly, she broke away from his kiss, shoved her palms flat against his chest and pushed.

White hot, the suspicion she'd once more played him for a rutting dog was born and as quickly died. Because as soon as he fell back, she rolled her leg over his hips, and rose, straddling his thighs.

For one intense moment she paused. Then, with a sigh of abandonment? Of distress? she lowered her head and placed her lips on his stomach.

CHAPTER 7

Allowing Ned to catch her had seemed her only possible choice if she was to get away. And she had to get away. She had to find John and warn him. At least, she had to try.

The only way that she could do that was to escape this room. And the only way Ned was going to let that happen was if he had no choice in the matter. If both his wrists were manacled.

But the moment he'd goaded her into striking him, all the frustrations and pain of the last months had overtaken her in a torrent of anguish that could only be expressed in violence. From that moment she'd been lost. And yet, when he'd kissed her, her body and her heart, already sensitized to his touch, had betrayed her all over again.

She wanted him. It was that easy, that simple, that horrifying. Her body sang to him, strained and flushed and swelled toward him.

She rubbed her cheek across his flat belly, the dark hairs silky beneath her cheeks. His belly dished in, leaving hard ridges beneath her lips. She nuzzled him. He smelled of soap and faintly of wood smoke and of masculine arousal, musky and warm.

She felt his hand hover above her head but he didn't touch her, didn't cradle her head with the destroying gentleness he once had shown her. She wanted that. She wanted too much and from this man and this man alone. Deftly, instantly developing expertise, her fingers worked the buttons of his trousers free. She heard him suck in a deep breath.

He'd never asked anything of her, never demanded anything. And she suddenly wanted to give him pleasure as much as she wanted it for herself. More. And she would have if . . . .

If things had been different . . . *If* he hadn't been intent on arresting her brother and ruining their lives. If there had been a future for them. The thought intruded with cruel insistence.

A lady did not do this with a gentleman with whom she had no intention of continuing a relationship. She hesitated. Of course, she thought desperately, a lady would not have done *any* of the things she and Ned had already—

"No," she heard him say. "Never with misgiving."

He gripped her beneath her arms and hauled her up his body. He'd misunderstood her hesitation, thought she had been persuading herself to commit an act she found repellant. She tried to tell him differently, but in dragging her up, her gown was dragged down.

Her breasts had sprung free of the small bodice. He cupped her shoulders and lifted her up, looking down at her naked breast with a smoldering gaze.

"You have the most beautiful breasts in the world," he said.

"Small." She seemed to have been rendered near mute by the expression in his face, for that was all she could manage.

"Perfect. Made for a man's—" He shifted her forward as easily as if she was a mannequin and held her suspended there.

Slowly he eased her down until his mouth was an inch from one puckering nipple. "—mouth."

The word sloughed over her breast in a warm rush and she shuddered.

Tenderly, he touched his lips to her. She jerked in reaction and he laughed, a pleased masculine sound. She scowled, glaring at him, her breath coming too rapidly, well past the point of schemes and plans.

Fine. She admitted it. He'd been right. She wanted him to dictate this. She wanted to relinquish control.

She'd always been strong, independent and proud of it. But strength and independence are bought only by keeping one's heart whole and unassailable, by being answerable to no one. And by never letting another close enough to threaten one's invulnerability.

She never wanted anyone to conquer her before, to claim complete control over her body. But she wanted Ned to. Because he would take her places she only dimly imagined, as both her guardian and guide. And she trusted him.

How perverse her heart must be, how convoluted her soul, if the only man she trusted was the only man she feared.

"I want you to want me, Philippa. I want you to feel some small measure of what you do to me, what I crave from you. Do you want me to touch you?" He already knew the answer.

"Yes."

"Like so?" He fastened his lips about the silky aureole and sucked. Hard and sudden. She jerked back again, gasping, and the inadvertent pull caused its own delicious sting of pleasure.

He smiled against her breast. "Or so?"

His tongue came out and performed a slow, languid lick across her nipple, the sensation at once soothing and exciting. Pleasure stabbed through her.

"Well?" His voice was Lucifer's, enticing, arrogant, and

commanding, rife with satisfaction but thick with longing, too. She was not alone in this tempest of need.

And that knowledge gave back part of the power she'd conferred on him.

"You'll not make me beg, Ned Masterson."

"We'll see." He laughed again, albeit in a voice shaking with passion, and rolled her under him, better availing himself of her body. He took her in his mouth and played with her, suckled and kissed her, beat little staccato tattoos with the tip of his tongue and drew so deeply on her that she cried out.

Only when he'd feasted long upon her did he finally release her, gazing down at her quaking form with lambent, sexually charged eyes, his face still.

Her gown was up about her thighs and his erection strained against her. He slid his hand under her skirt and found the juncture of her thighs. She was wet. Flagrantly so.

They'd ventured much in those months before she'd discovered his perfidy. They were healthy, willful, and hot-blooded. But while he'd pleasured her through a cloth barrier, he'd never touched her naked flesh before. They'd never gone this far before.

Deep beneath the mounting haze of expectation, she recalled where she was, what she'd meant to do. But it was fading, being devoured by sexual excitement.

She tried to wrench herself away but his free hand clamped her hip, keeping her still just long enough for his fingers to stroke her. His touch was deft, undeniable. She gave in, rising, moving in to his caress, wanton and wanting.

All the while his gaze remained riveted on her face, gauging her reaction. It had always been so. He'd always watched for her pleasure, never availed himself of her for his own use.

He did the same now, reading the slight parting of her lips, interpreting each jagged breath as his fingers slipped within her body and stroked her. He manipulated her with a thoroughness that had nothing to do with delicacy and everything to do with intuition, a raw, direct stimulation—like the man himself—the heel of his hand riding her mons, kneading her.

"Please . . ." That whimper couldn't be hers. But she'd heard the siren call of completion, and felt the first tendrils of pleasure seize her in its inexhaustible grip. She had one chance left to get away, to find her brother and warn him.

She fumbled awkwardly with the hand clasping her hip, prying it off and pushing it down toward where his free hand worked such magic.

He hesitated a moment and she stared wildly at his face. He'd broken into a sweat. His aristocratic face glistened, his expression was unreadable. "Please . . ."

"Yes," he whispered, delicately kissing her forehead. "Yes."

She stretched her fingers toward the loose manacle resting by her hip. She reached to secure it over his wrist. But before she could, it was snatched away. She heard a click and felt it close about her wrist.

CHAPTER 8

"You handcuffed me to you!"

"Yes." Ned relaxed on his side, propped up by one elbow and looked down at their hands. "Trumped you, sweetheart."

"You can't do that!"

"Why? It's only what you were attempting to do to me, was it not?" He grinned at her lazily, but the grin, she noted, did not quite reach his eyes. She decided that denying it would be ridiculous. "Besides, it will be easy enough to undo once we have hashed things out between us."

"Hashed out?" she shouted indignantly, rolling over and scooting off the side of the bed. She couldn't go too far, however, as Ned was not scooting anywhere.

In fact, as far as he would go to accommodate her was to raise his hand. Which made returning her breasts back beneath her bodice a very uncomfortable and embarrassing business and one which he took full advantage of, letting the backs of his fingers slide lightly over her skin. Her treacherous flesh tingled at the deliberate accident. She glared at him. His indolent smile didn't change.

Once she'd returned her dress to a semblance of respectability she didn't know what to do. So, she stood beside the bed with her hand hanging at her side while his rested on the mattress edge.

"Pleased with yourself?" she finally asked. She was near shaking with rage that he'd so adroitly manipulated her, frustration that the culmination she'd sought had been ripped away, leaving her wanting, flushed, and trembling. And that *he* looked like he'd just finished some slight exertion like a . . . like a brisk stroll!

"Hardly." He glanced tellingly at his crotch. "But you were the one groping for the manacles, love. And not being too subtle about it. Feeling a bit . . . randy were you?"

"You're loathsome."

"I'm right."

"What of it?" she demanded. "You've always had the power to make me feel things I shouldn't. Is the merry brotherhood of rakes giving out medals for that these days? Or are you simply trying to establish a record? How many other Trecombe women have you brought to the point and abandoned?"

Even as she spoke she was aware that she was making the same accusation against him which he'd earlier levied against her. In any other instance it would have been laughable. She didn't feel like laughing. She felt hot, her skin too tight, her heart wrestling with the imperatives of simple desire.

Simple? There was nothing simple about this situation, about the quagmire of emotion and conflicting needs that assailed her. And it *rather* irked her.

"If you want to be 'finished,' I'll be happy to oblige." With a gesture rife with mockery, Ned patted the mattress beside him.

She turned to stalk away, forgetting she was tethered to him and coming up short. With a strangled sound, she turned around and with all her might wrenched the bloody chain, jerking his arm straight out and jolting him flat on his back, his expression so comically astonished that Philippa laughed with triumph, enjoying the spectacle. She'd had precious few moments of mastery this evening. In fact, since the moment he'd opened his eyes, he'd had the upper hand.

His head swung in her direction, his green eyes glittered dangerously. Purposefully he rolled off the bed and slowly rose to his full height in front of her. But, she'd no fear left in her.

"What now?" she jeered. "You're going to beat me? Kiss me? Upbraid me for my loyalty to—"

He swooped down on her, his hand covering her mouth. "Don't. God, don't."

She wrenched her head free, pulling his hand away. "Don't what?" she demanded angrily.

"Don't say his name. I couldn't stand that." He meant it. It seemed Ned, too, had reached an end point. His expression was stripped of all pretense, his perfect, oh-so-carefully fashioned mask of cool composure was gone, leaving a stark expression of anguish. He looked raw, naked, and violable.

She didn't understand. It made no sense. And yet, for the first time she realized that this was hard for him, had been hard for him, that possibly he'd paid for their estrangement in the same painful coin as she. She'd hurt him, after all. The thought brought her no pleasure.

He stepped closer, lifted his hand and turned it over, stroking her cheek with his knuckles.

"Good God, Philippa," he murmured, his gaze roving in pained wonder over her face, "how much do you think I can take?"

His touch was exquisite, the more so for its trembling uncertainty. Her eyelids drifted shut. "I don't know what you mean."

She felt his head drop nearer hers, the warmth of his breath across her cheeks, her throat, as though he was tracing her features by scent. "How can you let me taste you, touch you, pleasure you, and then say his name to me?"

She barely heard him. The sensation, this muted desire was new and staggeringly sweet. She sighed, turning her head toward him, her eyes still closed. The movement brought her cheek against his lips. He did not move away. He pressed a kiss to her skin with tender fervency.

"It isn't just lust, you know." He spoke against her temple. She felt his hands slip up her arms, his long fingers circle her upper arms. "What you feel, it's more than a matter of craving release."

She needed no convincing. Regardless of what he thought, she well knew her heart. She always had. She'd never owned the art of self-delusion.

"You'll love me," he said. "I swear to God, you'll love."

The time for self-protection was past. She could not bear to hear the anguish in his voice. "I already do," she whispered.

The fingers around her arms tightened convulsively. "Don't taunt me."

Her eyelids flew open to find his head lowered, his eyes searching her face. "Don't lie to me. Not about that. You aren't the sort of woman that divides her heart between two men."

"I haven't. I don't."

Confusion chased across his features. His hands abruptly dropped. He raked his free hand through his hair, looking at her uncertainly.

"Forgive me, if I appear disconcerted," he said. "I am stunned by this sudden switch of loyalties. It has a taint of convenience."

"And I am beyond bemused," Philippa returned with a growing sense of injury. "I have switched no loyalties—" and then remembering John, she flushed. Ned must think she'd said she loved him in order to save her brother.

The moment her skin colored, Ned stepped back. His expression grew shuttered. If not for the heavy rise and fall of his chest, she would never have known she'd affected him in any manner. How strange that she, normally at the mercy of her emotions should be so drawn to a man who had mastered all of his.

Or had seemed to. She knew better now.

"I beg you, don't arrest him," she said quietly.

His head tilted back, his eyes briefly closed against some interior agony. "God, how can you ask that?"

"What choice do I have?" she asked plaintively. "He's my brother!"

He grabbed her arms, shaking her. "He's a *jackal,* Pip, a man without con—" He stopped. Stared. "What?"

"I love you, Ned. I don't deny it," she said tersely. "But loving you does not refute my other loyalties or affections. You would despise me if it did. He's my brother and I am begging you, as you have some affection for me—"

"Affection! God, nothing so tepid—" he broke in hoarsely.

"—as you have some affection for me," she went doggedly on, lifting her hands and cupping his lean, angular jaw between them, "do not arrest him."

"You think it is John I have been pursuing," he whispered as if to himself.

"I am not blind." She laughed without humor. "I guessed soon after I learned why you'd come to Trecombe. John is always leaving the house late at night on some pretext or another; he spends money we do not have; and he wastes his time at the local tavern associating with the sorriest lot on the coast."

She gazed earnestly into his eyes. "But he is a decent man,

Ned. I swear he would do no one a willing harm. Not coldly, not with planned malice. He is simply—"

"—headstrong, subject to his emotions, too willing to take risks. But fiercely loyal, dauntless and proud," he finished for her. At some point his free hand had slipped round her back. He pulled her close.

"Yes."

"I'm not after your brother, Pip. I never was."

She pulled back. "But, you were angry that I protected him. Indeed, derisive. You said—"

"Hal Minton," he broke in. "I thought you were protecting Hal Minton. I thought he was the man you were talking about when you said you were trying to save someone you loved. I thought—"

She tried to pull away. He wouldn't let her. "You thought Hal Minton and I were lovers!"

"I *thought* that is what you told me."

Her mind raced back, recalling bits and phrases from the evening. She never actually said John's name while several times Ned had mentioned Minton. But, as Hal Minton meant nothing to her, she'd simply discounted his name. And on more occasion than one, she *had* flaunted Minton before Ned.

Yes. She could see how he might misinterpret her words. All night, in every instant that mattered they'd spoken at cross-purposes. "Hal Minton means nothing to me."

"Good." Jealousy imbued the single tense syllable. "Because he is the leader of the smugglers I have been sent to arrest."

"Hal Minton." Her shock faded before a growing realization that Ned had only needed to tell her who he was and what he was doing for all the agony of the preceding months to have been averted. When the full impact of that realization hit her, she raised her hands and shoved him away with all her might.

For the third time that night, she caught him off guard. He fell back a step, his thighs hitting the edge of the bed, and tumbled onto the bed. She watched him fall with undeniable satisfaction but, as she was chained to him, her satisfaction was short-lived. Before she knew what was happening, she was falling atop him, caught in his embrace, cushioned by his body.

Shaking the hair from her eyes, she rose up, her arms braced on either side of him and glared at him.

"You could have told me!" she accused him. "You *should* have told me! Instead you let me think that you—Oh!"

He swept the hair back from her face. His gaze was glazed. He swallowed. "I couldn't." He sounded breathless. "God, Philippa, you have always been honest, sometimes disastrously so. Be honest in this. You could no more have kept the knowledge that Hal Minton was a smuggler secret than the sun can keep from shining."

"That's not fair," she denied hotly. "I can be trusted. If I swore not to speak, by all that's sacred I wouldn't have spoken."

He nodded, still with that strange look of forced concentration on his face. "I know you wouldn't have said a word. This is not about trust or keeping promise; it is about who you are, Pip. You would have condemned Minton with every scorching glance, every biting word, every dismissive gesture."

"How do you know?"

He smiled crookedly but it looked like it was an effort. "Because I've been scorched, bitten, and dismissed.

"My darling, everyone in Trecombe goes to great lengths to tell me how much you loathe me, and yet, I have it on the best authority that you have never actually told anyone so."

She sniffed, still glowering down at him. "I wouldn't do anything so déclassé."

"No. Yet every person in town knows your opinion of me.

It only took one meeting with you to realize I could not tell you who I was or for whom I was looking without risking not only my mission but the lives of the men working for me."

She could not dispute his charge. She was easy to read.

"Of course," he continued, his breathing choppy, "you were a good bit better at artifice than I had allowed. Because I had no idea you knew my mission until this night."

"Well, I had what I thought to be prime motivation to keep my knowledge secret from you." She could afford to be magnanimous. She had the upper hand here. It had finally dawned on her why Ned looked so uncomfortable. If she shifted a little she might even—oh, my! she could *definitely* feel the reason for his discomfort.

"I thought you were using me to get close to John and I thought if you knew that I knew who you were, you'd arrest him forthwith. I was simply trying to buy time to convince John to give up his criminal ways." She broke off, her eyes growing round. "Oh, no! Poor John! I've been preaching to him for months, accusing him of the worst things!"

"Don't worry about John," Ned said in a strangled voice, because when she'd risen up higher on her arms, her lower body had ground against his. And then, his lips compressed together and his face that of a man set to an arduous task, he lifted her off of him and rolled her to one side. She allowed the small distance. For the moment.

"It still seems a shabby sort of thing," she said, "first to court me and then—"

"Then nothing," he said grimly. "I wanted you. I wanted you then and God knows, I want you now. But *you* spurned *me,* sweetheart. Not the other way around. And if it makes you feel better, you have put me through hell."

"It does," she said.

He laughed, leaning in and dropping a quick, hard kiss on

her lips before hastily retreating. And why was he retreating? she wondered, frowning. She wanted more than that quick, brief touch. She'd been suspended on the edge of carnal satisfaction for hours and now she'd discovered that he didn't want to toss her brother in prison and he hadn't wanted to deceive her. She'd never given a rap for convention. But most important, she loved him. She loved him so much.

She wriggled closer and he flinched back.

"Don't you want to kiss me?"

He didn't answer, but a tremor rippled through his tensile body.

She used the weapons at hand. Casually she moved her manacled hand over her hip to the other side, by necessity dragging his hand with it. He could have stopped her. He was certainly stronger than she—*she* couldn't have moved this monolithic bed—but he didn't. When his hand was on her hip, she stopped pulling. His fingers curled around her hipbone, clasping her. She edged closer.

"Do I kiss poorly, then?" she asked, a feminine potency surging through her. *"Won't* you kiss me, Ned?"

His green gaze transfixed her. "I told you not to play games. Continue this and you'll reap the consequences," he said, his face tense but his voice even more so. "I've nothing left with which to resist and I've little will to do so."

"I want you."

"I know." He was breathing hard, his smooth naked chest rising and falling. "Marry me."

"Fine."

He drew back, startled and seized her arms pulling her close. "You'll marry me?" He looked so shocked, so gratified, so amazed that she could not help but smile.

"Of course," she replied simply. "I'd have no other. I'll *have* no other."

"I swear you'll not regret it," he vowed fervently and then with a rueful grin added, "not more than once or twice a week. And in between I'll make you glad you married me."

"But until then . . ." She raised her hand and traced her index finger down his sternum, over his pounding heart, across the compact muscles that leapt to life in his abdomen, lower over the soft swirl of hair low on his belly, to the narrow band of his trousers. Wickedly, she hooked her finger beneath the band and touched something blunt and silky smooth. He jerked back.

"No," he said desperately. "We must wait until we're wed."

"Why?"

He squeezed his eyes shut, raised his face in a manner beseeching the heavens. "Only you would ask such a question, Pip."

She took advantage of his closed eyes, leaning in and nibbling on his collarbone. His skin was hot. He tasted salty. Ah, yes, he'd endured his own trials this night—

He grabbed her and rolled her under him, his free hand cradling her head as he kissed her. It was a rough, uncontrolled kiss, the pressure driving her down into the mattress. She met it open-mouthed.

He was thoroughly aroused, a big hard mound between her thighs. He tore his lips from her. "There's no reason not to wait," he said desperately. "I'm not a scoundrel, Pip. I love you. I want you to realize that, to know it in your very soul. I'll prove it to you by any means, satisfy every convention with my dutiful respect."

Her heart bounded with joy. He loved her. He wanted her to know he loved her, to prove his love. But, she didn't need this sort of "proof." She already knew.

"I'm strong enough to handle a little self-denial," he said crookedly.

"Then I must be a scoundrel," she replied with a roguish smile. She fumbled with his trousers' remaining buttons, fighting them free of their holes. "And I most definitely cannot handle self-denial right now. And as for satisfaction, there are only two people you need worry about satisfying. Don't make me ask, Ned. Please—"

With a strangled sound, he reached down and jerked away the fabric between them, both her gown and his trousers, the chain dragging between them. "Touch me."

She complied, reaching down and wrapping her fingers around him. The intimate knowledge of his heat and size lanced through her. He bit off a sharp cry, swelling in her hand. Later she would explore more thoroughly this satiny smooth, rock hard enigma. Right now, they needed to finish what they had begun so many hours before, so many months before.

He grabbed her knee and pulled her leg up over his hip, spreading her legs. "Take me inside of you. Guide me"

He needed to know that she wanted him. It was there in his tense commands. Should she show any sign of pain, any alarm, exhibit the slightest second thoughts, she realized he would stop—even if it killed him. It made her want him even more. Unhesitatingly she set him at her threshold. He grabbed her hands, both manacled and free, and laced his fingers with hers, holding her hands down against the mattress on either side of her head. Deliberately, she tilted her hips up in age-old welcome.

He'd long since readied her. She felt herself stretching to accommodate the slow, nerve-rasping slide of his entry. He filled her slowly, thoroughly. The sensation was amazing. Wonderful. All the while he watched her, his face set as in stone, his eyes glittering and alive to every nuance of her expression, every check in her breathing, every contraction of every muscle. He watched her eyes as he took her.

"Move," he muttered thickly and she began to move, a slight, deliberate dance, her thighs locked around his trim hips.

A grimace crossed his aquiline features. He was holding back, letting her feel him, accustom herself to his presence with her. She didn't want him to hold back, part of this was about power, the give and take of uncontrollable forces. She wanted him to take her. She wanted to be taken.

"Move," she whispered and rocked her hips hard against him. He trembled.

"Move in me." She bucked, seating him deeper. His teeth clenched and he growled, abruptly sliding their two sets of hands up to her hips. He clasped her tightly and lifted, thrusting hard and deep into her. Sensual pleasure snaked through her body, pooling in her groin, seizing her in its inexhaustible grip.

Again and again, over and over, he drove into her and she reveled in the sensation, basked in the ferocity of his possession, hurling toward some summit, unforeseeable pinnacle of pleasure locked between her legs, plunging into her body, lifting and holding her, his body marble hard, hot, and immutable. She needed that. She moved with him, feeling her interior muscles clench. And still the pleasure kept building, the need for surcease as sharp as an addict's craving.

Only the end remained, a sun blazing just beyond her reach and she struggled . . . ! God, how she struggled. Her body strained for release. She squeezed her eyes shut, lights exploding against the swirling darkness, her body straining. . . . There! There. There.

Waves of pleasure flooded her body, inundated her; skin, pores, senses. She stretched, transfixed by gratification, her throat arching back, sobbing, her nails digging into his sides as the tremors rippled through her.

*   *   *

Her climax nearly killed him. He'd matched her thrust for thrust, ground his teeth against it, watching the waves build in her, feeling the moment she abandoned herself to the little death and felt his own body rise to partake of the feast. But he fought it, fought his climax, unwilling to let it go until he was sure, until every muscle in her body gripped him and the contractions had started to ebb. Only then did he allow himself release.

He came abruptly, scorching and inexorable, the power of it leaving him gasping, his arms bruising her, his throat raw with the sound torn from him. And when it was over and he collapsed above her, his face buried in the velvet lee of her throat, she wrapped her arms around him and pressed her lips to the base of his throat and gave him heaven by whispering, "I love you."

CHAPTER 9

It was a miracle he even heard the faint knock on the door. The night had turned into day before all the months of anger and heartbreak had been burned away by the intensity with which they loved. But then, perhaps it wasn't surprising that the smallest sound woke him. He had something to protect.

He stood up beside the bed, shielding her with his body. "Who is it?"

"It's John Jones, Captain."

"John?"

He swung around to find Philippa looking up at him from a nest of linens and blankets, tousled and infinitely desirable, her dark eyes wide and questioning.

He touched her lips. "Quietly, my love," he said in a low voice. "You may have no use for others' opinions, but I'd not care to have your name bandied about. I'm a bit rusty with a sword."

Twin lines appeared between her brows, the beautiful, willful brat, but she demurred without a sound.

"I came to see if all was right with you," John spoke through the door.

"Aye, I'm fine, John. What happened with the raid?"

"Caught him, sir." There was undeniable pride in John's voice. "He's in chains on his way to Glastonbury as we speak."

"My brother *works* for you?" Philippa said.

"Aye. And will try to make you a widow before you're even wed if you speak louder," he cautioned.

"What's that, Captain?" John asked.

"Good work, lad."

"Thank you, sir. But why is it you weren't there at the end after all you've been through chasing the devil to ground. Or rather I should say after my ill-tempered sister has put you through."

"The wretch!" Pip mouthed, her expression hot with affront. She started to sit up but Ned pushed her gently back.

"I'll not have you speak of her that way, John," he said.

John snorted. "Aye, you poor bastard—beggin' your pardon, Cap'n. I don't know why you don't just toss her on her—"

"That'll be enough, Jones," he said, his voice was deadly serious. "I'll speak with you later."

They heard John sigh loudly. "Aye, Cap'n. But you missed out on a rare good time. I hope whatever it was that kept you back was worth it."

Ned looked down at Pip. "Oh, it was."

"Then, as it appears I'm not going to be invited in, I'll report to you later, only . . ."

Her eyes had grown dark as she looked up at Ned and a pink blush bloomed in her cheeks. She'd lifted her arms up to him.

"Only what, John?" he grated out in exasperation.

"Only, please, Cap'n. I beg you to let me be there when you tell my sister who you are and what you've been doing and, more important, who I am and what I've been doing. I've had to listen to her sermons for near half a year. I think I deserve to be there."

"Maybe," Ned allowed, watching Pip's eyes narrow dangerously. "Now, go away, John."

"As you will, Cap'n."

With a sigh of relief, Ned turned to Pip. She was sitting up, the covers pooling around her hips, Venus arising from the sea. "You are the most exquisite woman—"

"Oh," Jones voice again. "One more thing I forgot."

Astonished, Ned swung toward the door. "What?" he thundered.

"Forgot to say, 'Morning, Pip.' " And with that he was gone, leaving Ned and Pip staring at each other.

"I believe," Pip finally said, her voice high and unnatural, "that my brother has just given his blessing to our union."

Her lips started to twitch and then she broke into a smile and finally she began laughing and she was irresistible when she laughed. Too irresistible. He reached down and swept her up into his arms, nuzzling the velvety skin at the nape of her neck, the chain that had bound them all night swinging lose against her shoulders. He released her. Her lips were parted in invitation, her eyes darkening with anticipation.

"You know, adept as I am with one hand chained, you would be amazed at what I am capable of doing with both hands free," he said, bending down and sweeping a long, lingering kiss against her mouth.

"Oh?"

"Yes. Why don't I demonstrate. Where's the key?"

"The key?" she asked.

He smiled. "Aye." He lifted their imprisoned hands and jangled the chain.

"The key!" The drowsiness flushed from her expression, her eyes grew round. "I was afraid you'd find it, so . . . so I threw it out the window last night."

She looked up at him, falsely repentant, but a tiny bit concerned, too.

"It doesn't matter," he said. "Sooner or later a maid will arrive and we'll send her for your fool brother who we will then send to find a bolt cutter."

"But, what will we do until then?" she asked.

"I can practice more of my one-handed technique, I suppose," he suggested, smiling rakishly. He looped one strong arm around her slight waist, hauling her close and nipping her throat, beginning the ancient dance again. "That is, if you're willing, my dark and wild Cornish beauty."

She was.

The Masterson bed is our last stop on the tour, so if you'll come this way . . ." With practiced ease, Laurel led the tourists downstairs to the neat little gift shop. "Because this is our last tour, everything except the books is half price." She smiled too brightly. "Buy lots."

"Even the weapons?" the teenager asked.

She started to answer, but Max got there before her. "Especially the weapons."

The tourists chuckled while she glared at him. She wanted to ask why he had followed them, but she thought she knew the answer. He wanted to annoy her for as long as was humanly possible. And he was doing a good job of it.

Then the tourists, scattered throughout the store, distracted her.

"Do you have different sizes on the T-shirts?" Meghan held up an extra large.

"Everything we have is on the shelves," Laurel answered.

Mrs. Stradling was scooping up the bumper stickers and the pencils. Brian went right to the glass-topped display of swords and battle-axes, and when his mother joined him, embroiled her in a heated discussion of why he needed one.

Laurel turned to watched the tourists, her heart in her throat. *The last tour.* For over a year she'd been living at Masterson Manor, cataloguing the contents, discovering the most marvelous diaries from years past, and visiting the archeological sites on the estate. Once a day, she led a tour group through the manor, showing them the rooms and the furniture and trying, so hard, to give them an appreciation of the history in this little corner of England.

Now it was all over. Mr. and Mrs. Barry had sold Masterson Manor, and the new owner not only wanted to live here, but to discontinue the tours. When Laurel had asked if she would be allowed to carry on her research, Mrs. Barry had shaken her head. The new owner had been most insistent that he would use Masterson Manor as his country home.

It wasn't easy to support such an old house, with its constant repairs and the need for improvements. Laurel didn't know how anyone could do it without the income from the tours, but it sounded as if the new owner was wealthy. So she had to face the facts. Her job was almost over. She had no choice but to secure another position close to a viable research site.

"Is this a replica of the Masterson estate?" Miss Ferguson peered through the glass at the three-dimensional scale model.

"It is." Laurel hurried to her side to point out the sights. "There's the manor. We're standing inside right here." She indicated the northeastern corner.

"Any ghosts in the manor?"

Smiling at Mrs. Stradling's enthusiasm, Laurel said, "None, I'm afraid. The inhabitants, at least all the ones I've researched, lived happy and healthy lives."

"Oh." Mrs. Stradling drooped with disappointment.

"There's the Masterson castle built on the cliff overlooking the ocean. Cromwell's men used cannonballs to knock the walls down, and the Cornish elements have done the rest."

Before Miss Ferguson could speak, Laurel added, "The motor coach will take you by there on your way out."

"I would hope so," Miss Ferguson said crisply. "I like castles."

"There's really not much to see." A recalcitrant wisp of hair fell out of the clip that held the slippery mass atop Laurel's head, and she tucked it back in. Indicating the cluster of houses close to the manor, she said, "There's the village of Trecombe."

Mrs. Stradling peered at crooked streets. "Very picturesque."

Brian pressed his finger on the glass over the square mound not far from the manor. "What's this?"

"It's the site of the medieval abbey. It was razed by Henry VIII and the monks scattered. The chapel became Anglican, of course, and it still stands as a fine example of Gothic construction."

"Is it still in use?"

"Absolutely. Father Ellis performs services every Sunday. You saw some of the church art which is scattered throughout the manor. St. Albion's cross is in the room with the Masterson bed, the reliquary in the great hall and the alabaster vases in the library." She frowned. She couldn't remember seeing the alabaster vases when they'd passed through the library.

Oh, no. Not again.

John wrapped his arm around Meghan's neck and kissed her forehead for no apparent reason other than he could.

Meghan closed her eyes and offered her mouth.

Laurel just wanted them to stop. Not because she envied them. Not at all. Because such behavior was inappropriate in . . . in a souvenir shop.

As if answering her appeal, they slipped out the outer door. Laurel sagged with relief.

"The reliquary is remarkable," Miss Ferguson said. "But I wonder who had the nerve to steal the jewels off of the lid."

In his most ironic voice, Max said, "Sold off to support the Masterson family in its dissipations, I'm sure."

"The Mastersons were a noble and honorable family," Laurel retorted.

"All of them?" His eyes gleamed. "They hatched no scoundrels at all?"

The hair on the back of Laurel's neck rose.

Abruptly, she was sick of putting up with him. His big feet, clomping around on the wooden floors. His big hands, deftly using hand tools to fix the plumbing and run modem cable and any of a hundred more jobs around the manor. His broad shoulders, at just the right height for a woman her size to rest her cheek on. His tight ass, the kind that gave blue jeans a good name. His tawny mane of hair, his crooked blade of a nose, his lips, too grim for a genuine smile. His green eyes, the kind that young women fell in love with.

It wasn't bad luck that had brought Max to Masterson Manor. Oh, no. Max had told her he made his own luck.

Well, so did she, and she didn't have to put up with this rat and his provocative remarks.

She smiled at the tourists in apparent benevolence, then turned to Max and in the tone of a lady of the manor dismissing a serf, said, "I don't require your help. You can go back to your odd jobs now."

Which should have put him very firmly in his place.

But Max looked at her, and something in his slight smile made her retreat.

He followed, draped his arm across her shoulders, and in a voice loud enough to stop every conversation, said, "But, darling, it's the last tour. We can tell them the truth." He looked over his head at the avid group. "Laurel and I are engaged to be married."

The Bed Wins All

MASTERSON MANOR, PRESENT DAY

CHAPTER 1

Furious, Laurel pulled away and swiveled to face Max.
Max, whose moss green eyes were watchful and wary.
"We are not engaged." She enunciated clearly, just in
case someone in the fascinated tour group was hard of hear-
ing. Or in case Max was, which he must be, because she'd
been saying this for two weeks.

He, too, used a crisp enunciation, and Englishmen always
won that game. "We should be."

The tourists gasped.

"Mom, does he mean they—" Brian pointed from one to
the other.

"I believe he does," Mrs. Plante answered.

Miss Ferguson whipped out her notebook and started
scribbling.

Laurel wanted to kill Max for making such a scene. "We're
not engaged, and I can't imagine two people with less in common."

"We've got one very important thing in common," Max
said.

Laurel narrowed her eyes as she glared.

Everyone leaned closer.

He gestured behind him. "This house."

The tourists exhaled in disgust.

"Not for long," Laurel snapped.

The outside door slammed as John and Meghan stepped back into the souvenir shop. Seeing the tense little group, Meghan stopped short. John bumped into her.

Everyone turned to look at them.

John's hair was mussed. Meghan's lips had that swollen, well-kissed appearance. Color climbed in both their faces, and they couldn't have looked more guilty.

They'd been outside kissing. They were always kissing, and smiling at each other, and holding hands. They were married, and they were in love.

And what did Laurel have? A duty-bound handyman chasing her around making fallacious claims on her ring finger.

"What's going on?" Meghan asked.

"Nothing's going on." Taking a long breath, Laurel turned to the fascinated tourists, and in her commanding, guidebook voice, said, "That completes your tour. Your bus is waiting." Striding briskly to the door, she opened it and relied on her standard, end-of-tour chatter. "It's a beautiful summer evening. I hope you enjoy your dinner, whatever it might be, and that the rest of your trip in England is delightful." As she talked, she walked toward the bus and they trailed after her, too polite to ask further questions—but their eyes gleamed with curiosity.

Curiosity destined to go unsatisfied. Max, smart man, had stayed inside, and Laurel waved the bus off alone. Turning toward the house, she stared up at its tall, white exterior. Masterson Manor was beautiful, a place where she could happily spend the rest of her life. But since that wasn't possible, she wished she could spend these last weeks in quiet communion with the house and its history.

But quiet communion was out of the question, and all because of that damned handyman. Max Ashton was a menace to her peace of mind. And, she reminded herself, it was all her fault.

That didn't make her any less grouchy.

Stalking into the souvenir shop, she slammed the door behind her. Unfortunately, Max missed her grand gesture. He'd slipped away to avoid her wrath.

That was just like him. Stir her up, then leave her to stew. Well, he wasn't getting away with it this time. They were going to have this out.

She locked the door, turned out the lights and headed to the place where she knew she would find Max. In the bedroom, working with his beloved tools.

But he wasn't working. He was stretched out full-length on the velvet counterpane, his arms tucked behind his head, his eyes closed, a big, dark, muscular, hairy pain in the rear who remained at Masterson Manor despite her repeated invitations to leave.

She ought to be feeling nostalgic and very much aware that this was the end of an era. Instead she could scarcely speak for outrage. "Get your boots off of that comforter."

Without opening his eyes, he smiled, and an amused curve played over his plush lips. "You sound like my mother."

"In fact, get off the bed."

His long lashes fluttered open, and he stared at her with that sexy, warm, bedroom look that reminded her, only too explicitly, of a moment when he'd stared like that and she'd gone into his arms. Like a lemming, she told herself, going over a cliff.

But sarcasm was no guard against the warmth that flooded her, bringing a flush to her cheeks, making her breasts ache with fullness, and down deep within her, that ache grew sharper. That ache never quite went away, no matter how much she ignored it. Her body wanted him.

But she was more than a body. She had quite a fine mind, one that was smart enough to recognize trouble stretched out, unmoving, before her. "Get off the bed." She didn't even know why it mattered so much. Perhaps it was because he looked so comfortable there, so at home, like some medieval knight weary from long days in the saddle.

She had to stop romanticizing this man. She had to concentrate on her grievances. "How dare you say that to the tourists?"

"You mean, tell them the truth?" He sat up on his elbows.

"We are not engaged. It is not the truth, and I don't even know why you want it to be. I can't think of one reason why you'd want to marry me."

He looked at her, just looked at her, long enough to make her nervous. "Can't you?" he asked softly.

Her stomach twisted in a combination of lust and . . . well, just lust. He'd always had that effect on her. And she . . . she knew better than to stand so close to him. He never hesitated to use the advantage size and strength gave him. "Why did you get yourself hired on here?"

"The Barrys advertised for a handyman." He shrugged smoothly. "I'm the best."

How could he lie like this? Right to her face? "You came here to be a handyman? To a wretched old house that ought to be bulldozed?" she asked sarcastically.

He glanced around. "I'm fixing it up."

She almost shrieked in frustration. "I was being sarcastic. The Masterson Manor is in beautiful shape."

"The plumbing is turn of the century, and I don't mean the twenty-first century."

Her hair fell around her face in wisps, and she blew at the

one that draped itself over her eye. "There is more to life than plumbing."

"You wouldn't say that if the loo didn't work." In the blink of an eye, he went from strictly practical back to their relationship. "I came to Cornwall because you were here."

"How romantic." Going to the window, she crossed her arms and stared out at the castle. "When I have a moment, I'll be impressed."

His low, deep, oh-so-English voice coaxed, "Why won't you give me a second chance?"

She whirled to face him. "For one thing—you're not a handyman."

"How can you say that?" He waved a hand at the box of tools on the floor. "Do you have complaints about my work?"

"Handymen do not buy antiques." And they'd met buying antiques. She'd been in Kent, chasing down a Victorian dressing table reputed to be originally from Masterson Manor, and he'd been seeking, well, just anything. He'd been abysmally ignorant of how to bid at an antique auction, and drove the prices up out of sight until she couldn't stand it anymore and offered to help him. She'd been doing a kindness—which went to prove that no good deed goes unpunished.

"You're a snob," he observed.

"If you were a handyman, you could buy antiques—but not for the prices you were paying." Where had his money come from? Why had he come here, now? She couldn't remain still. Not with these suspicions tormenting her. She paced back to the bed and stared down at him.

He stretched back out again, six feet two inches of confidence, strength, and proportioned muscles laid out for her inspection. "Fixing things pays very well."

"You're lying to me." She wanted to make a broad gesture, but she would have hit him with her hand. Which seemed like a good idea in theory, but in the two weeks he'd been here, she had been very very careful not to touch him in any way.

He had not been so scrupulous. He had taken her arm to help her stand, helped her clip her hair up. Little touches, nothing she could complain about, but irritating—and startling—to a woman who had been alone for too long.

"All right, I'll tell you the truth." He blinked at her with sleepy charm. "I'm a millionaire banker."

She wanted to grind her teeth. "Could you pick some middle ground?"

He ignored her derision and observed her, weighed her reactions, made her self-conscious about every blink, every grimace. "Is it so impossible that I'm a millionaire banker?"

"Yes. Millionaire bankers are smooth, suave, polite."

"I'm not polite?"

"Your manners are impeccable, as you very well know."

"Smooth? Suave?"

He was those things, too, but he had a rough edge to him, as if life hadn't always been easy. He was alert. He was wary. He seemed more like a predator than a banker or a handyman— and that frightened her. Carefully she chose her words. "I think if you were a millionaire banker, you would frighten your competitors to death."

He smiled, a slow, warm, approving smile that both warmed and alarmed her. "You're very astute. You're also tense. Why don't you rest on the bed with me?" Reaching over his head, he took the headboard in his hands. "I promise not to touch you."

Lying like this, he looked taller, broader, more tempting. His broad, big-boned wrists were too large for her to span with her fingers. She knew, because on *that* night she'd tried. She'd tried to touch him everywhere, drunk on the pleasure of throwing caution to the wind, of having a man beneath her to caress and explore. Color rose in her face, not just a smooth blush, but that prickly, uncomfortable kind of color that she knew turned her skin red and blotchy. Returning to the point she tried to make time and time again, she said, "We do not have a relationship."

"We slept together."

"Only once!"

"Actually . . ."

"Only one night." She gripped the bedpost and shook it. The sturdy old bed barely shivered. "A one-night stand does not a relationship make."

She saw his muscles bunch, realized her peril, but too late. Seizing her by the waist, he picked her up as if she were a petite thing, which she most certainly was not, and rolled her over the top of him and flat on her back in the middle of the bed. He lifted himself over her, the dominant male asserting himself over his woman.

He was so handsome. His broad cheekbones and wide chin were harsh and unyielding, but his mouth . . . she adored his mouth. Beautiful, rich, broad, the kind of mouth that promised a woman sensual satisfaction so intense . . . Laurel could scarcely catch her breath. The promise of that mouth had been fulfilled. She could have kissed him for hours . . . but then she would have missed all the other delights he had provided.

"I proposed," he said.

"Be still my heart." Which at his touch was pounding hard and irregularly.

"All right." His beautiful mouth was grim, his eyes serious. "It wasn't my finest moment, but I was in shock. I wasn't expecting a vir—"

She slapped her hand over his lips. "Do you have to keep saying that? Are virgins so rare in England?"

"You're the first one I've ever—"

"Yes, I know, or you'd already be married." She tried to roll away from him.

He wrapped her tighter against him.

"Your mother taught you never to debauch innocent young women, and to correct your mistakes when you make them, so 'Will you marry me, Laurel?'" As she quoted him, her mockery was fierce and scornful. She pretended to shiver. "Oo, I got a warm fuzzy from that proposal. I wonder how I had the presence of mind to turn it down."

"Have you thought that maybe it meant so much to me I botched it?"

"No."

"You're determined not to give an inch."

"If there are any inches to be given, they should come from you." At once she'd realized what she'd said, and closed her eyes against him.

For a long moment, he didn't say anything—she reluctantly gave him points for that—but then he stated, "Tonight I'll take you out for dinner."

Her eyes sprang open. "What?"

"I can't show you how willing I am to . . . cooperate if you won't go out with me."

"No."

"Then I'll stay in with you."

Persistence was his middle name. "Don't you get it? I'm not interested."

"If I believed that were true, I'd leave you alone. But we've got this." He swooped on her, kissing her with passion and a possessiveness that branded her as his. On that one night, he'd been a lover who had initiated her with such tenderness she'd spent all the time since wanting him. Fruitlessly, desperately wanting him. Now he took her mouth with the assurance of knowing he would be welcome. He held her beneath him, his leg draped over her hip, and tasted her, thrust his tongue into her mouth and demanded she answer him.

She did. She couldn't not. She'd waited for him all her life. As a lover, he was everything she'd ever dreamed of, and he was here. He was now. He kissed with the assurance that marked his every movement. Her hands crept up his chest, up his shoulders, into his hair. The straight strands were silk between her fingers as she held him to her. The scent of him enveloped her, setting her adrift in raw pleasure. His chest pressed against hers; his weight pushed her into the mattress. "My God, Laurel," he muttered against her lips. "How can you give this up?"

"We barely know each other," she whispered, but oh, how familiar and warm and wonderful this felt.

"Have dinner with me."

She was tempted. So tempted. Then . . .

"Here you two are!" Grace, the housekeeper, bustled in.

Laurel vaulted off the bed in a flurry of guilt and embarrassment. "Yes. Grace. What do you need?"

"I was just wondering where you wanted your tea—and I'd venture I got here just in the nick of time." The round-cheeked old lady frowned disapprovingly. She was tall, almost six foot, and raw-boned, but like every other grandmotherly-type in Trecombe she wore an apron over a blue flowered housedress, and stockings rolled down to her knees.

Kenneth, the butler, trailed along after her. "Maybe they want their tea in bed."

With a sniff, Grace announced, "I would not serve it there."

"Grace, you were young once, too." Kenneth was the same height as Grace, and was probably in his late sixties, too, but he hadn't aged well. Wrinkles scored his stubbled cheeks, his teeth were stained, and he walked as if each movement gave him pain. "A long time ago."

If Laurel left them alone, they'd start quarreling as only old enemies could do. "I'll take tea in the library," she said. "Mr. Ashton will take tea right here. He has a job to finish."

"She's a slavedriver," Max informed Grace.

"Aye, Mr. Max, but she's right. Everything's got to be done before the new owners arrive." Grace nodded over and over again, adoring Max as she had done since the first day he arrived. Max hadn't gone out of his way with the housekeeper; he'd just used his usual impeccable manners, opening doors, carrying loads, and escorting Grace back and forth from the village to the manor every day, and she rewarded him with worship. "I wouldn't want you to get a bad report. I'll bring your tea right to you."

Kenneth shot Laurel and Max a sharp glance. "It's not eating they're interested in."

Max sat up. "That's enough."

Kenneth glared.

Max stared him down.

With a snort, Kenneth shuffled out the door.

"Well!" Grace eyed Max with a new respect. "You're to be congratulated, sir. 'Tis not every man who can intimidate Kenneth." She nodded again. "I'll bring tea just as soon as I get the kettle boiling."

She bustled out, leaving Max and Laurel alone again. But this time the memory of that kiss was between them. Laurel shot him a glance, expecting to see an evil gleam of triumph. Instead, he watched her with all the intensity of a wolf who'd enjoyed the first taste of his prey. He didn't feel satisfaction at the first sign of her capitulation. He wouldn't be satisfied until he had his way about everything. Until she was in his bed, clinging to him, his ring on her finger and his body possessing hers.

Well, she might have suffered a moment of weakness, but he hadn't won yet. "Get your boots off the bed," she said.

"Yes, Ma'am." Standing, he walked toward her, and didn't stop until he stood toe to toe with her. Of course. She was willing to bet Max Ashton had never backed away from a challenge in his whole life. He wouldn't know how.

She stepped sideways until he no longer towered over her. "And get away from me."

He followed her, leaned down until his breath touched her face, and whispered, "Not ever."

CHAPTER 2

Y ou'll lock this door and set the security system as soon as we leave." Max didn't ask; he commanded.

"Yes. As I always do." Laurel would have snapped with quite a bit more irritation, but Grace hung with obvious adoration on Max's arm.

"I already checked the locks on the other doors and all the windows," he informed her.

Laurel hung on to her civility by the barest of threads. "Thank you."

"Max is right," Grace chirped. "You must keep yourself safe."

"And the antiques," Kenneth said in his hoarse, smoker's voice.

"Now, Kenneth, the contents of the house aren't as important as Miss Whitney's well-being. You know they aren't." Grace smiled and shook her head at Laurel. "Older men are so gruff, but he doesn't mean a thing by it."

Kenneth grunted and shuffled down the road.

Max looked at Laurel and repeated, "Lock the doors. Set the security system."

For the second time that day, Laurel slammed the door.

This time, she knew he'd heard her. But her satisfaction was short-lived. Max was standing on the other side, waiting to hear the solid clunk of the bolt in the lock, and she wanted so badly to wait him out.

But he wouldn't go away. He'd just come back in, and if she saw him one more time today, she would shriek like a frenzied cat. So she shot the bolt and set the security system, and told herself she should be grateful that he'd secured the other locks. The problem with Masterson Manor, the reason why it was so difficult to make safe, was that it boasted four different entrances—the servants' entrance into the kitchen, the door from the souvenir shop into the covered portico, the front door that led into the foyer, and a door that led from a narrow stairway into the bedroom that held the Masterson bed.

Heaven only knows which Masterson had added that, and why.

As she trudged to the kitchen and heated up the meal Grace had left her, she tried not to think that dinner with Max would have been entertaining and tasty . . . and would have ended up in bed. She'd already proved she had no resistance where he was concerned. She didn't need to test the matter again.

If only she hadn't kissed him as if he were the only man alive, or rather—the only man for her. Which, if she were truthful, he was. But what good was that when she was so obviously not the only woman for him?

He didn't talk about his past loves, but that meant only that he didn't kiss and tell. Of course there had been other women. A man didn't look like Max and walk like Max without suffering from a surfeit of lady friends to warm his bed. Laurel wouldn't care . . . if he loved her. But she was only a woman he took responsibility for.

Who would have thought in this day and age that a man would be cursed with such nineteenth-century values? According to her friends, guys didn't care about honor or commitment. In fact, the mere word commitment sent guys scurrying in the opposite direction.

Only Laurel, lucky Laurel, had discovered the one man who steadfastly believed in doing the right thing by a woman, even if the woman found the suggestion downright insulting.

Well. She had only two more weeks before the new owner appeared and she had to leave. She'd already started packing her belongings, and before long she'd be on to another location where she would find just as much information for her paper and feel just as much at home. Max would decide he had made a valiant effort, but since she still refused him, he was free to go his own way, and everything would be right with the world.

Somehow, that thought failed to cheer her.

By the time she'd cleaned up, checked the security system and the locks again, and located and hidden away each one of the valuable antiques in her care, darkness had fallen, and she was ready for bed. It was still early, a little before ten, but the emotional wear and tear of leading the last tour had taken its toll.

And the tussle with Max might have upset her a little, too.

In her bedroom, she strode to the window to shut the drapes and glanced out across the pitch black darkness that separated her from the castle and the cliff.

With a sharp intake of breath, she leaned into the window. There, up by the ruins, a red light was blinking.

The signal. Just like before.

Violence and fury rose and mixed in Laurel's head. She hated these thieves who sold their past for a profit. Every year, thousands of artifacts from every corner of the world disappeared into private collections, never to be seen again, and she wouldn't let it happen here.

At least—not again.

Her hand hovered over the telephone. Surely . . . but no. Last time she'd called the police, Frank Shelbourn had answered and he'd been worse than useless. He'd been insulting.

Catching up her navy blue windbreaker, her cell phone, and a flashlight, she headed down the stairs at top speed. Groping her way through the darkness, she found her way to the door. She set the security system, slipped out onto the terrace, and locked up.

The half-moon was low on the eastern horizon. Ragged clouds slipped across the sky, and the breeze blew off the ocean.

It was a perfect night for smuggling.

And for sneaking up on the smugglers. She set out across the field toward the castle, stubbing her toes on rocks and stumbling into rabbit holes. But she kept walking, her eyes fixed on that blinking red light. It seemed stationary. And . . . oh, look. There were two lights now. The second beam glowed steadily. It wasn't moving. It was white.

Had the smugglers left? Or were they watching out to sea as a small boat motored in, took the loot and motored out again?

Clutching her cell phone, she climbed the small hill to the tumbled ruins. Except for the sound of the waves, it was silent here: abandoned, ancient, dead. If there were ghosts in Trecombe, surely they resided here.

As she stepped into the midst of the ruins, she could hear nothing. Was someone standing in the shadow of a tall stone column and watching as she entered? Was she in danger of attack? The hair on the back of her neck rose, and she stepped into the deepest shadow she could find. The remains of the medieval tower rose above her, the rocks shaped and set by the hands of a workman long dead. She knew pieces of the tower walls littered the uneven ground. Grass grew liberally between them, and each step she took was hazardous.

As the moon rose, she scrutinized the cliff, but no figures stood silhouetted against the moonlight. Nothing moved in the ruins. Senses on alert, she worked her way toward the red light.

The large lamp rested on a grassy hummock just inside the wall and had been set to flash. The other light, a flashlight, had been placed on a broken column higher than she could reach.

She prowled the length and breadth of the castle, and found nothing. There was no one here. No one at all. At last she ventured out into the open and paced toward the blinking light. She reached out to flip the switch. Either she'd missed the smugglers, or—

An arm wrapped around her neck, tightened and lifted her off of her feet. "Got you!"

She screamed in pure fright.

"Laurel?" The arm fell away. "Bloody hell. Laurel!"

She leaped into the air, turning around to face her assailant—Max!—and came down on a stone, stumbling and falling backward in an ignominious heap.

He took one long step and stood over her, the red blinking of the light making him look like a demon at a stoplight. "What are you doing here?" He spoke quietly, shooting words at her.

She answered the same way. "What are *you* doing here?" Dressed all in black, like a thief or a . . . smuggler?

He embodied everything she feared.

He extended a black gloved hand.

She ignored it and scrambled upright, prepared to flee. "What *are* you doing here?"

As if sensing her intention, he clasped her upper arm. "I asked first."

She couldn't lie. What was the point? He held her, and he could outrun her. Her only hope was to play dumb. "I saw lights."

"You saw lights." He sounded patient, but he pulled her around the corner into a shadow so deep she could see nothing but the gleam of his eyes. "You came haring up here after admitting to your tourists that you knew smugglers still prowled this coast?"

"Yes."

"You put your life at risk because the smugglers are stealing England's national heritage?"

"It's true!"

He sounded cold, clear, resolute. "I ought to beat you for this."

"I beg your pardon!" She rubbed her already bruised rear. "You're the one who scared me. If there is violence to be done, I get to do it."

"I could have been one of the smugglers."

She hesitated a second.

"Hell and damnation." He took her shoulders. "You think I'm one of the smugglers!"

That crisp English scorn certainly drove her toward insanity, or at the least, rage, and she shrugged him away.

"It would serve you right if I was." Walking to the blinking light, he flipped it off.

She followed him; oddly enough, she felt safer close to him than alone.

"Do you have no sense of self-preservation?" he demanded.

"I do, so I brought . . . oh, no." She started groping at her pockets.

"What's the matter?"

"I dropped my cell phone."

The waves crashed against the beach below. The scent of the ocean filled the air. And Max's silence was awesome. "You thought if you stumbled on some smugglers, you'd be able to call the ambulance while you were bleeding to death because they'd shot you?"

"You're overreacting." And if he was a thief and a smuggler, he was hiding the fact well. Either that or he really wanted to marry her for her expertise at antiques.

She had to get a grip on her imagination. "I was supposed to call the police if I found smugglers."

"What bright soul suggested this to you?"

"Frank Shelbourn. The constable."

That shut Max up. She could see him in the moonlight, and his expression could only be called astonished. "Let me see if I've got this straight. The village constable told you to come up to the castle ruins, see if there were smugglers working in the area, and call him on your cell phone?"

"That's it."

"You must have misunderstood him."

She enjoyed setting Max straight. "Trust me. That was his idea, which came right after I reported having seen lights on the cliff and he accused me of having PMS-related hallucinations."

"My God." Max sounded awed.

"I love being a girl."

"I can see it carries previously unimagined difficulties." Leaning down, he picked something up and handed it to her.

It was her cell phone. She debated calling the police, then decided she was safer with Max than with the idiots in the village. She slipped her cell phone into her jacket pocket.

"Laurel, tell me the truth." He spoke slowly and carefully, as if he worried for her intelligence. "Have you realized the smugglers are stealing antiques from Masterson Manor?"

Her harsh breath was clearly audible in the silence.

"You have, then."

"But how did you know?"

Making his way to the outer edge of the castle, he looked out toward the sea. "Interpol."

"Interpol?" She fumbled for the cell phone again.

She could see his profile in the moonlight: sharply etched as stone, and as cold. "I've got a friend who works for them in France."

"A friend?" She invested the word with doubt and painstakingly dialed the emergency number.

"We went to Oxford together."

"A lowly handyman," she muttered.

"A millionaire banker," he corrected. "Dennis said objects from Masterson Manor are selling on the international market. He wanted to know what I intended to do about it."

She hesitated, her finger hovering above the *send* button. "Why would he call you?"

"Actually, we were chatting, and I told him I was involved with you, and he asked how well I knew you."

"And you told him we were engaged." Then Max's meaning sank in. "Why did he ask how well you knew me?"

"Because Interpol believes you're the one selling the antiques."

"Me?" She realized she had squawked, and in a lower tone, repeated, "Me?"

"You've got access, and a knowledge of what's valuable."

"My God." The pit of her stomach dropped to her toes. "I'm never going to get my thesis done."

"Your thesis?" He turned on her like an attacking beast. "If you don't clear yourself, you're going to jail."

"Don't be silly. I've got no money. If I'd sold those antiques, I'd have money."

"There are ways to hide profits."

"Millionaire banker." Come to think of it, in Somerset, he had looked like a millionaire banker on vacation. But he was a very good handyman, and millionaire bankers didn't know how to run electric cable.

Yet she had believed Max was not what he claimed. Could he be a government agent instead? Had he been following her in Somerset and lured her to speak to him? A horrible thought occurred to her, and she clutched at her chest. "Did you seduce me to get all my secrets?"

In that decisive British accent that made almost anything sound respectable, he said, "No, love, I seduced you to get in your knickers."

"You're . . . crude," she sputtered. Yet he sounded so amused, she was perversely comforted. "So you're not a spy?"

"No."

"And you're not a smuggler?"

"No. If I were a smuggler . . ."

His cold tone sent a chill up her spine. "Yes?"

"I would already have pushed you off the cliff."

Shivering, she zipped up her windbreaker. "You really have a way with words."

"Think about it. You're not Indiana Jones, and this stuff is not the Lost Ark."

"It's important!"

"The fate of the world does not depend on what happens to a sixteenth-century chalice. But the fate of my world does depend on you."

She didn't know what to say. Was he insinuating he . . . loved her? He certainly hadn't given her any indication of adoration before. Friendship, yes. An appreciation for her face and figure, certainly. Passion . . . oh, my, yes. But the man had been chary of showing affection, and she . . . she felt too much affection for him to settle for anything less.

Going to the second flashlight, he extinguished it and took it off of the column. "At least *this* eliminates you from the suspect lineup."

Alarmed by his grim satisfaction, she asked, "What do you mean?"

"You couldn't have got the flashlight up this high by yourself." He tucked it into his bag. "Whoever did this had to be a man. Come on. There's no one out here except us. We might as well go back to the manor." He took her arm firmly in his and they worked their way across the meadow. His head turned as he scanned the area; he was watching for more than just rabbit holes. He observed the terrain, scrutinized the manor, yet he spoke to her with every evidence of attention. "I really do make a lot of money."

"Okay." Where had that come from?

"I can support you very nicely."

Exasperated, she asked, "How do you do that?"

"What?"

"Turn every conversation to marriage." She stopped and faced him. "You're not solely responsible for what we did. You didn't rape me, you know."

His lips quirked in an unaccustomed smile, and he stroked his cheek with his fingers. "I know."

When he spoke in that deep, smooth, utterly male and satisfied voice, she remembered that night. The silky sheets, his warm, welcoming body, his male scent enveloping her. The madness of passion, the pain, and the slow rebuilding of desire as he brought her back to him, over and over, until she moaned with the agony and the pleasure. When she thought about that night, she suffered such an ache in the area of her heart, she could scarcely breathe. She wanted to fling herself into his arms and beg that he satisfy all the glorious urgings of her body.

But she'd done that once and it had proved disastrous. No one could say Laurel Whitney didn't learn from her mistakes. "All this talk about virgins and marriage is nonsense. We enjoyed a night of mutually pleasurable passion, and the fact I was untried is immaterial." She lifted her chin. "Everyone has to have a first time. Even you, Mr. Ashton."

"Yes, but mine was at home—alone."

She gurgled with surprised laughter. How did he do that? She was standing on her dignity, making good points of logic, and he made her laugh. It wasn't fair—and at the same time, she knew that, no matter what she said or how eloquently she made her point, he would pay her no heed. He adhered to some archaic moral code which said a man married a virgin he had despoiled, and by God he would marry her, whether she wished it or not.

The problem was . . . she did wish it.

She loved him.

She started back toward Masterson Manor.

With a considerable lowering of spirits, she admitted she loved him, or she would never have slept with him. She loved the way he listened when she lectured about history. She loved that air of command that worked so well on hoteliers and maître d's. She loved the way he dressed, the way he looked, the way he smelled . . . she shouldn't think about those things or she'd fling herself at him and he'd know he'd won. She was not going to be married because of her maidenhead or lack of one.

She flung back at him, "Millionaire banker or handyman, I wouldn't marry you for your money."

He caught up with her and took her arm once more. "I know. That makes you all the more attractive."

"I'm not trying to make myself attractive to you!" The manor loomed before them.

"And yet you succeed at every turn." He led her toward the front of the house where the shadows were deeper.

The gravel walk crunched beneath their feet. The nicotiana blossoms gave up their strong, sweet scent. Max and Laurel mounted the steps.

Lowering his already quiet voice, he said, "Give me the key."

She knew why he wanted it, and as she pulled her key out of her pocket, she said, "I can open the door myself."

He caught her hand. "No, you can't."

"Listen—"

"Did it never occur to you that those lights might have been a diversion to get you out of the manor while thieves stole the rest of the valuables?"

"Yes." That had occurred to her up at the castle, right before he'd grabbed her. "The burglars might be in there now. We should call the police, not go in ourselves."

"I wouldn't call the local constables to catch a stray dog."

One other possibility existed. "Constable Shelbourn might be in on the take."

"There is that."

Obviously, he already suspected that. Perhaps he hadn't wanted to frighten her, and if she had good sense, she would be frightened. Instead, the thought made her furious. If it was true, if Shelbourn was part of a smuggling ring, she wanted nothing more than to thwart him and drag him to justice.

But Max made her just as angry—and twice as worried. "Why should I let you go in and risk your life alone?"

Wrapping his arms around her waist, he leaned against the wall and pulled her so that her whole body rested against his. "Because I'm your man and you're my woman, and I will protect you, whether you wish me to or not."

Her hands pressed against his shoulders, her head tilted up toward his.

He kissed her, without hesitation, without a single doubt about his welcome. He opened her lips and made himself at home.

She pushed against him, tried to get away—and collapsed against the wall in a heap of tangled emotions. He tasted so good, like fragrant wine and rich cakes and desperate passion. He wrapped her in warmth, his body radiating heat like a furnace. Her hands kneaded his shoulders, her breasts pressed against his chest.

How many weeks had it been since she'd left him? Weeks of tossing in her lonely bed, remembering his touch, his taste, the way he brought her to completion again and again. She'd been shy. He'd been bold, insistent, demanding everything from her and receiving everything . . . and more. All his skill and all her desire conspired against her then, as it conspired against her now.

Right now, if he chose, he could strip off her slacks and take her against the wall.

When her knees had collapsed and she was nothing but a puddle of desperately unsatisfied womanhood, he kissed her one last time. "Now tell me the security code and give me the key."

CHAPTER 3

Laurel still hesitated, and Max wanted to shake her. But he was learning that Laurel would not be coerced, and for a man used to having his own way, it was a hard lesson indeed. Placing one hand on the wall on either side of her head, he leaned close enough to whisper in her ear, "Humor me. If you go in there with me, I wouldn't protect myself, I'd protect you."

"Humph." She pushed his head aside and dropped the key into his shirt pocket. "Be careful."

He would have been happier if her wish hadn't been so plainly torn from her by guilt. "I might go in there and never come out." He bent down, his lips almost touching hers. "Make a man's last moments memorable."

She ducked out from under his arm. "Go away."

He grinned. She made him happy in a way he hadn't been since . . . well, he didn't ever remember being so happy. She was smart and funny, passionate and dedicated to her work. And he wanted a little of that passion and that dedication for himself. He would win her. He would have her. But first, he had to discover who was making her life hell by stealing from Masterson Manor—and from him.

For Masterson Manor was his house. That was why he'd been at an antique auction. That was why he'd met Laurel. That was why Dennis had called from Interpol to tell him about the smugglers.

Max was the mysterious new owner.

Moving with a stealth he'd learned in his early years on the rough side of town, he set the key in the lock. He turned it. The latch clicked; it had been locked, and he breathed a sigh of relief. Perhaps whoever had set those lights hadn't had time to get into the manor . . . or maybe they'd come in a different door. Stepping inside, he checked the security system. Everything was blinking. Everything looked normal.

But the security system was at least five years old, antiquated as only old technology could be. If he had a readout of who had entered, and when, and a video record . . . he'd already ordered the new system. It would be in place as soon as he took possession.

Silently he moved through the empty rooms, looking for an intruder or evidence of one. When he confirmed no one was in the house, he stripped off his gloves and thrust them in his pocket. Flipping open his cell phone, he punched in a number.

A very grouchy French-accented voice answered.

Max grinned. "Dennis, old man, did I wake you?"

"Max? Whatever it is, couldn't it have waited until tomorrow? I have a lovely *jeune fille* here, awaiting my attentions."

"She'll thank me for the call. You Frenchmen always hurry these delicate matters along."

Dennis's snort was both Gallic and expressive. "This had better be good."

"It is." Max told him about the evening, about seeing the lights at the castle, about finding Laurel and no other sign of smugglers. Most important, he told Dennis about Constable Frank Shelbourn and his outrageous suggestion that Laurel investigate the smugglers herself.

In a second, Dennis went from disgruntled lover to professional investigator. "His name again? Frank Shelbourn, heh? Ask your Laurel if he has the code for the security system. The actual key he doesn't need; the police have picklock tools. He's in a good position to smuggle things out of the country, too. Yes . . . very interesting. I'll check this out and be back with you tomorrow." His voice grew sly and teasing. "If he is the culprit, your Laurel is off the hook, *oui?* Will I be dancing at your wedding soon?"

Max hesitated an instant too long.

"Non?" Dennis shouted with laughter. "She doesn't want you?"

"Shut up and find out about Shelbourn."

"I will." Dennis sobered. "In the meantime, you'd better keep an eye on your darling *demoiselle."*

"Believe me. I have no intention of leaving her alone." Max cut the connection and went back to the front door for Laurel. Damn Dennis and his sense of humor. He'd better come through, and fast. Max wanted this riddle solved and their safety ensured so he could concentrate on Laurel to the exclusion of all else. Sweet, defiant, lovely Laurel, who stood huddled against the wall, her arms wrapped around her chest, her head down.

He turned on the lights.

Her head jerked up.

"Come in." He held the door. "No one's here."

She gave a sigh of relief. "Good."

As she passed in front of him, he experienced a flash of satisfaction so intense, it took his breath away. *His* woman, willingly stepping across the threshold into *his* house. Did she know what this meant to him? No, of course she didn't. She didn't know . . . so much.

He wouldn't tell her, either. The pain of his early years were not to be shared. He had put those memories aside, and instead concentrated on the present and the future. Eventually she'd realize he was telling the truth about his profession, and perhaps she'd be pleased. Perhaps not—Laurel would be just as happy being the wife of a handyman as a banker. Possibly happier, for he didn't imagine she would enjoy the social events he was required to attend. But if he had to, he would bribe her with the house and all the money she needed to restore it to its original glory, and the time to work on her thesis.

No, it wasn't necessary for him to tell Laurel about his past, for surely she would despise him.

He must have been staring at her like Dracula at his next victim, for she backed away from him. "Why are you looking at me like that?"

Glibly, he answered, "Because you look so beautiful."

She rolled her eyes. "Sure." Stripping off her windbreaker, she tossed it on a chair. Then she did the female thing, the one which drove him wild with desire. Loosening the clip from her hair, she shook the long, straight, shining black locks free. The strands floated about her face. Lifting her arms, she caught up the exquisite mass, twisted it into a knot, and displayed all the sleekness of her body for his pleasure. He wanted to take advantage of her vulnerability. He wanted to wrap his arms around her waist and pull her against him, kiss her long neck, slide his hands under her sweater . . .

All unaware, she fastened her hair and dropped her arms. "So no one has been in here tonight."

Shaken from his fantasy, he was crisp, like a man waking from a sound sleep. "Many pieces are missing."

Smiling, she shook her head. "No, they're not. Or—at

least—not the smaller pieces. I put away the ones I could lift."

Charmed, relieved, he asked, "Did you?"

"I've been doing it every night since I realized . . ." She strolled toward the stairway. "I feel so stupid. I didn't grasp what was happening until I did an inventory for the new owners."

"Three weeks ago."

She whirled on him. "How do you know that?"

"That's when the Barrys asked me to work for them." He raised his eyebrows with mock innocence. "No one does repair work until they've sold the house."

Leaning against the Regency era table, she scrutinized him, her long lashes drooping over her blue eyes. The oversized cream-colored cashmere sweater clung in all the right spots. Her navy slacks hugged her thighs.

She was still suspicious, poor lass, wondering who her real friends were. If all went well, by tomorrow night she would know. Sliding his arm around her waist, he turned her back toward the stairs. "But how clever you are to hide the antiques!"

She went reluctantly. "What else could I do? The Barrys depended on me, and I've failed them. I had to save what I could. I have to try to find out who is stealing so many irreplaceable objects."

If he weren't careful, her sense of responsibility would get her killed. "Who has the key and code for the security system?" he asked.

"Too many people. The Barrys, of course. Kenneth and Grace."

Of course. The servants were so often at the heart of these robberies. "They both live in Trecombe," he said, "and they have the advantage of knowing where everything is and what it's worth. It would be easy enough for one of them to come back here and take what they wanted."

"That's an awful thought!" Laurel's eyes flashed with indignation. "Grace is sweet, if a little too fond of sermonizing—"

"She never sermonizes to me."

"You're a man. She thinks you're perfect." Clearly, Laurel didn't suffer from that misapprehension. "Kenneth is . . . well, surely he's too old to steal."

"You *are* a babe if you believe that. Who else has a key?"

"Father Ellis at the church."

"Unlikely." Father Ellis's arthritis made it hard for him to walk.

They reached the stairway. "And the police," she said.

"Our likeliest suspect." He made to start up the stairs with her.

She halted, her hand on the banister. "Where do you think you're going?"

"Upstairs." He tried to urge her along.

Her eyes turned from blue to a flinty gray. "Not with me, you're not."

Tonight, she had lost the right to make that decision. "If you like, you can keep your almost virgin bed. Although . . . I am of course available should you change your mind."

"You're not staying here."

He'd perfected a facial expression that he used to ruthlessly quash unruly board members. He donned it now, and lowered his voice to a menacing whisper. "Do you have any idea how angry I am that you knew about the robberies, and you stayed here, alone, at night, anyway?"

She climbed the first step, as if wanting the advantage the extra height would give her. "If I'd abandoned my post, the thieves would never be apprehended."

"And you, my pet, would be out of harm's way." She still

wasn't taller than he was, and he moved in on her, letting her see how his eyes gleamed with fury. "Do you think I give a damn about the antiquities in this house, or any other, when compared to your safety?"

"You would care if they were yours."

He gripped the banister until his knuckles turned white.

She backed up another step.

He followed, crowding her, furious that she thought he would dismiss her safety in the interests of ownership.

She took another step, and another.

He followed, pushing upward, step by step, until they reached the landing. Taking her shoulders, he lifted her onto her toes and stared straight into her wary blue eyes. "Find me a bedroom. I'm moving in."

CHAPTER 4

The great hall, a remnant of Masterson Manor's medieval origins, stretched the length of the center wing. Its high ceilings soared out of sight, the tall windows were impossible to clean, and the fireplace stood taller than Max. The morning sun slipped through the east windows, slanting its light across the long, narrow banquet table where, every morning at precisely eight o'clock, Kenneth and Grace served breakfast to Laurel.

But this morning, although Laurel sat at her usual place in the master's chair at the end of the table, Max sat at her right hand, looking wide-awake and disgustingly cheerful. Of course, he would, Laurel thought sourly. He had got his own way.

"I don't approve, miss." Grace stood beside Laurel's chair, her hands wrapped in her apron, her spine stiff. "A young man and a young woman, living here with nary a soul to chaperone them. It's not proper, it's not."

Before Laurel could answer her, Max usurped the conversation. "We're in love, Miss Grace. We're going to get married."

Laurel opened her mouth to deny it.

Max laid his hand over hers and squeezed, and smiled at her with every outward appearance of affection. Only Laurel saw the warning glint in his eyes. This was his plan. He would move in, claim they were madly in love and preparing to marry, when in reality he'd be protecting her life. She hadn't liked it. She had forcefully protested, but he had been positively menacing about the risks she'd taken with her life. Last night, capitulation had seemed the better part of valor.

This morning, dislodging him was impossible.

"In my day"—Grace was still talking to Laurel—"young people waited until the ceremony to live together."

Kenneth arrived in time to hear Grace's comment. He set a steaming basket of scones between Max and Laurel, and said, "In your day, Moses was a whippersnapper." Flinging back his head, he wheezed with laughter.

"Very funny," Grace huffed. "A hot scone, Mr. Max?"

Laurel wanted to shriek. The housekeeper reproached her as if she were the one responsible for Max's residing here, which *she* most certainly was not, and at the same time urged food on Max as if he were totally innocent, which *he* most certainly was not.

"Current scones, heh, Miss Grace?" Max helped himself to one. "My favorite."

"I know, sir. I baked them just for you."

"No one does them better. It's a marvelous breakfast." He gazed at the sausages, the porridge, the sliced peaches clotted cream, the homemade raspberry jam in a silver pot. "I haven't seen a spread like this since the last time I visited my mother."

Laurel hadn't either. Grace didn't prepare meals like this for Laurel.

Grace beamed. "I like to see a young man with a good appetite."

"She's been cooking since five-thirty this morning," Kenneth groused. "Bloody pain, she is."

Ignoring him, Grace patted Laurel on the shoulder. "If you can actually catch Mr. Max, Miss Laurel, you'll have a good man."

"Based on his appetite?" Laurel watched Max take a bowl of porridge and sprinkle it with sugar.

"There's nothing wan about this one. He's hearty. He'll last. He'll breed well." Grace sighed heavily. "But why should he buy the cow when he's getting the cream for free?"

Max choked on a slice of peach.

Kenneth smacked him vigorously on the back.

Laurel could scarcely contain her irritation. "I put him in the lavender bedroom, and that's where he's sleeping."

"It's true, Grace." Max waved Kenneth away, took Laurel's hand again, and this time he raised it to his lips and pressed a kiss on her knuckles. "I am."

"Oh, that'll convince her," Laurel muttered.

Kenneth cackled.

Max wore the same black shirt and jeans he'd worn last night, and he rubbed his hand over the golden stubble on his chin. "I have to go collect my clothes this morning. They're still at the inn."

Couldn't the man be grumpy in the morning, or have bad breath? For rumpled or not, stubbled or not, he still looked too damned fine for Laurel's comfort.

"Remember, Miss Laurel, temptation is ever present in the weak," Grace pronounced.

"Amen," Laurel agreed silently.

Lifting one of the silver covers, Grace said, "Try the manor eggs with haddock, Mr. Max. They've got fresh tarragon in them."

"Um, marvelous." He spooned some on Laurel's plate first, then on his own.

Laurel knew better than to say she hated tarragon.

"There's gammon," Grace said, "and leftover steak and kidney pie."

Suffering from a surfeit of both food and advice, Laurel said, "Thank you, Grace, Kenneth. That will be all." She waited only until they'd left the room before looking menacingly at Max and tapping her spoon on the table in an aggravated motion.

"Grace is a lovely person," Max said. "Kenneth . . . is not."

Laurel didn't answer; she just kept tapping. Nothing could muffle the clink of her silverware: not the velvet draperies, plush antique rugs, nor ancient, the smoke-encrusted wood beams.

"All right." Max put down his fork. "I apologize."

"For what?" For which of his many perfidies was he apologizing?

"For whatever it is you're irate about."

He didn't even know, and that made her angrier.

"Because Grace likes men better than women," he speculated. "Because you don't like scones with currants."

Laurel smacked the spoon onto the table. "Guess again."

He gazed directly at her. "I won't apologize for telling them we're engaged. That's the course we agreed on last night."

"*We* did not agree on that. You took over just because you thought . . . you said you thought I was in danger."

"What other reason would I have for insisting that I stay in this house with you?" He grinned. "Beside the chance to lead you into temptation?"

She ignored that as she had resolved to ignore any and all sexual allusions. "I do everything to make the house secure, so I'm safe."

"Treasures are disappearing, so you are not safe."

She ignored that, too. Better not to get in a quarrel with Max. He had a tendency to win. "I don't understand how someone is stealing my antiques. That's why I went out last night, or at least one of the reasons."

"You're not going to convince me that your going out at night when thieves are abroad is a good idea."

Forgetting she didn't want to quarrel, she snapped, "I don't care if I convince you of anything. I'm paid to housesit at Masterson Manor. Artifacts are disappearing while under my care, and my professional reputation will be ruined." Gloomily, she said, "I'll never get another job."

He stroked her arm, a long, slow caress that gave her goosebumps. "Once we've found our burglar, you'll be known as the historian who broke up the smuggling ring."

She hadn't thought of it that way. She might acquire a good reputation out of this mess, after all. Shaking off his touch, she tasted the porridge.

Which apparently irritated him, for his tone got low and menacing. "But you *are* a professional. You know what goes on in the world of smuggling. You know people kill for these things, and yet when I think you went out there looking for trouble . . ." He was breathing hard. His eyes glowed green. "You're lucky I haven't set up camp in your bedroom where I can watch you all night long."

She stared at him and wished she could insist that she wasn't in danger. But she was—although not from the thief.

She was in danger from Max.

She couldn't believe it. She'd kissed Max. And not just kissed him. She'd embraced him. She'd clutched at him. She'd stuck her tongue in his mouth and accepted his into hers. Women who were trying to discourage a prospective husband did not act like that. Men with Max's determination and drive would view such acts as a positive sign.

Men like Max would view the fact that she was breathing as a positive sign.

She had to stop thinking about him.

Why had she kissed him? She was supposed to be smart enough to resist him. And she had. These last two weeks, she'd ignored his deep rumbly voice, his green, bedroom eyes, watching, always watching her, with a kind of flattering hunger . . .

Yes, she'd done a good job of ignoring him . . . until they'd kissed.

She had to stop thinking about him, about those beautiful, magnificent kisses and the wonderful time they'd had in Kent. But how could she?

Especially when it seemed he was thinking about the same thing—or perhaps he saw the involuntary softening in her expression. "You can't blame me for caring. I'll never forget the first time I noticed you. We were at that antique auction and you made that throat-cutting gesture at me."

Without meaning to, she relaxed. "You were driving the prices out of sight."

"You were staring at me as if I were insane." He chuckled, a deep, affectionate chuckle that made her toes curl in her shoes.

"You were insane. Everyone recognizes that wild look people get the first time they bid. And you were bidding on that horrible tablecloth." She shook her head. "It was from the fifties, for pete's sake!"

"The eighteen fifties?"

"The nineteen fifties. It was vinyl. How many vinyl table-cloths did they make in the . . ." She saw his smirk, and sighed. "You're pulling my leg."

What was she doing, indulging in memories and banter with him? She was pretty sure his scent got to her, weakening her resolve, making her receptive to him. He used mint shampoo, and lately, whenever he walked past her, she caught an enticing whiff of mint.

But more than that was just how his skin smelled. Those three days when they'd traveled from auction to shop, she'd wanted to bury her nose in his chest and just breathe. He smelled warm and fresh and there was always that faint promise of . . . oh, she didn't know . . . hot sex. Pheromones, she supposed. Little tiny pointy chemical hormones that signaled he was a prime candidate for mating, and each point aimed right at her.

She pinched the bridge of her nose. What was she going to do about him? She was leaving Masterson Manor soon, but she didn't make the mistake of assuming he would just go away. He might not love her, but she loved him, and the danger was—she was starting to think she should marry him. Surely, if she loved him hard enough, he'd come to love her.

She grimaced. And that was every ex-wife's worst mistake. Assuming she could change the man she married.

"Try the scone." Breaking off a piece, he held it to her lips until she opened her mouth and accepted it.

"Good," she mumbled.

He watched her chew as if the sight of her eating his food gave him some weird satisfaction. "I remember everything you taught me about antiques," he said.

She swallowed. "Someone had to take you in hand."

"I'm glad it was you." He looked as if he were going to place a slice of peach in her mouth.

Hastily she filled her mouth with sausage.

He leaned close enough to speak softly. "Today, when I go into the village, I'm going to spread the word around that the owner asked that I change the security code and the locks. That will put pressure on our thief. So here's the important question—if this is his last chance, what will he steal?"

She didn't hesitate. "St. Albion's cross." She pictured the glittering cross in her mind. "Although it's heavy, it's transportable and by far the most valuable of all those pieces."

"Why haven't they taken it before?"

"It would immediately be missed. It holds a position of prominence by the Masterson bed. It even has a spotlight shining directly on it."

"All right." He pushed a wisp of hair off of her cheek. "The cross will be safe, I promise you."

"How? Who . . .?"

"I'll tell you tonight. Try not to worry. I'm not going to disappoint you. I know your passion."

Wary and confused, she sat back.

He pretended not to notice. "After all, I spent three days with you, digging around through every barn and auction for miles. When you talk about history and antiquities, you burn with a most glorious fire."

His amusement was almost insulting. "I love antiques. You don't." She asked the question that had bothered her ever since she had met him. "So why were you collecting them?"

"Do you still think I'm one of the smugglers?"

"No. As you rightly pointed out last night, if you were, you would have killed me." And he didn't look as if he wanted to kill her. More like he wanted to eat her.

He tilted her cheek toward the light. "You're blushing quite delightfully. What are you thinking?"

What was *he* thinking? Where was he from? This last twenty-four hours had made her realize how little she knew about him. For those three days as they moved from auction to art gallery, he had asked her questions about herself, but when she asked him, he turned the subject. He'd just done it again. She'd asked him why he was collecting antiques. He'd answered a question with a question.

"Since I love antiques so much, why are you so sure I wouldn't steal them?" she asked.

"You have morals."

"Most people have morals."

"Um . . . some people have some morals." Leaning back in his chair, he sipped his hot chocolate. "But how many twenty-four-year-old virgins are there in England?"

"One less," she snapped.

Softly, seductively, he said, "Let me make an honest woman out of you."

She took in a deep breath to blast him, then let it go with an exasperated sigh. Max was impervious to slights, to hints, to direct frontal attacks. "I'm as honest as I ever was." Pushing back her chair, she stood. "And I intend to stay that way."

CHAPTER 5

It's not right, Miss Laurel. It's not proper, that's all I know, and your mother would be horrified if she knew." Grace fired her parting shot before she shuffled down the road toward the village. She'd stalled until long after serving them dinner, trying every tactic imaginable to dislodge Max.

Naturally, nothing had worked on him.

But Laurel knew she was right; her mother *would* be horrified if she knew.

Kenneth leered at the couple standing in the doorway. "Don't pay any attention to the old besom. You two just spend the evening doing what young people do." He headed down the road, too, then turned and added, "Might as well. Everyone in the village is gossiping about it."

Laurel stabbed her elbow into Max's side to remove him. As his arm dropped from her shoulders, she said, "Great. I've always wanted to be the whore of Babylon."

Max sounded patient. Overly patient, to Laurel's intolerant ears. "No one thinks you're the whore of Babylon."

"Grace does."

"Well . . . yes. But all the other ladies in the village think you've done very well for yourself."

She faced him. The setting sun gilded his tawny hair and turned his green eyes to a beautiful moss, and sculpted his face with the sheen of a precious metal. He was smiling, a whimsical smile that put a cleft in his cheek and, no doubt, charmed women for miles. "That's what I like about you. You don't suffer from a lack of conceit."

"A man should know his worth." He slipped his arm over her shoulders again and hugged her to him. "Women like a man who can unstop a toilet."

"Yes, and run a bank, too."

"That, too."

She debated jabbing him with her elbow again. He was leading her down the corridor, and she rather resentfully noted how often and well he guided her wherever he wanted her to go. He was like a stallion, herding his chosen mare. "What are we doing?" she asked.

He raised his brows at her truculent tone. "Going to the library. Isn't that where you spend your evenings?"

Of course he was right, and that didn't make her any happier. She'd spent the day sorting through the Masterson papers, making lists, trying to decide which of the diaries and accounts would be most important to her thesis. She was ready to relax—but how could she relax with Max in the house?

Oh, and the smugglers on the prowl, too. How could she have forgotten the smugglers?

Then, as Laurel stepped through the door of the library, she felt the room embrace her. Going to the lamps that stood in every corner and by every chair, she turned them on and, as night deepened outside, warm highlights shone off the light oak shelves that rose from floor to ceiling. So many of these dusty volumes had yielded their knowledge to her. Thousands of books filled the shelves, some so old she handled them with the care of a child for her beloved grandmother. Others were brand-new, kick-your-heels-back adult fiction, made for whiling away an evening. Of course Harry Potter had his own shelf. Here and there, a painting hung on the wall or a spun glass vase reflected the light. She slithered into the depths of the great, over-stuffed chair she had commandeered as her own, and sighed.

Max stood, hands on hips, watching her with a satisfaction that reminded her of last night. Why did he like seeing her here in Masterson Manor? What perverse happiness did he get from seeing her cross the threshold in this domain? In witnessing her pleasure in the homiest of the library? She didn't understand anything about him. He was a different kind of man than she'd ever met before. Perhaps that was why she loved him. Certainly that was why she couldn't marry him. One didn't marry a man one didn't know.

He cleaned up well. When he wore his well-worn, faded-to-white jeans and denim shirt, and a tool belt sat low on his hips, he looked like every wife's dream of a handyman; qualified to perform any repair, capable of cleaning up after himself, and given to taking off his shirt if the heat got too much.

In more formal wear, he looked like every woman's dream date, with shoulders broad enough and pectorals big enough to be identified through his shirt, beautiful long legs, and the kind of sincere, commanding smile that made for polar cap meltdown. He wore black again this evening; black slacks, this time, and a black short-sleeved silk sweater that clung to his shoulders and proved decisively that he lifted weights. Add to that the damp, combed-back blond hair, and his fresh washed scent of soap and sex appeal, and he made an irresistible package.

She took a long breath. She would resist.

She wore her softest gray workout pants, drawstring tied at her waist, a sleeveless blue zip-up sweatshirt, and no shoes. She was no match for his elegance, but then, she didn't want to be. "Are you going to chase after smugglers?" she asked.

"Why do you ask?"

He had answered a question with a question, not providing information, yet diverting her attention. Or rather . . . always before he had diverted her attention. "You're wearing black."

He looked down at himself. "I live in London. Everyone wears black there."

"So they do." Still no answer to her query. *What was going on?* She stood. "You know, I don't think I'll sit here tonight. I think I'll wander around the house—"

He moved to block her. "No!"

She put her hand on her hip and jutted it out. "No? Why not?"

His eyes narrowed.

"Are you perhaps a smuggler after all?"

"Do you think I am?"

"I think you are an expert at evading my questions, and why you imagine I would marry someone about whom I know nothing, I can't imagine." She could see him thinking, weighing his options, trying to decide how to handle this situation. How to handle her. "When you and I spent those three days together, I told you everything about myself. About my parents in Idaho, about going to school in California, about getting my degree. I told you that this was my dream job. I told you all my hopes and dreams for the future."

With a whimsical smile, he said, "Those were the best three days of my life."

He was trying to cajole her. She wasn't interested. "You told me nothing."

"I knew about myself. I wanted to know about you."

She moved past him.

He caught her arm. He didn't move, but she could see him choosing his words. "I really am a banker."

She looked at his hand, then looked at him, eyebrows raised. "I suspected that."

He was a smart man who comprehended very well that she was blackmailing him. She wanted an exchange of information for her continued presence in the library. She could see him weighing the consequences and deciding on his course.

"I was born in Liverpool thirty-two years ago." All expression smoothed from his face. "My parents weren't married. My father abandoned my mother before I was even born."

The clock ticked. Around the casement windows, the breeze off the ocean whistled softly. He looked straight into her face, waiting patiently for her to . . . to what? To reject him because of what he had been subjected to in his childhood—the laughter of other children, the taunting of relatives, and poverty, no doubt, for raising a child alone was difficult in any city, in any land.

And he knew Laurel's childhood had been ordinary. Positively homespun. A mother and father, a farm with haystacks and barnyards, a school bus, a lunch bucket. Public school and college, and always the unending support of both parents.

Well. At least now she knew why he didn't talk about his past. But she didn't show sympathy. He didn't want that. In fact, she would have sworn he feared her pity more than her scorn. Quietly, afraid she might drive him away with the wrong tone, the wrong words, she said, "That must have been rough for you."

He let out his breath. "Won't you sit down?"

She did, walking back to her favorite overstuffed chair.

He opened the wine cabinet. "Could I get you something to drink?"

"A pinot noir would be lovely."

Kneeling, he rummaged through the bottles. "I was tough. I was okay. But we were poor. You can't imagine how poor we were. Without a pot to pee in or a window to throw it out of, my mother used to say." He laughed, but there was no merriment in the sound. "She's a good woman. Too good for that kind of treatment."

"Oh." Oh. No wonder he was so insistent that she marry him. His mother had been an innocent, abandoned by her lover. Max would not be a man like his father.

Max brought forth a bottle and after an examination of the label, he pulled the cork with an elegant twist of his wrist. "All my childhood she worked too hard, trying to put money away so I could have a chance in the world. All she wanted was for me to go to university and make something of myself." He poured a bit in one glass, lifted the ruby liquid to the light, sniffed it, and tasted. "I think you'll like this."

Laurel accepted the glass he offered. "Does your father know who you are? What you've become?"

"He's dead. Killed, thrown from a horse during a foxhunt. He was a minor aristocrat, you see, impoverished but far too good for my mother, or me." Max sneered as elegantly as any English aristocrat who ever graced a portrait.

"He was stupid, then," Laurel said briskly.

Max blinked as if taken aback.

"Your mother must be very proud of you."

"So she is. I bought her a house. I was going to get her a place in the country, but she said no, she liked London. She's lived in a city all her life, and she'd miss it." He chuckled, and pulled one of the upright wooden chairs to sit right in front of

Laurel. He seated himself. "She likes to check up on me. She's quite a character." He lifted his glass in a toast.

Laurel loved the look of pride and affection that lit his features. She clinked her glass against his. "I'd like to meet her." Before he could make anything of that, she asked, "How did a banker learn to be a handyman?"

"I learned to be a handyman first. When I was a lad, I worked to help out."

Yes, he would work from the moment he was big enough. Anything to help his mother. The man burned with ambition. Laurel sipped the wine. Lean, ripe, and tasting of currant and cherry, it was just what she needed as she struggled between jubilation and dismay. Jubilation that he trusted her enough to tell her about himself. Dismay that her heart was melting.

She had wanted to know about him. She had needed to know about his past and why he was the way he was. Now . . . now it seemed indulging her curiosity was not such a good idea. The things he had told her about himself only made him more attractive. The expression on his face, that wariness, as if past experience had taught him to expect rejection . . . as if he expected her to turn from him with disgust, when in fact his confession had done nothing more than make her admire him more than ever. "Are you really a millionaire?"

"What do you think?"

"I think . . . you're a multimillionaire."

"And I think you're smart."

She loved him. She loved his face, his body . . . his expression, his character . . . but she couldn't marry him. Not for *that* reason. She didn't know how to say it with any finesse, so finally she just blurted, "I'm not pregnant, if that's what you're worried about."

Very gently, he said, "If you were pregnant, I would be very upset with some quite famous pharmaceutical companies. I take extensive precautions."

"Oh. Of course you do." He wouldn't take a chance of fathering an illegitimate child of his own. She stared down at the wine. "Do you . . . like children?"

"Very much. I'd like to have kids someday. When I'm married." He moved his chair closer, until his knees touched hers. "Laurel." His voice ached with longing.

Like the fool she was, she responded. She placed her glass on the end table. She took his glass and put it beside hers. Leaning forward, she took his face in her hands, and she kissed him. This was not simple lust. She put her heart into that kiss, showing him how much she admired him, loved him . . . he accepted each gentle touch with such appreciation, she couldn't stop. She slanted her head to seal their mouths together. In a rush of daring, she touched him with her tongue.

His lips opened and he welcomed her inside.

She slid her hands around his neck.

He slipped his fingers up her arms. He slid under her sleeves to massage her shoulders. He moaned slightly, as if the feel of her skin beneath his hands gave him such sensual pleasure, he couldn't keep it to himself.

Was he really so affected? Did her kiss mean so much to him?

She rubbed his earlobes with her thumbs. She loved touching him; he was gorgeous, sexy, gentle . . . ruthless, determined, unstoppable . . .

From upstairs, a sharp noise blasted through the house.

They sprang apart.

"What was that?" she shouted.

Before she had finished the question, Max leaped up. He knocked over his chair, and ran for the door.

She jumped to her feet. "Was that a gunshot?" she yelled after him.

He pulled the library door shut behind him.

"Damn you." By the time she got it open again, he was pounding up the stairs.

She followed, chasing after him like a demented woman. From inside the Masterson bedroom, she could hear shouts and thumping. She burst through the door to see Max wade into the knot of four struggling men and drive his fist into Constable Frank Shelbourn's face. Frank's head jerked back. His knees sagged. He hit the floor.

One of the other men grabbed Max's arm, and indicated the chips of wood scattered across the floor. "No, *mon ami*. He shot only the Masterson bed."

Max nodded, once, brusquely. Leaning down, he picked Frank up by the shirt front. Frank's head rolled back. His eyes squinted open. Max said, "You little coward. I'll kill you if you ever—"

"Max!" she said.

He turned his head, and she saw a facet of Max she had only suspected. His expression was grim, deadly. If left alone, he would have murdered Frank.

"Max," she said again.

Max looked down into Frank's bloody face. "Don't you ever come near her again." He dropped Frank to the floor and straightened up. His lethal look had vanished as if it never existed. Spreading his hands, he said, "I'm sorry, darling. He shot the Masterson bed."

CHAPTER 6

Max saw Dennis and the other Interpol agents off, Frank in tow, and went looking for Laurel. The library was dark. She wasn't in her bedroom. And really, where else would she go after an evening like this?

He strolled down the corridor to the room where the Masterson bed stood in all its regal glory.

Laurel sat on the bed, on top of the comforter, the pillows propped up behind her, her arms crossed behind her head. She still wore her sleeveless zippered sweatshirt and gray sweat pants, and she managed to imbue those pedestrian garments with a lean elegance that tugged at his senses. The lone spotlight that lit the glittering gold cross provided all the illumination in the room, leaving the wooden behemoth—and Laurel's face—in shadow.

He walked to the side of the bed, slid his hands into his pockets, and tried to gauge her mood. Her face was placid as she stared at the cross, at the array of Masterson portraits on the wall, at everything but him. She was giving nothing away. And, obviously, she wasn't going to start the conversation. "How did the Masterson bed survive this latest assault?" he asked.

"The bullet's buried in the footboard, but it didn't really hurt anything." She sounded almost dispassionate. "This old bed has survived worse."

"You're right." He nodded. "Of course it has."

She said nothing.

"Fires. Raids. Other smugglers. Other thieves . . ."

Still nothing.

He ventured, "I'm relieved we caught the thief."

"Yes." She paused. A clock ticked on the nightstand, the only sound in the quiet room. "I wish I'd known what was going to happen ahead of time, but I suppose Interpol considered me a threat to international security."

"I didn't want you involved."

"Of course not." Her tranquil mask slipped. "Why should the primary suspect be involved in clearing her name?"

He tried to reassure her. "You were only the primary suspect for Interpol. I always knew you were innocent."

"That makes it all better." She was testy. Definitely testy.

The silence fell again.

He rocked on his heels and watched her. Her black hair tumbled around her shoulders. Her lean, strong body glowed with health. Her skin had the fine grain of pale porcelain. Never mind her informal wear; with her arms behind her head and her ankles crossed, she looked like some ancient queen relaxing on her royal divan. He wanted to be her consort. He would be her king. "I wonder what you think of the things I told you earlier."

"About you?" She looked him over as if the sight of him irresistibly drew her gaze. Then she looked away, but her breathing quickened. "I thought it was a start."

"A start?" He'd bared his soul, and she called it a start?

"You can't sum up thirty-two years in a few terse sentences. I don't know where you live now, what your hobbies are, if you have pets . . ."

More? She wanted more? He didn't want to talk about himself—but if he had to, he would turn it to his advantage. With the decisiveness that marked all his best tactical moves, he said, "Okay. Scoot over."

"Wha . . . ?"

"In fact, hop off for a second." He scooped her up and stood her on her feet, then peeled back the comforter and the blankets to expose the white sheets. "Now." Picking her up, he deposited her back on the bed. He took off his shoes and climbed in beside her.

The whole operation had taken less than a minute, and while she was still formulating her objections and he was arranging the pillows, he said, "When I met you, I was buying antiques for my new house."

Her jaw sagged. She forgot all about protesting his high-handed treatment. "You have a new house? Where? What is it? When did you buy it?"

"I started negotiations about six months ago. I thought the owners might be willing to sell; it's an old place, and the upkeep is always hell. The owners made a lot of noise about family and living in the country, but I knew right away they'd give it up. They knew I would pay a premium price, and I've seen that voracious look often enough in my career." He reclined on the bed and sighed with pleasure. The mattress was really quite comfortable. He turned his head and looked straight at her from across the pillow. "So I started shopping for antiques."

As he spoke, her eyes were narrowing.

She knew. She finally knew.

He continued, "I wanted to find the original antiques that had been in the house—"

She bounced up on her knees. *"You're* the new owner of Masterson Manor?"

"Yes, but I could have been hired as the handyman on my own merit."

"Let me get this straight. You made an offer on the house, you went looking for the old furniture and knickknacks, you met me." She ticked off the facts one by one on her fingers. "We spent three days together. You knew I was from Masterson Manor, and you never said a word?"

He couldn't help but smile.

That did not seem to ease her ire.

Hastily, he said, "You were so charming, so happy in your job and so pleased to be teaching me everything about antiques. I just couldn't tell you I would probably soon own Masterson Manor—"

"—And fire me?" Her eyes flashed. "I can see that would have put a crimp in your style."

He sat up, faced her and leaned forward aggressively. "I have not fired you. I simply wish you to assume a different post in the house."

She backed up, her brow knit warily. Apparently she decided she didn't want to broach that subject, for she said, "No wonder Interpol told you that the antiques were on the international market. They were your antiques."

"Yes, but Interpol has more important matters to deal with these days than the theft of a few relics. Dennis called me because of our friendship."

She nodded as she absorbed that, then gestured around at the room with its ancient bed and its antique furnishings. "Why Masterson Manor? Why here?"

"Because . . ." But he found he couldn't quite say it yet. Instead he said the next best thing. "I'm a bastard boy whose only family is my mum. I wanted someplace with a past." Still Laurel considered him, and he feared she was about to ask questions he didn't want to answer. So he asked one of his own. "I've told you my secret. Are you afraid to marry a man with a background like mine?"

Swift as a snake striking, she smacked him on the shoulder as hard as she could.

"Hey!" He grabbed the sore spot and rubbed it. "What'd you do that for?"

"Is that what you think of me? That I'm so shallow? That all that matters to me is who your family is?" She tapped her chest. "I'm a farm girl from Idaho. I'm scarcely the person to be putting on airs."

"Perhaps you fear I'd abandon you."

She sighed in exasperation. "If I could have easily gotten rid of you, you'd not be here now."

"Our children could as irresponsible as . . . my father," he said.

"Or worse, they could be as stupid as you." Whoops. That was a mistake. "*If* we had children, which isn't going to happen."

Too late. He rose over her and toppled her onto the bed. "If I haven't given you a disgust of me with my background, then . . . won't you give me a second chance?"

"Just because you finally got around to telling me about yourself doesn't mean you've fulfilled all my dreams, or even a little of them."

"I could."

She didn't believe the nerve of the man, thinking she would melt just because he gave her a hint of who he was. Of course, she couldn't believe that he was here, trying to please her, to convince her to give him another chance. She couldn't believe . . . that she was tempted.

"Why?" she asked. "Why are you doing this? Am I like some possession that got away?"

She thought he might be offended, but he only snorted. "If I thought that, I would have come for you at once."

She knew that. She really did, but she still didn't know why.

He stared into her eyes, holding her gaze. "You're right. When you left me, I thought . . . I thought I would be okay. You left me. Fine. I'd done my duty. I'd asked you to marry me. I thought . . . you were just a woman, and I could find another woman."

Pain grew and twisted in her. She understood what he was saying. She'd even thought just that—that she'd been easily replaced.

"The thing was"—he wasn't looking at her now, instead he watched his hand as he stroked her hair back from her forehead—"I got a lot of work done, because I couldn't find any women who interested me. I did date." He glanced at her.

She wanted to hit him again. "Yeah?"

"They were always too tall or too short or too loud or too quiet or too sophisticated or too dumb. They didn't talk like you or look like you or smell like you." He closed his eyes. "I hated it. I fought it." He pinned her with his green gaze. "It's been a damned hard lesson for me to learn, but you are the only woman I want. I want you to be my wife."

And Max kissed Laurel.

Not like this morning, when he'd been coaxing, teasing, alternately sweet and passionate. Now he took her lips like a man in desperate need, without respect for her wishes or desires.

Trouble was . . . it felt good. It felt right. He thrust his tongue into her mouth, explored her teeth, bit gently at her lips. He slid his fingers through her hair, tilted her head, held her where he wanted her, and kissed her yet more.

She gasped, and gasped again, trying to think when all she could do was feel . . . so much.

Her breasts tightened, and deep within her, she softened, melted, wanted. It had been so long, months and months. She had been so alone. The weight of his body on hers filled a need she had pretended did not exist.

At last she gave in and welcomed him, kissed him back. The taste of him filled her mouth, making her hungry for more. He overwhelmed her with the way his hips moved on hers. She wrapped her legs around him, lifted herself to him, the seam of her sweats and the bulge in his pants rubbing her into a frenzy.

He tore his mouth away from hers. "Tell me . . ." His chest heaved, his breath labored. "Tell me that you want me."

She looked up at him. At his square jaw, shaved so smooth. His tawny hair, tousled around his face. His strong neck, corded with restraint. She did want him. Of course she wanted him. How could she not? She loved him. No matter how far she ran, no matter how long they were apart, still she loved him.

She would always love him.

Stroking the backs of her fingers across his cheeks, she said, "I do want you. I want you all the time."

A smile dawned across his face: a slow, mighty lifting of his lips, a twinkle of his eyes, a gleam of his teeth.

She recognized triumph when she saw it. "I am too weak," she mourned.

"You?" He kissed her, the smile still on his face. "No, you're too strong, too stubborn, but I'll make you happy. I swear it."

"I know you will." She meant now, in bed.

He shook his head, as if she didn't understand, but he wanted more than talk now. He kissed her again, then sat up to straddle her. He unzipped her sweatshirt.

She laughed tremulously and tried to take over, but he brushed her hands aside. "Let me."

She kept laughing. His fingers were trembling, and when she smoothed her hands across his chest, he muttered, "God, Laurel. I can't wait."

When he spread her shirt open, he stopped and stared. "Since when did you give up wearing a bra?"

"Since I don't sleep in one. I'm not wearing . . . any underwear." She gave the last word a breathy intonation.

He turned a searing shade of red. "You are the most wonderful woman in the world."

"Cheap compliments." She couldn't laugh anymore. Not when he gazed on her as if she were a miracle—or a dream come true.

He skinned her out of the pants in a single, swift movement.

Except for her blue sweatshirt, hanging off her arms, she was naked, and judging from the expression on his face, desirable. And when he lowered his head to her stomach and kissed her, then turned to his cheek and rested there, she couldn't resist the chance to run her fingers through his hair.

Could he be telling the truth? Had he suffered loneliness and heartache without her?

He rose up and the light behind him revealed a silhouette of sculpted masculinity. His hair glinted about his head, a halo with hints of gold. His shoulders and arms rippled with muscles. His body narrowed nicely to his hips, and something about that shape made other women—not just Laurel—stop and stare. But he said he was hers, and right now, this minute, he was.

Settling himself over her hips, he removed his sweater.

If his chest made the sweater a noble item of apparel, his chest stripped of clothing was worthy of worship. A thin line of blond hair slid down the middle toward his trousers. Nothing distracted from the smooth skin of his pectorals and the small male nipples that made her mouth water. His abs rippled like water over rocks, and when she slid her fingers down toward his waistband, his stomach contracted and he caught her wrist.

"If you touch me," he said, "I'll be finished right now."

"Really?" She was surprised to hear a sultry tone in her voice. When had she learned sultry? "So I should brace myself for disappointment?"

"You should definitely brace yourself."

"I mean . . . it won't be long?"

In a voice warm with enjoyment, he said, "As long as it always was, sweetheart."

"Smart-ass." With her other hand, she caught at the button on his trousers and popped it free—and brushed her fingers against the bulge in his pants.

He audibly sucked in air. He jumped to his feet and stood on the mattress. He unzipped, displaying a pair of black underwear she saw only as he slid them off. He fished a foil packet out of his pocket. He stepped out of his pants, kicked them off the bed and fell to his knees between her legs.

He wasn't kidding. He was horny to the point of—

"My God." Gripping the rails on the headboard, she felt in one hand the worn silkiness of the wood, in the other the rough abrasion from those long-ago manacles. Anticipation thrummed through her veins.

He tore open the packet with his teeth, fitted himself with its contents. Lifting her hips, he positioned himself and pushed.

She'd been without a man—without him—for three months, and while at first her muscles parted reluctantly, her body soon welcomed him. The pleasure of his entry drove her to scream, a scream so intense she bit the back of her hand to stop it. Using his hand to stroke her and hold himself, he worked himself inside—slowly. Sliding forward, pulling back. Touching her. Caressing her clitoris until she wanted to grab him and force him all the way in.

Instead she spread her legs, arched her back, raised her hips.

"No. Don't. No." But his discipline collapsed under her urging. With both his hands clasping her hips, he surged forward, all the way in.

He touched the deepest part of her, and for one agonized moment they looked into each others' eyes. She didn't know what he saw, but she saw her man. Her lover.

Her fate.

Then he pulled back and plunged forward, as desperate to take possession as she was to give it to him. Together they took up the frenzied rhythm, surging toward satisfaction, toward orgasm, toward that moment of blessed union where they were one and would never be alone again. They'd never been there before, but this time, for all the passion, she knew . . .

And then it took them. Picked them up like victims of a storm and forced them toward each other. Toward desperation. Toward a pleasure that united . . . forever.

As she rose toward him, carried by a wave of climax so great she could only scream his name, he hammered into her, his features contorted, his fingers digging into her skin. Pleasure dripped from his pores, and he called out her name. "Laurel!"

CHAPTER 7

Max fell on her, a magnificent, heavy weight, and Laurel stroked his damp shoulders before her arms lost their strength and fell away. She wanted to hold him, she really did, but she could scarcely wiggle her toes.

In fact, she wasn't sure she had toes.

But she had other parts, for he filled her still.

In a weak voice, he told her, "That was the most fabulous moment of my life." He kissed her cheek, then slowly, he withdrew from her body.

For a brief moment, she tried to hold him, but she couldn't. He was growing soft. She had to let him go.

Falling back on the pillows, he groaned. "That's it. I'm done. That was the best sex in the history of the world, and I'll never be able to get a woody again."

Exhausted, still shivering with the remnants of her orgasm, she groaned at the thought of him getting another erection.

The way he would loom over her. The size of him as he entered her. The way she would wrap her legs around him, hold him close, lift her hips to meet each thrust.

Then she whimpered at the thought of him *not* getting another erection. Feebly, she said, "That would mean . . . that would mean we've deprived the world of its most magnificent natural occurrence. That would be like . . . plugging all the volcanoes or stopping the tsunamis."

"Destructive elements."

"But primal and beautiful in their untamed power."

"And I suppose there's not a chance we would ever bury Pompeii or drown a village."

"No." She managed to raise her hand and wipe her damp eyes. "Do you suppose 'National Geographic' will want to do a special on us?"

"It doesn't matter. I'm finished. Through." He sounded absolutely and totally convinced. "I can never get it up again."

Someone had to help the poor man, and that someone was her. She would have to force herself to abandon her afterglow and demonstrate to Max that he could, indeed, once more achieve erection.

It took a few moments and several deep breaths before she rolled toward him, threw her leg over his hips—he might, after all, try to escape—and leaned on his chest, her left breast conveniently close to his left hand.

He didn't move. He acted as if he wasn't even aware that he was naked, that she was naked, and that she had crawled half over him.

Right.

She loved the feel of her skin against his. Warmth curled up from everywhere they touched, the warmth of intimacy.

She studied his face: muscles relaxed, eyes closed, lips slightly apart and demanding to be kissed.

So she complied. She kissed him softly, stroking her lips across his, enjoying the sensation of being in control. His chest rose and fell in long, smooth breaths that deepened as she touched him, and she rode him like a wave. When she circled his mouth with her tongue, his breath halted for one startled moment. She wanted to chuckle with delight, but she wanted to kiss him more. She sealed their lips together, kissed him deeply, filling his mouth, ravishing him with her tongue. His arm, the one beneath her, rose, trembled, then slid around her waist. His hand weighed heavily on the small of her back, and he kneaded her muscles. The combined pleasures—from their kiss, from his touch—made her want to stretch and claw like a cat.

When he tried to take over, when he thrust his tongue toward hers, she pulled back. "You're incapable," she whispered. "Remember?"

His head dropped back on the pillow, and his eyes were slits as he watched her kiss his shoulder, then bite it, just a little. Just enough to leave a dent in his skin, then smooth it away.

He tensed, but she murmured, "Relax. I won't hurt you."

"It's not the pain I fear. It's the torment."

"I can't torment you. You're feeble." She kissed her way down his chest, pausing at each of his small male nipples to lave them with her tongue.

His knee rose and his hip rolled toward her.

A glance proved that his previous information was incorrect. His penis was stirring.

He cupped her breast in his free hand, and stroked her nipple with his thumb. The pleasure was so intense, she paused and closed her eyes. She winced with disappointment when he took his hand away. Then his finger was back, wet from his mouth, and he circled her nipple, over and over, while it puckered with chill and delight.

Slowly, reluctantly, she pulled away. With eyes still closed, she lowered her head and kissed his stomach. Beneath her lips, the muscles rippled and rolled. She stroked his sides, finding pleasure in the skin and muscle over his ribs, in the graceful dip of his waist and the hard thrust of his hips.

He was a creation of God, a glory of human pulchritude. If he had been Adam to her Eve, she would have needed no temptation to seduce him; she would have done it freely and gladly, whatever the consequences.

She opened her eyes, used her fingertip to trace her way down the path of downy golden hair to his groin. "Why, look." She managed to inject wonder into her voice. "What's this?"

His penis had grown and lengthened with every kiss, with every touch. Carefully, she traced its length. The blue veins. The polished skin. A little drop of semen formed, and with her fingertip she picked it up, looked into his eyes, and deliberately licked it off.

His penis rose off his body as if seeking her mouth.

Nothing could have kept the smile from her lips. She stroked her hands up his legs. Here the hair was thick, rough, and beneath it were the muscles that gave him the strength to thrust and thrust like some young stallion on his first mare.

She kissed the base of his penis, a chaste kiss with lips closed.

His toes curled.

She kissed again, adding a quick flick of the tongue.

He groaned.

Damn, he was easy to please. In slow increments, she worked her way up toward the head, alternately kissing and licking until his back was arched and he clutched the sheets in his fists.

Such power was intoxicating.

She swirled her tongue around the head. She slipped her mouth around him, and slowly worked her way down.

"Dear . . . Laurel, you . . . anything, please."

She loved the taste of his skin, the way he flinched as if he were in pain, the groans and half-spoken phrases. Heady with intoxication, she lightly scraped her teeth along his length, then soothed and sucked. She rubbed her hand up and down where her mouth couldn't reach.

And when he was writhing beneath her, begging her to stop, to give him surcease, to somehow bring him to ecstasy, she slid her mouth away and looked down at his damp, rosy penis. Curling her hand around his erection, she looked up at him. "Resurrection," she said.

He pulled her up and over him. He fit them together. "That is why, in ancient times, men were worshipped as gods." As he slid inside her, he said hoarsely, "And rightly so."

"I admit it. I am a mere sycophant to the womanhood that is you." Exhausted by the long, slow, meticulous lovemaking Laurel had subjected him to, Max flung himself face down on the bed. "You make the earth move, the sun shine, the tides rise and fall. You are the living embodiment of a goddess."

She rubbed her thighs and watched him with a knowing smile. "Damned right."

What a woman she was. She had ridden him—tortured him—until he would have given her anything just for the ecstasy of finishing hard and fast.

Not that she wanted anything. They'd done this, had wonderful sex, and she had not uttered one word about forever.

Not one word about love.

He was going to have to tell her everything.

CHAPTER 8

A harsh scraping sound brought Laurel from deepest slumber to tense awareness. Without opening her eyes, she knew Max was gone, and had been for a while. It was morning, very early morning.

And someone else—a stranger—was in the room with her.

Where was Max? She was in danger. She knew she was. Her jaw was locked, her muscles clenched. Moving slowly, each joint aching with the effort, she peeked over the edge of the comforter.

The only light in the room shone on the spot where St. Albion's cross had stood . . . but the cross was gone. Cradled in the arms of . . .

Holding the covers to her naked chest, she sat up. "Kenneth, what are you doing?"

The tall old butler spun around. "Why, Miss Laurel. I didn't see you there in the shadows." He hunched over the cross, trying to keep it from her sight. "What are you doing, sleeping in the Masterson bed?"

"I was . . ." Wait a minute. She didn't owe him an explanation, and she could never explain anyway. "Never mind that. What are *you* doing with St. Albion's cross?"

"It . . . occurred to me . . . that this might be . . . the next piece the thieves would come after . . . so I'm taking it to a safe place."

His hesitations told a different tale. He was thinking up the story as he spoke. "Kenneth, put it down." She reached for the alarm panel at the head of the bed.

He pulled a pistol from his pocket and pointed it straight at her.

She gasped. Her heart gave a hard thump, then raced in panic. She clutched the covers tighter.

"Why did you have to be there? Why did you have to wake up?" His voice rumbled as it always had. He sounded no more and no less like the crabby old butler she'd come to know. But he looked . . . altered. Cold. Indifferent. As if he knew how to use the gun, and had no qualms about using it on her.

She didn't know what to say. She didn't know what to do. *Where was Max?*

"You should have kept sleeping. What you didn't know wouldn't hurt you." Kenneth apprehensively glanced around. "Where's your man?"

"My . . . who?" Max. He meant Max. She glanced at the clock. "I don't know. It's five o'clock in the morning. He's sleeping in his bed, I suppose."

"That's good. Now what am I going to do with you?" Kenneth glared as if his crime was her fault.

"Wh . . . why . . . are you . . . stealing St. Albion's cross?" She couldn't believe it. "Why are you?"

"You know why." His gray brows lowered, his bulbous nose quivered.

"Is it the gambling?"

"Is it the gambling?" he mimicked savagely. "Aye, it's the gambling. I'm old. I've got no family. I deserve a little fun."

Gun or no gun, that was nonsense. Such sophistry made her blood boil. "Not if it involves stealing your own English heritage and selling it."

She'd seen Kenneth sneer many times, but never had his condescension been so openly directed at her. "Please, Miss! You're a romantic." His gaze sharpened on her, his lips grinned, and she knew he'd realized she was bare beneath the covers. "You should know only the rich can afford morals."

"I should know nothing of the sort." But he obviously had no morals of any kind.

He snorted. "I've been helping myself, a little bit at a time, for years. It could have gone on forever, only now the manor's been sold to a mean as hell businessman."

Yes. Max. *Where was he?*

"The bugger's installing a good security system," Kenneth said. "I've got no more time."

She couldn't tear her gaze away from the unwavering gun that was pointed at her chest. "We thought it was Frank."

"It is Frank. He helps me get the pieces past the inspectors. And Georgie from the pub, and Miss Howard, the schoolmistress."

She found herself breathing hard. Panic had her in its grip. She was so afraid he was going to kill her. He had to kill her, or else be revealed. But there had to be a way out. And even if there wasn't . . . she had to speak out. She had to. "Look, Kenneth. I'm responsible for making sure the manor and its contents are delivered to its new owner intact. You have to put the cross back."

He laughed, a grating horrific guffaw. "A pretty girl like you isn't going to get in trouble." He stared hard, his faded brown eyes moving over her bare shoulders. "In fact, I'll help you out. I'll tie you up so *they* know you're not involved."

Her fingers tightened on the covers. Max had disappeared,

she didn't know where, but clearly she had to get herself out of this. She couldn't allow Kenneth to tie her up, then shoot her. A germ of an idea took root and grew. "Yes. I suppose." She had to appear reluctant. She had to nonplus him. It took a real effort of will to loosen her fingers from that one corner of the covers, but she did, and pretended not to notice when it slipped down her chest, almost off her breast. "That's a good idea." She glanced at the windows beside the bed. "Why don't you use the tiebacks?"

"Aye, why don't I?"

The old leech was distracted, thinking he would get an eyeful—or more. He placed the cross back on the highboy.

She made sure the comforter was untucked and free of constraint.

Pistol in hand, the old fool swaggered toward the bed. Toward the window. He reached behind the curtains to loosen the tieback.

Comforter in her grip, she sprang on him, flinging it over his head.

He staggered under her weight. Windmilled his arms to rid himself of the comforter. Shouted in fury.

Another shout sounded near her ear. Something, someone— Max!—tackled them. Clad in only his trousers, he knocked her aside. Dragging the cover tighter over Kenneth, he threw him to the floor and landed on him.

Beneath the comforter, the pistol went off.

It was after eight when Max shoved Dennis, Dennis's men, and the handcuffed Kenneth out the door and headed back to the Masterson bed. To the bed, and to Laurel. By God, when he thought of how she'd jumped on Kenneth, nude and armed with nothing but a comforter, he almost fainted from fear. And when he'd heard that pistol go off . . . he pressed his hand to his chest above his poor, abused heart.

If the bullet had struck her instead of the bed, she would have died.

Instead feathers had flown across the room, the comforter had smoldered, and she . . . she had gasped and reached for him with the same panic and fear he felt for her.

She loved him. He knew she did.

But he loved her, too. If there had been any doubt in his mind, that bullet had cleared it away. He couldn't survive without her. Now all he wanted was to hold Laurel in his arms, make sure that she was healthy—and his, in every way it was possible for a woman to belong to a man.

Running up the stairs, he burst into the Masterson bedroom, announcing, "I'm done with all this diplomacy and political correctness. You're going to—" He stopped, and stared in a different kind of horror.

Laurel sat on the bed, her back pressed against the headboard, facing his mother on one side and Grace on the other.

Without thinking, he blurted out, "Mum! What are you doing here?"

His mother turned disapproving brown eyes on him.

At once he was aware he'd been less than gracious. Also, his feet were bare, his trousers and shirt rumpled.

Laurel was dressed in her sweat suit, thank God, but she looked harassed. Poor girl, she'd been dealing with both of those bloody-minded women . . . both of whom believed sex must result in marriage.

He pasted on a belated smile. "Good to see you, Mum! Grace, you too."

"Good morning, Mr. Max." Grace greeted him fondly—a lot more fondly than his own mother—and started out the door. "I'll start your breakfast."

Her departure left Max squirming beneath his mother's glare and Laurel's silent, panicked appeal. "Mum, really. I know that you're an early riser, and I was trying to call you earlier."

"Why, son?" Mum's deep, smoker's voice demanded an explanation . . . for everything, and her toe was tapping.

"To tell you I've found the girl I want to marry."

With a sigh, Laurel sagged against the pillows and covered her eyes.

Mum embraced him. "About time. Have you convinced the girl?"

"Almost."

Laurel looked up and glowered.

He amended it to, "I'm trying. She's stubborn." He released his mother and walked toward the bed, trying to tell Laurel how he felt without actually saying those difficult, impossible words. "She's also brave and lovely and more than I ever hoped for, and unless she marries me, I can never be happy."

Laurel lowered her hands and in an unloverlike tone, inquired, "Why not? You're rich, you're handsome, you own Masterson Manor. You've got a mother who loves you and I think banking suits you, so you must enjoy it. Why do you need me to be happy?"

"I rather like her, dear," his mother said.

"That's nice, Mum," he said absentmindedly. He knew someday he'd be pleased, but right now Laurel demanded all of his attention, all of his tact . . . and those difficult, impossible words.

"I'll be in the kitchen with Grace, cooking your breakfast," Mum said. "Don't be long."

She left them, and he was alone with nothing but himself to offer to the one woman to whom he wanted to give everything. "Laurel . . . Laurel, please marry me. I need you." He wanted to buy her gifts, take her in his arms, shower her with adoration, but he had only a single stark truth to offer her. "I love you."

"I love you, too," Laurel whispered.

And at last, he could breathe again. He grabbed her, embraced her, as if he would never let her go.

Laurel laughed breathlessly. She kissed his chest, his wrist, anything she could reach. Then she stared into his eyes, touched his cheek, smiled tremulously. He held her as if she embodied every need, every desire of his body and his heart. And he . . . he was more than just love to her. He was safety and exhilaration. Family and sexuality. With him, she could be free and be wild, all at the same time. Together, the two of them . . . she blinked.

His eyes.

Those brilliant, green eyes.

Where had she seen them before?

"My God," she whispered. She glanced at the family portraits on the wall—the formal portrait of Lord Rion Masterson, the more carefree portrait of Lord Sterling Masterson, and even a darkened, stylized sketch of Sir Nicholas Masterson, the founder of the family. And she said, "You're a Masterson."

He dropped his head. "Damn."

"You are. You're a Masterson!"

"Yes, I'm a Masterson." The resemblance between him and his ancestors was uncanny. "My father was a Masterson, but since he never married my mother, I have her last name."

Laurel didn't know whether to laugh or cry. Whether to tell him or not.

"I bought the manor to thumb my nose at the father and the family that rejected me. My whole purpose was a kind of vengeful satisfaction that I had done so well while they were decadent to the bone and scattered to the winds." He kissed her hair. "Then I met you, and all that became unimportant.

Only you mattered. Having you. Loving you. You've brought me home."

Blinking against tears, she smiled at him. "I've brought you a lot more than that."

He must have grasped her turmoil, for his arms tightened around her. "What? Tell me what's wrong."

The rope scrolling on the bedposts gleamed with dark walnut wood hints of light, and the open fretwork around the wooden canopy warmed her heart. This bed signified everything she loved about the great old manor, its contents, and the history enclosed within its walls. And it worked its own magic . . . as it had throughout the ages.

Resting her head on his shoulder, Laurel started to laugh. "You're a Masterson, and that last time . . . that last time we made love, we didn't use birth control."

"I know. Darling, I do know." He tilted her head up to look into her eyes. "But I lost my head. I swear to you, I've never done that before. I couldn't think of anything but being inside you. And . . . I know I haven't the right to make such a decision, but when I did remember, I felt pleased. Proud, like some strutting peacock. I want to have a family with you." He lifted his brows questioningly. "Are you furious with me?"

"Stop blaming yourself. I was swept away, too." She went off into a bigger gale of laughter. "It's the bed. I've done a lot of research here. A lot of research. About the Mastersons. And the bed." She knocked her knuckles on the walnut headboard, then shook her bruised hand. "The Masterson bed."

"Yeah?" He watched her warily.

"It has a reputation. There's a legend . . ." She laughed helplessly at his guarded expression. He obviously thought she'd gone mad. "Whenever . . . whenever a Masterson and the love of his life unite in the Masterson bed, the result nine months later is . . . the Masterson heir."

A hint of a smile curved his lips. "Really?" He unzipped her sweatshirt. "Really?"

"What are you doing?" As if she didn't know.

"The Masterson bed is old." He slid her free of her clothing. "The charm might be worn out. We need to give it another chance to work."

She looped her arms around his neck. "It worked."

"We must make certain."

He stared at her so proudly, and caressed her belly with such awe, that the last of her doubts slid away.

"I'm certain." She kissed him, long, slow, moist, intimate. "As long as the Mastersons have a bed, the master will always have a son."

THE END

Afterword

All right. I'll admit it at last. The idea for *Once Upon a Pillow* came not from me, but from my husband. The man is the vice president of an engineering firm, but living with a writer has rubbed off on him. He's the one I call when I am stuck for a plot twist, and occasionally he pops up with a new idea so stupendous, I'm in awe of his creativity. *Once Upon a Pillow* was one of those ideas.

Of course, Connie recognized his genius at once and we were ready to write. But with a bed that spans the history of England, which time periods should we use?

We knew the Masterson Bed was built in Medieval times, so Connie wrote that tale. Then it was my turn to pick, and I jumped at the chance to write, once more, about Elizabethan England. It was such a time of romance, vigor, and drama, I couldn't wait to create Helwin and Rion and a mischance big enough to bring the unlikely pair together.

Before I was published, I wrote historical and contemporary novels and loved them both. I've since published historicals, but I've wanted once again to set a story in my own time, to show people I might meet on today's streets engaged in a tale of adventure and romance. Writing about Laurel and Max was just as much fun as I anticipated, and I hope you enjoyed discovering the secrets of the magnificent Masterson Bed.

May all your dreams come true.

Christina Dodd

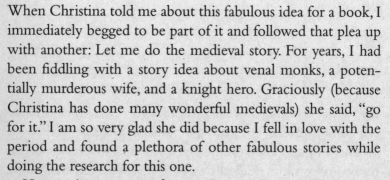

When Christina told me about this fabulous idea for a book, I immediately begged to be part of it and followed that plea up with another: Let me do the medieval story. For years, I had been fiddling with a story idea about venal monks, a potentially murderous wife, and a knight hero. Graciously (because Christina has done many wonderful medievals) she said, "go for it." I am so very glad she did because I fell in love with the period and found a plethora of other fabulous stories while doing the research for this one.

Happy circumstances for me. Because I was to begin the book that meant I could choose between two eras for my second story—the Regency or Victorian. Now, I love the Victorian but it had been many years since I had written in the time period of my first love, the Regency, so I jumped at the opportunity. As for the story, having written a battle-weary, patient hero and an emotionally pent-up heroine for the medieval, I knew at once that my Regency couple must be their polar opposites, and so Ned Masterson emerged from my imagination passionate, willful, and completely obsessed with the equally fiery (and stupendously forthcoming) Philippa. I hope you enjoy them.

Sweet Dreams!

Connie Brockway